I0760555

Blood Ties

The
Dream Diaries
Book 2

BECCA C. SMITH

Published by Red Frog Publishing, a division of Red Frog Media

Visit our website at www.redfrogpublishing.com

First published in 2021

Cover by Stephan Fleet

ISBN 9781949877380

Printed in the United States of America

Dedicated to three amazing women:

Heather Mattern for giving me the confidence to share the first Dream Diaries book, which ultimately inspired me to write this sequel! I will forever be grateful for your kindness and support!

Heidi Epp for reminding me I had finished drafting this second book after NaNoWriMo! Your enthusiasm and excitement for the first book and the possibility of a second book pushed me to finish the first draft of Blood Ties! Thank you so much!

And Emily Bourne. You are such a light in my life. Without you, this book would not be published. You encouraged me when I was certain I didn't want Blood Ties to see the light of day. It was because of you I was able to find my passion for this book again. Thank you, Emily, for being my friend and inspiring me every day to write and share my stories! You are amazing!

Dream Entry #1

I'm visiting Adam again tomorrow, and I'm both nervous and excited. In person, I mean. In actuality, Adam and I see each other almost every night when we find each other in our dreams. Sometimes I go to his dreams (a lot harder! I'm not as good at it as he is), but mostly he visits mine. It's weird to write about this like it's something normal, but I'm coming to accept that, for whatever reason, doing crazy things in dreamland is *my "normal." I had never met anyone like me before Adam. Truth be told, I didn't find out about Adam and his dreams until it was too late to save him from what he did. I still can't believe it's been two years since it all happened. Since Adam killed three people.*

Adam had been fully manipulated by Robert Garner for eight years before Robert finally convinced Adam to kill the "bad men." And the three men he killed were as bad as they come: one was a child beater (Robert's own father), another a child rapist, and the third was a foster parent who'd beaten Adam's friend to death.

I don't want to admit it to Adam, but I'm still not sure how I feel about what happened. In a vigilante world, what he did makes perfect sense, but I still can't wrap my head around it.

Adam's staying at Evergreen Moon, a psychiatric facility. I've been able to visit him twice a month for the last year (the first year, he wasn't allowed any visitors), and I'm just happy I've gotten to see him at all in person. He fully confessed and was sent there with the conviction of temporary insanity. I guess that's hard to prove, but Adam was a textbook case according to Agent Piper. And since he helped take down Robert Garner by getting himself shot in the gut, the court opted for leniency in its sentencing. It was obvious to the justice system that Adam had been systematically manipulated and abused by Robert, by his father, and by the handful of foster parents he'd had over the years. To say Adam had it rough was an understatement. Robert was the only one who showed him any decency in his life, so it made sense for Adam to trust him. Adam told me it wasn't until he met me that he began to understand right from wrong. I was his beacon (no pressure at all!). The fact that he dreams like me only makes our bond stronger.

***

Mara placed her journal on the table next to her bed. Glancing over at the empty bed across the room, she knew she was lucky she had an entire dorm room to herself, but she was also a little sad. Starting out her sophomore year at the University of Washington was a lot less nerve-wracking than her freshman year, but no one wanted to share a room with the girl who was dating a serial killer, especially knowing he was going to be released. The whole trial had been so public: Mara was still recognized on the streets at least three or four times a week. Weirdly, most people were supportive of Adam and what he went through, but when it came to spending the night with his girlfriend (who the world now knew had psychic dreams about murderers), that was a little too much for anyone. Luckily, Mara had gotten permission from the district attorney and the university to have Adam stay with her for a few weeks. The DA put Adam's psychiatrist in touch with the dean, and after a two-hour phone call, the dean was convinced that Adam was no threat to anyone on campus.

Sometimes she wished she had gone with Zia to college in New York since the chances were higher that no one would recognize her there. Mara just couldn't though. She wanted to be near Adam. Instead, she accepted her admittance to the University of Washington.

So many confusing emotions were tied up with Adam. Mara still wasn't sure how to process them all. Her parents kept pushing therapy on her, but Mara wasn't ready for that yet. They mainly wanted her to go to therapy because they were convinced that once their daughter got "help," she'd suddenly "wake up" and dump Adam. It truly annoyed her that they were so transparent about the whole thing. At least her sister, Josie, was on her side, though it was as likely as not to be motivated by Josie's natural inclination to be rebellious or contrary. It didn't matter though. Mara would take it. She hadn't seen or talked to her parents in a couple of weeks because she didn't want to hear another lecture from them.

Mara hated that her parents viewed Adam only as a killer, but what could she do?

After two years of psychiatric help, Adam's team of doctors

had recommended that he be released back into society. If professionals believed in him, why couldn't her parents?

Mara shook her head and snuggled deep into her comforter. The soft, cozy fabric of the down blanket wrapped around her and instantly warmed up her entire body. Closing her eyes, she hoped sleep would come fast.

Maybe she'd see Adam tonight.

***

Mara was dreaming.

She was in high school. Not her old high school but some other school she didn't recognize. A group of teenagers sat around the classroom, their eyes focused on three very pretty girls standing at the front of the room with a whiteboard behind them. Written on the board were the words: "Homecoming Dance Ideas."

It was daytime, so Mara knew she wasn't dreaming about it as it was happening. This was a good thing, because if the dream was happening at the same time Mara was sleeping, usually that meant she was witnessing some kind of horrific death. Mara could tell by the feel of the dream that it was real, though. She could differentiate between a normal dream and a psychic dream pretty easily. There was always an intensity about psychic dreams that made them stand out. They felt tangible, as if right this moment Mara physically stood in this very classroom with all these kids, from the hardness of the floor beneath her feet to reaching down and pinching herself. Everything felt as if she were awake and really there.

So why was she standing in a mundane high school classroom with a bunch of kids talking about the homecoming dance?

A girl caught her eye. She sat in the back of the room, her

stance positioned to bolt if necessary. Mara noticed several people glancing her way as if they were shocked that she was there.

Interesting.

A scrawny sixteen-year-old boy with a face full of acne sidled up to the girl with a smile. “Lucy Tildon, you’re my hero.” His voice was awed as he continued, “I can’t believe you came.”

The girl, Lucy, replied, “I can’t either. I think I should leave.”

That explained the girl’s stance of “wanting to run away” Mara had noticed earlier, but it made Mara curious as to why this Lucy girl wouldn’t be welcome at a homecoming dance meeting.

Lucy shrugged. “What do you think I should do, Barry?”

The scrawny kid named Barry shrugged back. “Samantha Perkins was pretty clear she didn’t want you here, but she’s just trying to intimidate you.”

Lucy rolled her eyes. “Per usual. I’m sick of it.” She motioned to her surroundings dramatically. “I don’t even like dances. I don’t even go to dances. But the fact that Sam told me I was dead if I showed up?” Lucy paused, obviously still shaken by the memory, then finally she continued, “I couldn’t let her scare me anymore.”

One of the pretty girls from the front gave Lucy the stink eye. “Lucy, no one wants you here, especially if you’re going to bother Barry. Samantha warned you not to come.”

Mara cringed.

Lucy was basically *her* in high school—and it sounded like this Samantha girl was like Kimiko, Mara’s own personal bully. Kimiko had made high school brutal for Mara.

Lucy responded, “Well, I don’t see Samantha here, so obviously *she* couldn’t care less about this dance either.”

Mara was strangely fascinated by what was happening. She

still had no idea why she connected to this particular girl. There were millions of girls and guys across the world who were bullied. It wasn't as if this was an uncommon event. So why Lucy Tildon?

A slow twisting of her gut.

Maybe Lucy was going to die.

Everyone and everything froze in place as soon as Mara had the thought.

Another girl popped into the dream, standing a few feet away from Mara.

She was beautiful and strangely familiar.

Her body began to glitch, as if she were a TV picture with a bad signal.

Mara immediately regretted bingeing old Japanese horror films a few nights ago, as she was sure this new arrival was about to crawl back into a well or . . . desk . . . or something scary.

Then it hit Mara: this newest girl was FBI Agent Raven Piper, but as a teenage girl. Instantly, it made her relax. This must be turning into a dream-dream and not the vision Mara had just witnessed with Lucy Tildon.

It was strange though because the girl in front of her felt as real as Lucy had, as if she were really standing there, as if *she* had been the one who stopped the dream in its tracks. It reminded Mara of what it felt like when Adam entered her dreams. He'd materialize out of nowhere and join Mara in whatever dream landscape she happened to be in.

The girl didn't speak, she simply stared at Mara.

"Agent Piper?" Mara asked, not sure of what her response would be.

"It's coming, and you won't be ready," the younger Piper

answered.

"What's coming?" Mara's bones chilled.

"Judgment."

***

Mara woke with a start.

Daylight poured through her window, though it was muted from the cloud cover. Another overcast day in Seattle. Shocker.

The intensity of Mara's dream lingered for a few moments, but since no one had died, she found herself snapping out of it a lot quicker than one of her other more violent dreams.

Mara had to assume from her vision that something was most likely going to happen to Lucy and that she should tell Raven about it. Why else would she dream about the FBI agent?

And *judgment*? Judgment of what? Mara was really tired of not being ready for things.

Deciding to let that dream percolate, Mara crawled out of bed and began to get ready for her Neuroscience 101 class. Yet another event she wasn't ready for. Her teacher, Dr. Jonathan Laurence, was a jerk. Mara couldn't think of any other way to describe him. She had decided to take the neuroscience course since she wanted to know if there was some kind of scientific explanation for why she dreamt the way she did.

But so far Dr. Laurence had made her scared to even broach the topic of her dreams, simply because he was so mean about any possibility of psychic dreams being real. He used the words quacks, fakes, charlatans, and con artists a lot. The worst part was that anytime he'd say one of these words, he'd stare straight at Mara. It was obvious he knew about her and Adam because of their press and internet fame, but every time she sat in class, it was as if he was daring her to bring up her dreams.

It was intimidating.

And it was humiliating.

Everyone in that classroom knew who she was, so everyone in that classroom knew that his comments were directed toward her. It was an attack Mara had no defense against. One of the main reasons she never told anybody about her dreams before was because she had been terrified of this very thing happening. To be ridiculed and basically called a liar for something she had no control over was . . . paralyzing.

Zia wanted her to transfer to another class, but Dr. Laurence was the only one teaching Neuroscience 101, and it was a requirement in order to take any other neuroscience classes. Dr. Laurence knew he was in a position of power and relished the control.

At least it was her only class today. And besides, she had visiting Adam to look forward to. It wouldn't be until three p.m., so she just needed to think of class as stalling for time until she could go see her boy.

Thinking about Adam reminded her that he hadn't visited her dreams last night. Maybe because she was in a vision? He'd visited her psychic dreams before, though, so Mara wasn't sure why this particular dream would be different. Maybe he couldn't sleep? She'd have to ask him about it today.

Mara finished dressing and made her way out of the room. Passing by a few other students on her way, Mara waved a simple hello, then hurried across campus toward the science buildings. Mara loved the UW campus. As she walked by a row of cherry blossom trees, she couldn't wait for spring when they'd be in full bloom. The entire quad would be stunning, with pink petals as far as the eye could see. Truly breathtaking. Right now, though, the leaves were falling to the ground, and soon they'd be bare branches. Fall and winter always made Mara think of death. She was more of a spring girl. It was difficult living in a place with seasons sometimes. The cold was cold. Someday Mara wanted to move to a city like Los Angeles or San Diego, someplace warm all year round. Maybe her dreams wouldn't bother her as much if everything around her wasn't dying.

Quickly entering the science building, Mara walked to Dr. Laurence's classroom. She still had about fifteen minutes to spare but wanted to go in early to find a seat near the back—but not so far that she would stand out. Blending in was the key factor for her. If Dr. Laurence couldn't readily find her, then he wouldn't be able to single her out. So far it hadn't worked, but Mara had to keep on trying.

Watching the other students file in after her, Mara smiled at a couple of friendly faces. She had known taking a class like this would draw attention because of her reputation, but she'd had no idea that people would have cared *so* much. Sometimes she wished she would have just bought *Neuroscience for Dummies* to satisfy her curiosity and then called it a day. But no, Mara didn't want to be afraid of what people thought or how they acted toward her. She had dealt with that kind of fear and intimidation all through high school with her resident bully, Kimiko Thompson, and Mara had felt so helpless back then. She didn't want to be helpless now.

So she wasn't going to.

Mara wanted answers.

And Dr. Laurence was going to have to give them to her.

Mara sat a little straighter as the class came to order and Dr. Laurence addressed the students. He wore a dress shirt and tie (like always), and he spoke with a condescending, smug little expression on his face. He looked older than her dad, so in all probability he wasn't open to anything new or different. He was stuck in his old, stupid ways.

Okay. Mara didn't want to go down that rabbit hole. Though it was so easy to with Dr. Laurence's snarky, annoying voice . . .

Stop.

Think of a question. Think of a question that Dr. Laurence might be able to answer. Might be able to help with. He was an expert in his field, and Mara had taken this class to learn more about where her dreams might come from. Just because Dr. Laurence made it his mission to demean Mara and basically call her a liar didn't mean she couldn't come up with a question he could answer that might help.

Mara remembered what moment had propelled her to take the class in the first place. She had been watching a talk show on the subject of neuroscience and mediums. When the doctor showed a before-and-after brain scan of the medium's brain, the scan showed little to no activity when the medium was contacting the dead, which the doctor said could be due to the fact that mediums "turned off their brain" in order to channel the other side. Mara wasn't sure how that applied to her—she didn't really channel dead people, she mainly dreamt about murder victims—but it made her want to learn more. What was her brain doing while she slept? A part of her had hoped her neuroscience teacher would be so excited and curious about the prospect that Mara could volunteer for brain scanning tests.

Wishful thinking.

As Dr. Laurence continued to lecture, Mara's confidence slowly started to wane, frustration building in her chest. Always letting her fear of being embarrassed or looking stupid hold her back from life, it seemed. She wished she could be bold like Zia. Zia would have had Dr. Laurence eating out of the palm of her hand. Mara so badly wanted to be confident in life, but anytime she tried, it always blew up in her face.

Although, to be fair, she rarely tried. She always *assumed* it would blow up in her face.

Mara took a deep breath.

This was important to her.

She had to take a chance.

Worst-case scenario, if things went horribly wrong, Mara never had to come back to this class again.

Yeah, great attitude.

Time slowly slipped by. Only five minutes left in class. Dr. Laurence was wrapping up his lecture. Unfortunately, Mara had only half paid attention since her brain had been obsessing over what she was going to ask the teacher or whether or not she was going to talk at all.

Finally, Dr. Laurence asked if anyone had any questions.

There would never be a clearer opening than that.

Mara nearly puked as she raised her hand.

When Dr. Laurence's eyes met hers, they widened slightly in surprise. Then, to Mara's dread, his expression turned to one of amusement.

He was ready to embarrass her, as if he'd been waiting for

this day.

Crawling under her desk sounded really good right then, but it was too late now. The entire class stared at her, morbid anticipation lighting up their faces.

"Yes, Ms. Johnson? You have a question?" Dr. Laurence might as well have sneered.

Why did Mara think this was a good idea?

Steadying her voice so it wouldn't squeak in fear (yes, this was a thing), she uttered, "I was wondering about dreams." Mara was proud that she'd said that much.

But her stomach sank when Dr. Laurence responded, "What about them?"

"Um." Did she really just say *um*? Think. Think. Think of something intelligent to say. "I wondered where they come from?"

Dr. Laurence guffawed. "Well, they don't come from the land of *psychics* or fairies. The whole brain is active when we dream, but I would guess that *your* dreams come from the cortex since that's where we invent monsters and imaginary events."

Mara was pretty sure the class gasped—or maybe that was her heart seizing up. She couldn't really tell at the moment. It was the first time Mara wished she was in one of her visions. At least there she was a bystander. Here, she was the center of everyone's attention. And they were all waiting for her to say something back.

Even Dr. Laurence cocked his head to one side as if daring Mara to retort in some kind of witty comeback that he could slam down.

But Mara just sat there, staring at him. She had absolutely

no idea what to say. He was telling her and the whole class that he thought Mara was a fraud. He acted as if her taking this class was some kind of publicity stunt, which was ridiculous because it wasn't as if there were any cameras around.

Dr. Laurence smiled smugly and opened his mouth to say something when a familiar voice sounded from the very back of the classroom.

Mara's eyes widened as she recognized . . .

Kimiko.

What was she doing here?

But Mara was stunned even more when Kimiko said, "Dr. Laurence, I find it interesting that you completely disregard the possibility that someone could have intuitive or psychic dreams. I mean, how would I know *this* if *I* wasn't psychic? You dreamt last night that you were playing in the state chess tournament at your high school, and Roberta Jackson kept checkmating you. Do you want me to tell the class what you did to Miss Jackson after the fifth time she beat you at chess?"

The class laughed. It was a kind of nervous laugh, as if they weren't quite sure if Kimiko was serious or not.

Dr. Laurence's face turned three shades whiter, his eyes a little too wide. He shook his head, indicating Kimiko should not continue sharing his dream to the students.

Kimiko had nailed it.

Mara had known that Kimiko had a gift similar to hers, but she had no idea Kimiko could dream jump. The whole situation was surreal. Kimiko. Mara's high school bully. Was here. In class.

Defending her?

It was too much to comprehend.

Kimiko had the confidence that Mara envied as she smiled with just as much smugness as Dr. Laurence had shown before. "Now, Dr. Laurence, if psychic dreams are *fake* or *make-believe*, then how did I know with precise detail what you dreamt of last night?" She raised her eyebrow with curiosity. "That *was* your dream, right? And right about now, you're trying to remember if you told anyone about it. That maybe I overheard you. But you know you'd never tell anyone about *this* dream." Kimiko shrugged. "I wouldn't either, considering what you did to Roberta."

The class laughed in an uproar.

Kimiko yelled over the class, "Oh, look. Time's up."

Dr. Laurence didn't reprimand Kimiko. He didn't say a word. He simply stood there as the students laughed and talked, making their way out of the classroom.

Mara was as shell-shocked as Dr. Laurence. She had barely recovered from him ridiculing her; now she had to recover from Kimiko ridiculing *him* . . . and being in her class. In her college!

And acting like . . .

A friend?

Was Mara dreaming? She gathered her things and practically ran out the door.

Kimiko caught up to her pretty fast. "Mara."

Mara stopped, still unsure what to say or do. "Kimiko," was all that came out.

"How are you?" Kimiko smiled.

And it was a real smile. A genuine smile. Mara couldn't seem to tell her brain to smile back or to respond in any shape or form.

Kimiko appeared to understand though. Her expression softened. "I just transferred in from Central. I honestly didn't know you were taking this class. I mean, I knew you went here, but I thought I'd be able to keep out of your way. But when Dr. Shmucko said those things to you, I had to say something."

There was an uncomfortable pause between them as Mara couldn't think of anything to say.

Finally finding her voice when her curiosity got the best of her, Mara asked, "How did you know? About what he dreamt of, I mean." Seeing Kimiko acting . . . like a human . . . was a new experience. It was taking her a few moments to adjust.

"I wasn't in his dreams or anything. I could just see it in his head while I was sitting there in class. Clear as day. He kept playing it over and over on repeat. That boy really had a thing for this Roberta chick." Kimiko grimaced slightly, disgusted at having to relive Dr. Laurence's sex dream. Then she continued, "It happens sometimes. I can hear someone's exact thoughts or see some random image or scene that they're thinking."

"I've had that happen before, too, but I've never been brave enough to tell anyone about it. I always thought I might be wrong, and then they'd think I was crazy," Mara admitted.

She still couldn't quite grasp the fact that she was having an actual conversation with Kimiko Thompson, and a civil one at that.

"I figure you've probably experienced everything. You're a lot like my grandmother in that way." Kimiko spoke softly at the mention of her grandmother.

Mara had witnessed the brutal murder of Kimiko's grandma a few years ago in a dream, and when Kimiko found out about it, she still treated Mara like crap. But Mara could see that Kimiko was genuinely trying to make a sincere effort at being nice, and she wasn't about to bring up old wounds.

Kimiko added, "I'm trying to be more like her. She told me to be kind to you, and I was horrible instead. I'm . . . I'm really sorry."

Wow.

Mara wasn't expecting that. She wasn't expecting any of this.

"Thanks," Mara sputtered. Lame, but she didn't know what else to say. She wasn't sure that she actually accepted Kimiko's apology; after all, there were a lot of years of torture to make up for. But standing in front of her old bully, after Kimiko had humiliated their teacher *for* Mara, Mara found that she'd rather have this Kimiko than the one she shared three years of high school with.

"Anyway." Kimiko turned her eyes away. "Maybe I'll see you around campus. I'm not sure Dr. Laurence will let me back into his class."

Then the unexpected happened.

They both laughed.

It was small, but it felt good.

Mara smiled. "I'm not sure I want to go back. He really is an a-hole."

Kimiko smiled as well. "That's an understatement. What did he say to you? *I would guess that your dreams come from the cortex since that's where we invent monsters and imaginary events.* What a dick. I had to say something, especially since he was being such a pervy nerd in his head."

"Well, I'm glad you did. You made a horrible situation quite enjoyable," Mara said, and she meant it.

"The exact opposite of every moment of every encounter we've ever had together, huh?" Kimiko's eyes darted away, then swung back around to meet Mara's. "Anyway, I'd like to make it up to you . . . if you'll let me."

Another shock. Mara didn't know how many more of these she could take. But she wasn't the kind of person who said no to someone who was genuinely trying to change for the better.

Slowly, Mara nodded. "Okay. That sounds . . . I'm not sure how it sounds, but I'd like to try."

Kimiko laughed and nodded toward the exit doors. "Why don't we start with a coffee and something sugary?"

A strange elation flooded through Mara at the turn of events. She smiled back. "As long as it's chocolate."

Kimiko held the door for Mara. "Duh."

Mara smiled and as she began to walk out the door . . . Kimiko's face shifted into someone else's.

It was so quick, Mara froze for a second in surprise.

Kimiko kept the door held open, but her eyebrows crinkled in worry. "What is it? You saw something."

Knowing Kimiko had a gift similar to hers, Mara decided honesty was the best policy. "For a second, your face turned into someone else's."

"Whose?" Kimiko didn't doubt or question Mara's sanity, which was nice.

"I don't know. It looked like a high schooler. She was

young, pretty, a redhead. It was so fast though." Mara shook her head, not sure of what it meant.

Kimiko nodded for Mara to continue to walk through the door since she still held it open, and they headed toward the campus café.

"What do you think it meant?" Kimiko asked.

"I really don't know," Mara answered honestly.

But the hairs on the back of her neck still hadn't gone down.

Dream Entry #2

I'm sitting here on the bus that leads to Adam's psychiatric facility, and my mind is racing. Who was that girl I saw in Kimiko's face? It was . . . chilling. I can't describe it any other way. I don't know what was weirder, seeing some strange girl's face in Kimiko's—or the fact that I was forming some kind of . . . what? Friendship?

With Zia in New York and Adam in a psych ward, I've been feeling isolated. My support system has been stripped. Now, having my old bully show up in my life? It makes me worried for some reason. I feel like I can't trust it because if I do, and Kimiko ends up being the monster she was in the past, then I don't think I'll be able to recover. With my parents being psycho, I don't have much access to Josie. Plus, she's dealing with being a senior in high school right now; I don't want to mess anything up for her. And Zia isn't here at all. FaceTime is good, but nothing like having my best friend by my side. I miss her so much it hurts.

And can I believe that Kimiko's change of attitude in life is real? I know it's been two years since I've seen her, but still. Do people really change? After Colt killed himself, Kimiko transferred out of Forest High our senior year, and I haven't seen her since. At the time, I was relieved she was gone, but relief had turned into a kind of regret. It was almost as if I wanted to explain more of what had happened to Colt. Not that I could. I had already told Kimiko everything I knew about his death, but I never felt like she truly understood how much Colt loved her. It was always weird when dreaming of dead people because, after all, it was actually his ghost *who told me to tell her . . . I could never really tell the difference in a dream, especially if I didn't know the person was dead in the first place.*

Anyway, coffee with Kimiko went surprisingly well. She told me about what she's been up to for the last two years. It sounds like a lot of soul searching. Her last year in high school was spent by herself. She didn't do cheerleading or anything extracurricular like she had in our school. She said her biggest regret was how she had treated me. I was the reason she left Forest High.

Me.

Two years of trying to be a better person. Two years of trying to come to terms with how she had acted.

I could see how much pain she was in. I desperately want to believe she's telling the truth. She said she had been exploring her abilities as well and that was what got her interested in neuroscience. Honing her talent of mind reading made me nervous though. I couldn't figure out if she was reading my mind or trying to read my mind. The whole thing was crazy. I kept waiting for the other shoe to drop, or pig's blood to fall on me like in Carrie, *but it never happened. We parted with an awkward goodbye, and let's face it, I still don't trust her—but it was a start. A start to what? I have no idea.*

I'm seriously getting car sick writing in my journal while bumping around in this bus. Write more later.

***

Mara placed her journal in her messenger bag and rubbed her eyes to soothe the growing nausea in her stomach. It wasn't just writing and driving that made her sick. Her nerves were adding to the queasiness. It was a constant battle between anxiousness and excitement when Mara was about to see Adam.

Plus, there was always the possibility that one or both of her parents would be there, ready to ambush her. It had happened before, and it had been pretty ugly. Luckily, Adam didn't have to witness any of it. The confrontation happened before he was brought to the visiting area, and Mara was grateful for that. It was the first time she understood the extent of how much her parents wanted her nowhere near Adam. They had called him every horrible name Mara could imagine and then some: psychotic, sociopath, murderer, psycho, serial killer. The list went on and on. Their tirade only ended when the head of the facility, Dr. Cushner, eventually kicked her parents out.

Mara was just happy that she hadn't been banned as well, but Dr. Cushner was one of Adam's biggest supporters, and she didn't like hearing what Ben and Claire Johnson had to say either. Strangely, the moment had been deeply satisfying for Mara, watching her parents being reprimanded for their harsh, close-minded judgment of Adam. Ben and Claire had been mortified at being treated as if they were in the wrong. And it hadn't changed their minds any. Later, they unsuccessfully tried to get a restraining order to keep Adam away from Mara.

Mara hated that she hadn't talked to her parents in a couple of weeks, but she also hated that they were so full of . . . *hate.* Another support system stripped from her. Though, after everything they'd done to hurt Adam, Mara wasn't sure she wanted her parents back in her life. It was a hard truth that ate away at her.

It made her furious that they couldn't see Adam's side. That they didn't possess an ounce of compassion for anything he'd been through. Or if they did, they certainly weren't showing it. Their judgment was because Mara was *with* Adam. She knew that logically, but it still didn't stop her anger, her hurt.

The bus came to a stop, interrupting her thoughts. Mara and the three other people on the vehicle made their way toward the exit. Peeking through the windows loomed the gray building of Evergreen Moon. As Mara stepped out into the open, she breathed in a deep breath of the cold early evening breeze. She knew that coming to see Adam the day before he was released was kind of silly. Why couldn't she just wait until tomorrow? A part of her was afraid she'd jinx his release if she waited. That if she waited, it was somehow putting all her eggs in one basket.

Adam was Mara's only support.

Zia was gone. Her parents and sister were gone.

Tomorrow, Adam would be released and Mara wouldn't be alone anymore.

It filled her with a comforting warmth she was terrified of losing.

So, in a weird way, seeing Adam today ensured that she would see him tomorrow. It didn't make any sense, but the isolation was getting to her, and Mara didn't want to do anything that might jeopardize her chances of being with Adam in person.

As far as mental health facilities went, this one seemed to be a step above the others. The walls were a deep gray, but mostly the structure was made of glass. Mara always thought it resembled some kind of swanky office building that should have a giant Apple logo on it or something. A good place to heal: lots of light and the comfort of everything feeling new and clean. The building itself was only five years old. It had been built by a private citizen who wanted to help the mentally ill.

Or people like Adam.

He was the only convicted murderer in the joint. The owner had made an exception after hearing Adam's case. He had a soft spot for abused children.

Mara grumbled to herself. If a complete stranger had faith in Adam and his recovery, why couldn't her parents, who'd known and spent time with him? It was so ignorant and selfish of them.

Following the others to the front entrance, Mara lagged slightly behind, trying to peer through the glass doors and hoping she wouldn't see her parents. When the double doors were opened wide, Mara could see that she was in the clear. She was surprised to feel a mixture of relief and disappointment. She hated to admit it, but she really did miss her mom and dad. It was like having two limbs ripped off her body sometimes. Adam had no idea Mara wasn't talking to them anymore, and he'd freak if he found out. He never wanted to come between Mara and her family.

Pushing aside her complicated feelings about Claire and Ben Johnson, Mara walked over to the front desk.

Flora, the receptionist, smiled at Mara when it was her turn in line. "Here to see Adam Layton?"

Mara nodded as Flora handed her a sticker labeled "Visitor."

"Thanks, Flora," Mara said politely.

Flora smiled back. "We're going to miss Adam when he leaves."

Mara knew the feeling. She had been missing him for two years now. And yet again, Flora's affection toward Adam only showed how he wasn't the sociopath her parents kept claiming he was.

Mara could debate the topic round and round in her head, but it still wouldn't change the fact that her parents would never be okay with their daughter dating a killer. And Mara had to admit, it was a hard position to defend. But if Mara was being honest with herself, she *did* think those men deserved to die. Did she wish it had been done legally through the justice system and not poisoned by her boyfriend? Yes, definitely. It didn't change the fact that Mara believed the world was a better place without those men living in it though.

Knowing the way by heart, Mara headed toward the visitation room. The hallway floors were made of a polished cement in contrast to the glass walls and windows. "Industrial chic" was what one of the nurses had called it. It reminded Mara of a modern art museum with the strange sculptures and abstract artwork scattered throughout each room and corridor.

Finally, Mara reached the solid metal door marked "Visitor Center" in a fancy chalk-drawing-style font. If there was a home design magazine for psychiatric care facilities, this one would be on their front cover.

A heavyset guard stood next to the door. Upon seeing Mara, he reached into his pocket to fish out his security badge. After swiping it on the scan-pad, he opened the door, nodding a hello to Mara.

Once inside the room, Mara's heart skipped a beat. Adam sat at one of the ten round, glass-and-metal tables inside. There were two other patients waiting at tables, but Mara only had eyes for Adam.

His whole face lit up as she hurried toward him. She couldn't get to him fast enough. As Mara reached his side, Adam's arms wrapped around her and everything felt right. All of Mara's fears, insecurities, and doubts melted away as they embraced each other. As they pulled away, Adam's eyes met Mara's, and there were tears there.

"I know it's only been a couple of weeks, but I missed you so much," Adam said as he held Mara's face in his hands. His sparkling eyes beheld her as if she were the most precious person in the world.

Mara's chest swelled with emotion. She never felt more connected to anyone in her entire life. Adam leaned down, and his lips pressed against hers. Every nerve in her body tingled as Adam's kiss intensified. The walls around them melted away. Now it was just the two of them, alone in the light of their embrace. Everything around them forgotten. No past, no future, simply living in the present moment of this one kiss.

"Break it up," a gruff voice interrupted them.

Mara was jolted out of the serene moment with a jarring impact.

The voice came from a passing guard. Though his tone had

been stern, he gave them a slight nod of support.

Adam smiled back, but his eyes returned to Mara's. His hands wrapped around hers, and he motioned for her to sit with a nod of his head. They sat across from each other, hands still clasped together.

"I missed you too, by the way." Mara grinned.

Adam's smile was disarming. He seemed so much happier and healthier than she'd ever seen him.

"I can't believe I'm going to be let go." Adam's expression turned somber suddenly. "I still don't think I deserve it. I'm guilty, Mara. I killed those men. I should be in jail for the rest of my life."

"Stop it. You're doing it again. Allowing yourself to be happy, then immediately putting yourself in never-forgive-myself mode." Mara knew the feeling. She wrestled with the same thing.

"You feel it too. I can tell. I would completely understand if you never wanted to see me again. I can't ask you to be with me. Not with what I've done." Adam looked downright petrified. He said the words, that he'd understand, but his face revealed true terror that Mara would take him up on the offer.

"We've been together in our dreams almost every night since they took you in. You know me. You know I'm with you for life whether you get sick of me or not." Mara tried to lighten the mood. Whether Adam was good for her or bad for her, Mara didn't care. She loved him with everything she had, and she would never let him go.

And from the sparkle in his eyes, Adam felt the same way.

"What should I expect from your friends and family when I'm out? Give me a lowdown." Adam's deep breath indicated that he was prepared to hear bad news, so Mara decided to be honest and not sugarcoat it for him. He'd find out anyway. Mara doubted her parents were going to give up their pursuit to break them up any time soon. It was a topic Mara and Adam had never discussed in their dreams. It wasn't like they avoided it, but neither of them had known how quickly Adam would be released, so neither wanted to dredge it up.

Taking a deep breath, Mara said, "My parents tried to get a restraining order against you for me, so they're not in support of us in any way. Josie and Zia are on board, though I haven't heard from Josie in a while. It's her senior year, so I want her to enjoy it and not worry about me. Zia took a little bit of time, but she got to know you better than my parents did, so she supports us too."

Adam tried to hide his crestfallen expression, but Mara still caught it. He forced a smile. "Like I said, I'm guilty. Your parents are looking out for you. I'm sure I wasn't the kind of guy they dreamed about for you. Maybe you should listen to them. I could leave you alone."

"Adam, just stop. I'm telling you because I don't want you to be caught off guard if my parents show up and try to bully you or something. Not that they will, but well . . . they might. They're really adamant about us not being together. But I think in time they'll come around. You'll be able to show them who you are. They'll be able to see that you're not a monster. Robert was the monster," Mara said with as much conviction as she could muster.

Adam's hand squeezed hers a little bit tighter for emphasis. "But I *am* a monster, Mara. I *did* those things. I *killed* those men. Not out of self-defense, but murder. I played the executioner."

"And you've served your time," Mara answered.

"Two years is not a lot of time." Adam's voice shook slightly. He was scared.

"Are you afraid you'll do it again?" Mara asked the question she had thought she'd be too scared to ask.

Adam's eyes met hers, and they were steady. "No. Never. Even the thought . . ." He shook his head. "Never."

An invisible weight lifted off Mara's chest. Not that she thought Adam would kill anyone again, but she guessed a part of her was a little scared. Her parents had drilled into her head that Adam couldn't change. That once a killer had the taste for blood, they could never shut that part of their brain off. It also didn't help that Mara had binge-watched every season of *Dexter* after Adam was put away. She knew it was fictional, but one point they made clear on that show: once a killer, always a killer.

But Mara knew Adam's mind, his heart, his soul. As cheesy as it sounded, Mara trusted Adam as much as she trusted herself. She was afraid, though, of the pressure of everyone around him, expecting him to do something horrible again, a pressure that would then push him to . . . do something horrible again.

Hearing Adam's conviction and knowing who he was as a human being subdued any doubts in Mara's mind. She simply wished her parents could see and feel what she did. One thing Adam needed most was love, especially from a parent figure, and the only two he had exposure to wanted to lock him up for life.

Mara squeezed his hands back. "I love you, and I believe in you."

Adam reached over the table and kissed her gently. Mara desperately wanted to embrace him again, and she wished they were alone, but both of them pulled away before the guard could break them up again.

"I love you, too," Adam said with such intensity it made Mara's knees buckle—and she was sitting down. He glanced up at the digital clock above the doorway. "We don't have much time left."

Mara nodded somberly. "At least we only have to wait until tomorrow. Then you're free from this place."

Adam's hands stayed locked to Mara's, and she found that she'd be perfectly happy if they stayed that way forever.

Then a thought occurred to her. "Why didn't you visit me in my dreams last night?"

Adam turned thoughtful. "I was having a vision. It was intense. I couldn't seem to leave."

"I had a vision last night too," Mara confessed.

Adam shifted to Mara. "What was yours? Maybe it was the same girl. Red hair? Pretty? Her name was Samantha?"

Mara's breath caught in her throat. "Samantha Perkins?"

Adam's eyes lit up. "Yes! I knew you dreamt about her too!"

"You said she has red hair and is pretty?" Mara remembered the girl that appeared in Kimiko's face for just an instant.

"Well, you know. You saw her, popular-girl material, right? I don't know if you got a good look, but she was in bad shape from what I could see. That guy is torturing her. Did you get a good look at his face? I couldn't see him at all." Adam's shoulders slumped.

The guard announced to the room, "Two-minute call."

Mara knew she didn't have much time, but she also knew something very strange happened to the two of them last night. "Adam, I didn't dream about Samantha. I dreamt about a girl named Lucy who's being bullied by a girl named Samantha Perkins. This Lucy girl showed up to some kind of homecoming dance meeting after Samantha had threatened her not to go. Then a young version of Agent Piper showed up and told me that judgment was coming and I wouldn't be ready." Mara shook her head. "I didn't even know anything happened to Samantha. From my end of the vision, she was a bully that didn't show up to a school dance meeting."

Adam took a deep breath at hearing the news. "Well, she was taken by some guy. He had a mask on. He had her in his basement and tied her up by the wrists, dangling her from the ceiling. Last I saw her, he was cutting the backs of her ankles and she was screaming."

Mara shuddered. "Why would I be dreaming of the girl that's safe? The one Samantha's bullying at school? And why would I see Samantha's face in Kimiko's today?"

"Wait, what? Rewind. You saw Kimiko? And her *face* was this Samantha girl's?" Adam reared his head back.

The guard's voice echoed through the room like the bringer of doom, "Time's up. Everyone out."

Adam and Mara stood, and they kissed one last time.

Mara replied quickly, "I'll find you tonight in your dreams and tell you everything. Don't worry, it's not bad, Kimiko was actually . . . nice." Mara found the word *nice* hard to say when referring to Kimiko, but it was the actual truth.

From the expression on Adam's face, he found it a bit hard to believe as well, but he nodded. "I'll make sure I'm open to you, even if I'm in a vision." Then he paused and smiled. "It's my last night here."

Mara kissed him one last time. "I love you."

"I love you." Adam touched her face briefly, then followed an attendant back with the other patients toward their living quarters.

Mara followed the other visitors back in the opposite direction, through the hallways of the facility until she was outside under the cold, overcast sky. The bus was waiting for her and the others. Without talking to anyone, Mara sat near the front of the bus, thinking about everything that had happened.

Her mystery gears were cranking up again, she could feel it. Two psychics: one dreams about a girl who has been taken, the other about a girl who is being bullied by the girl that has been taken. It was strange to be dreaming about two girls who were clearly connected, but only one was in danger. Mara was determined to research Samantha Perkins as soon as she got home to her dorm. At least they had a full name. That was more than Mara normally received from dreamland in cases like these. She guessed she should be relieved that she didn't dream of Samantha, but the part of her that wanted to help was a little disappointed.

Having Agent Piper's younger self make an appearance—and her warning to Mara—didn't clear up matters much either. Was her subconscious telling her to call the FBI agent so she could help find this Samantha girl?

The pine trees whizzed by as the bus drove down the road.

Both she and Adam were connected to this case.

It was the first time in a long time that Mara felt as if she had a purpose.

Getting into research mode, Mara prepared herself for what was coming next. She was going to save Samantha Perkins whether she deserved it or not.

And Adam was going to help her. In person. A rush of happiness flooded through her body.

Tomorrow.

Adam was coming home.

Dream Entry #3

I haven't done much research, but I found enough to make my head spin. I really hate living alone, especially when researching kidnapped teenage girls. I almost invited Kimiko over to not feel freaked out. Almost! I must be getting desperate. I tried to FaceTime Zia, but with the three-hour time difference, she was already asleep. So here I am, alone, in my dorm room, writing in this journal like it will protect me somehow.

I still can't believe Adam will be here in my dorm room tomorrow night. I'm so happy the dean agreed to let him stay, especially since he's not a student here. I have no idea what Adam's psychiatrist said in that two-hour conversation with the dean, but I'm just thrilled he ended up being okay with it. Honestly, I'm just happy everyone knows. This way, Adam can't get into any trouble for living in my room with me. Besides, according to the law, he served his time and now he's a citizen again. And in the terms of Adam's release, he's required see a psychiatrist for the rest of his life, but Adam wants to do that anyway.

I have to stop worrying about it. I need to concentrate on Samantha Perkins.

The only thing I could find on Samantha was that she was indeed missing, and no one had any clues as to where she was. I wasn't too surprised that Samantha and Lucy only lived thirty miles away, in Everett. It usually works that way with me. The closer in proximity I am to a victim, the stronger the visions. That was how I was able to be in Adam's head with such clarity when he was . . . well . . . when he was killing. I hate that I wrote that. But Adam isn't trying to pretend he didn't kill those three people, so I shouldn't either.

Why can't I be like those characters in vampire romances where the girl doesn't care that her vampire boyfriend has killed hundreds of people and she loves him anyway? No one ever questions the girl's logic for being with the vampire! It's freaking expected by almost every teenage girl!

Anyway, onto my investigation:

I did find a photo of Samantha in an article that talked about her kidnapping, and it is definitely the same face that was on Kimiko's. Right now, my running theory is that the reason Samantha's face was on Kimiko is because Kimiko used to be a bully herself. Or maybe she still is? Maybe it's a warning that Kimiko hasn't changed at all? Or maybe it's a warning that Kimiko is next? I have no idea.

One thing at a time.

Even though I'm going to see Adam in person tomorrow, we still plan on seeing each other in our dreams tonight. I need to give him the confirmation of Samantha Perkins being kidnapped. It's ten p.m. now, and I'm wired from too much coffee and a little bit of fear, but

I really want to tell Adam everything. I think I'll put my chair under the doorknob to make myself feel a little safer. I know I'm being paranoid, but this bad guy that took Samantha is a kidnapper, and that totally freaks me out.

Okay. Signing off.

***

Mara felt like her eyes were permanently pried open. She didn't know if it was possible for her to sleep at this point. She chastised herself for drinking the venti mocha with three extra shots. It sounded so good at the time, and she had thought she'd be up late researching, until all she could really look up was Samantha Perkins and Lucy Tildon. Searching their Instagram accounts and Twitter feeds was the best way to piece together their ongoing rivalry. Though Mara saw it for what it was: Samantha was a mean girl and Lucy was her number one target.

Some of the things Samantha tweeted about Lucy were way worse than anything Kimiko had ever said to Mara. Mara was grateful she had Zia as a friend since Kimiko had wanted Zia to be a part of her pack. That alone had restrained the wrath of Kimiko. She never wanted to go too public with her hatred of Mara for fear of Zia finding out. It was almost as if Mara had an imaginary bully that she could never prove existed. That was why Zia would always attempt to defend Kimiko. Eventually, Mara had given up trying to convince Zia. She ignored Kimiko's taunts as best she could.

But Lucy? She didn't have a Zia buffer. Samantha was relentless on all the social media outlets. Mara could only imagine how much worse Samantha was in person! From taking a humiliating picture of Lucy in the locker room naked and posting it all over

Instagram and Twitter to constantly telling Lucy she should do the world a favor and kill herself. It was amazing how Lucy had the self-confidence she did in Mara's vision. The fact that Samantha had expressly told Lucy not to go to the homecoming dance meeting, but she went anyway, showed Mara that Lucy had a certain "steel" in her that was impressive.

It also made Mara not want to help Samantha Perkins at all.

She hated that she felt that way, but reading Samantha's tweet after tweet berating Lucy made Mara seethe with anger. It was hard not to think that Samantha was getting exactly what she deserved.

It was also hard not to suspect, for just a second, that Lucy had something to do with it. Familiar feelings of vigilante justice began to creep into Mara's thoughts. It was the same emotion that allowed her to understand and even empathize with Adam over his crimes. If Lucy had anything to do with Samantha's kidnapping, Mara was having a really hard time finding much fault in that. But there was nothing pointing to that conclusion. At least not on the internet.

So that left dreamtime with Adam.

And Mara was wired.

She breathed a huge sigh of frustration and grabbed a box of chamomile tea. Turning on her portable teapot, Mara boiled water and poured it into the waiting cup with the tea bag inside. Maybe if she steeped it for an hour it would be strong enough to counteract the caffeine. Not likely, but she had to try something.

Mara let the tea steep and went back to her laptop. Opening up the Word document labeled "case notes," Mara began to write down all the random thoughts she had about Samantha and

Lucy's situation.

Who were Samantha's enemies besides Lucy? A lot, Mara assumed, but who would want to kidnap and torture her? A straight-up serial killer after a pretty girl? Samantha fit that victim profile too. Mara couldn't count how many episodes of *Criminal Minds* had the old she's-hot-let's-kill-her plotline. Someone who hated bullies? Someone who was bullied?

Like Lucy.

It kept going back to Lucy.

Why else would Mara dream of Lucy and Adam dream of Samantha? On psychic principle alone, Lucy seemed guilty. But Adam had said it was a man who had Samantha, and Mara didn't pick up any I-just-kidnapped-my-mortal-enemy vibes from Lucy either.

A pang of familiarity swept through Mara. When her neighbor Ed Garner was killed and Mara had known the details because she saw them all in her dreams, Detective Jennifer Nicholson had thought Mara was guilty. Frankly, if Mara had been separated from the case, she would have thought the same thing. Mara didn't feel in her gut that Lucy was guilty, but she knew the authorities might think otherwise. It made sense. If in ten minutes Mara was able to find all the horrible posts Samantha had inflicted on Lucy, the police wouldn't be far behind.

Lucy Tildon will be their number one suspect. Of that, Mara was certain.

So maybe Mara was dreaming about Lucy because she was supposed to help her. Help prove her innocence.

And the young Agent Piper showing up, randomly warning Mara that "judgment" was coming and that she would "not be ready for it" made total sense if Mara was expected to help defend Lucy. Though, coming to that conclusion in itself might not make her "ready," but it at least made her better prepared for it.

Mara knew she'd learn more if she could go to sleep!

Giving up on waiting, Mara practically chugged down her chamomile tea, then drank a giant glass of water. Maybe she could pee her way out of the mass amounts of caffeine running through her body. To be fair, it had been a good four hours since she consumed the coffee. She definitely wasn't as amped up as she was right after drinking it.

Feeling like a science experiment on how to flush out caffeine, Mara made one last trip to the bathroom, hoping she was relaxed enough to go to bed. Lying down on her mattress, she closed her eyes and began her breathing techniques to try to relax. It was difficult at first, what with an antsy feeling in her legs that made her want to jump up and run around the quad a few times, but after a half hour or so, she physically began to relax.

Keeping her eyes closed, Mara tried to clear her overactive mind. It was difficult, so many thoughts weaving in and out of her brain. Turning scenario after scenario over and over, then thinking of Adam and the fact that he was going to be free tomorrow, then Kimiko and how strange it was that she was not only acting like a friend but was a full-on psychic as well. Mara had never had a psychic friend before. Now she had Adam and potentially Kimiko.

Stop.

Mara forcefully pushed all the random, rotating thoughts out of her head. She pictured them as clouds floating away. Sometimes this worked amazingly well, but tonight it made her think of the weather and how cold it had been the last couple of days. She wondered if her parents . . .

Stop.

Mara breathed in deep.

She had to go for the tried-and-true method that worked almost every time. As she breathed in, she focused only on the word *relax*—breathing out, she focused only on the word *sleep*. Relax and sleep. Relax and sleep. Relax and sleep . . .

***

"Hey." Adam smiled at her.

Mara was asleep. Finally! They were in their favorite dream spot, Disneyland. Neither of them had been there in real life, so they kind of had to make one up on their own based on pictures and videos they'd seen. Mara was sure their Disneyland was way better than the real thing simply because they didn't have to wait in any lines and had the whole place to themselves. The rides were a blast too since they created those to their liking as well.

In the waking world, Mara almost didn't want to go to the real place for fear of disappointment, but Adam didn't feel that way. He was gung-ho on going with her someday. It had been the dream destination for Adam and his mom when they were planning to escape together from his abusive father all those years ago. Then she disappeared, and it had been devastating for Adam to believe his mother abandoned him to live in Los Angeles alone. Now, after having time to sit with the knowledge that Robert had murdered his mom and that she hadn't left him at all, Adam wanted to connect with her in some way. That was how "Dream Disneyland" they currently stood in had started, as a kind of therapeutic way for Adam to remember his mom with love instead of the bitterness he'd carried inside all that time Robert had been deceiving him.

Pulling Adam toward her, Mara kissed him deeply. It was amazing that even though she was dreaming, everything felt as real as if she were awake and Adam stood in her dorm room. This time they didn't have to worry about any guards breaking them up. In their dreams they were truly free. Only the two of them. Sometimes Mara wished this was the real world, but it would be soon enough.

Adam pulled away, his face beaming. "I can't wait to do this in person." He turned thoughtful. "I'm afraid that something will happen right as I'm leaving, and they'll make me go back in."

Mara had the same fear, but she didn't want Adam to see it, so she smiled as convincingly as she could and said, "I'm *going* to see you tomorrow. You're *going* to stay with me in my dorm, and that's that. No more doubts. No more worries. Just accept that this is going to happen. The fact that the DA gave permission for you to stay in my dorm should be proof enough." Then she laughed. "We're both psychics, for crying out loud. I don't have any bad feelings. Do you?"

Adam slowly shook his head. "No, I guess not." He grinned again, and Mara found it infectious. He was happy, and that made her smile inside and out. Gently taking her hand, Adam led the two of them toward the Magic Castle. "So, tell me about Kimiko. How in the heck did you run into her?"

Mara still had trouble believing it herself as she told Adam the entire story: from Kimiko defending her in class, to seeing Samantha's face on Kimiko, to having a cup of coffee and talking about Kimiko's psychic gifts.

Adam looked as amazed as Mara felt. "Wow. That's insane."

Mara shrugged. "The more I kept thinking about it, the more I thought it must have been how you felt about Colt at first. He went from being your bully to being your friend."

Adam nodded. "True, but Colt and I were being manipulated by Robert. He bonded us over our fathers' abuse. Kimiko . . . she seems to be trying to be a better person all on her own. If she's really telling the truth, then that's a pretty great thing."

"Yeah, I was thinking that too. It's the not-trusting-her part that has me leery," Mara agreed.

"We'll keep an eye on her. See what happens." Adam stopped for a second, then smiled. "*We.*" He shook his head. "I still can't believe it."

Adam reached down and kissed Mara again until her toes went numb.

TUG!

Mara's body yanked backward.

Adam was a few feet away with an expression of surprise. "What was that?"

"I don't know," Mara answered, a little freaked.

TUG!

Mara was pulled back a few more feet.

Adam hurried to her side, grabbing her hand. "Where you go, I go. I think you're being pulled into a vision."

"This has never happened to me before," Mara admitted. "Am I doing this?"

"I don't know, but I'd relax into it. Let's see where it takes us." Adam grinned widely with excitement and tightened his hold on her hand.

Mara knew better. Being torn out of a dream, especially one of her and Adam's making, would take serious mojo. Mara had thought she was growing stronger in her control over her dreams—but now she felt helpless, like a puppet, with someone pulling her dream strings and there was nothing she could do to stop it.

YANK!

This time they both went flying backward.

Dream Disneyland dissolved in front of them and turned to blackness. Mara could feel Adam's hand slipping away from hers.

Feeling this too, Adam wrapped his arms around Mara, holding her tight to his chest. "I won't let you go."

Mara felt safe in his arms but scared about where they were headed.

The blackness began to take shape around them as they hurtled through the nothingness. Though the colors became brighter, the shapes around them were still dark and silhouetted.

With a last jerk of their bodies, Mara's and Adam's feet hit solid ground.

Looking around, Adam said, "This is where Samantha was in my vision."

"Are we in a vision?" Mara asked, not sure.

It felt like a vision, but being pulled around like this made Mara suspect that someone was behind this. Someone with psychic gifts far more powerful than hers. It scared her more than seeing Samantha tied up.

Speaking of which, Mara pointed at Samantha huddled in a corner, chained to a wall. Samantha was a wreck. The ends of her hair were crusty with dried blood. Her arms and neck were covered in bruises. She had a long, thin cut down her right cheek, and her left eye was swollen shut.

Adam eyed the girl with sympathy. "At least she's not dangling from the ceiling anymore, but she looks a lot worse than she did. Do you think this guy will kill her? We need to help her." He began to examine the room, trying to find anything distinguishable. Adam turned to Mara. "Is there any way to figure out where we are?"

Mara helped him search, but they both came up with nothing. The room itself was obviously a basement. There was a rickety wooden staircase against the far wall, leading up to a metal door with three deadbolts sealing the room shut. There didn't seem to be any windows, at least not that Mara could see in the nighttime darkness. There wasn't much in terms of furniture, just some old empty boxes, a desk with three legs propped against the wall, a stack of fold-up chairs and . . . Samantha. She hardly moved, but she was breathing.

"Do you think we're *here*-here, or do you think we're seeing what happened earlier?" Adam asked Mara. "You're the only one I've ever been in the present with when dreaming. I'm not sure how to tell the difference."

Adam appeared genuinely curious, but even though Mara had been having visions of murders her entire life, it was still difficult for her.

Mara walked over to Samantha, Adam next to her. Samantha cried softly, as if she had run out of energy to cry at all. It was beyond difficult seeing the kind of abuse she was enduring. And all those feelings of thinking that Samantha somehow deserved to be here washed away in a tidal wave of guilt for entertaining the thought. "I don't know. It feels like we're here, but who brought us here? We didn't. I'm certain of that."

It scared Mara that someone could rip her out of her dreams and into a vision of a girl that was kidnapped and being tortured.

"You really think we were *brought* here?"

Mara nodded. "We didn't come here on our own. Unless you think you might have by accident?" she asked, really hoping that had been the case.

"I don't think I did. Remember, you got tugged first, I just hung on for the ride."

He was right. She had been pulled first. So if someone was powerful enough to do that, why wouldn't they be waiting here for her? They must have thought bringing Mara to this location would accomplish something, but what? Mara couldn't tell where they were. There was nothing in all the garbage around them that provided any kind of identifying information. Not even an old newspaper to give them a date or location. What if this kidnapper didn't live in Everett? What if he lived far away, but he took Samantha from her school?

Two good questions. But nothing in this basement would give her answers to either one of them.

"Can we get past the door?" Adam's eyes were focused on the metal door.

"You mean walk through it?" Mara nodded. "Might as well try, right?"

Adam held on to Mara's hand, and they walked up the wooden stairs until they reached the door. Mara placed her free hand out and tried to push it through the door, but it was a solid surface.

Reaching out himself, Adam tried as well, but his hand stopped at the door also. "Seems weird we can't go through when this is a dream."

"It's more than that." Mara couldn't shake the cold in her veins. Something was wrong. Something was off. "Can we leave here?" Sudden panic gripped her. What if they were stuck with Samantha in this basement forever and no one could wake them up on the outside. They could be in comas because some mind-master-psychic-villain had them trapped inside his vision!

Okay, that was paranoid even for Mara.

A popping noise sounded behind them.

Mara and Adam turned to see the younger version of Agent Piper standing next to Samantha.

Her image flashed in and out of existence, as she had before in Mara's vision.

"You see her, right?" Mara asked Adam.

"She keeps disappearing. Is that happening for you too?" Adam asked.

"Yeah, it's like she's a radio station that won't tune in all the way." Mara wished the girl would become solid permanently. Seeing her shift in and out of reality was beyond creepy.

"Who is she?" Adam wondered aloud.

"It's Agent Piper, isn't it, but younger?" Mara suddenly doubted herself.

Adam nodded. "She looks like her, but she doesn't. I don't think that's her. She's too young."

"You don't think that's why she keeps shifting in and out of existence? I thought it might be the younger version of Piper. Like my subconscious is telling me I need to tell her what we've seen?" Mara explained.

"We should definitely tell Piper what we've seen, but I really don't think that's her. I can feel it. That's a person, a real person, and there's something different about her, something odd." Adam lowered his voice to a whisper, and even though it was a dream, it gave Mara the sensation of hairs rising on her neck.

He was right.

There *was* something different about her, and it wasn't just the fact that she couldn't seem to stay in solid form. Mara had wanted to ignore it because . . .

Because this girl scared her.

Looking at the girl staring back at Mara, in that instant Mara knew she had brought them there.

Swallowing her fear, Mara led Adam down the stairs to confront the girl.

When they were face-to-face, Mara asked her, "Who are you? Why did you bring us here?"

The girl's body became solid, then radiated with bright flashes of static electricity.

And Mara could tell . . . the girl was angry.

The girl stared at Adam as if he were the scourge of the earth and screamed, "Killer!"

Her hand flew up and pointed at Adam, electric sparks flying off her fingers.

Adam lost his grip on Mara and his body flew backward, through the wall behind them, and he was gone.

"No killers!" the girl yelled at Mara.

Terror raced through Mara's veins. She knew Adam would be okay since this was a dream, but she wasn't so sure about herself.

Mara wanted to wake up, but it felt as if the girl held her with invisible strings, preventing Mara from leaving.

"Are you Raven Piper?" Mara tried to use a soft voice, hoping it would help calm the girl down.

At this point she was positive it wasn't Agent Piper, but the fact that they resembled each other so much was uncanny.

The girl steadied herself, at least to the point where the electricity bolts weren't happening anymore, but she still fizzled in and out of view as she glanced down at Samantha.

"I'm Terry," she said, then Terry's eyes grew wide with anger and she shouted, "Keep her safe!"

***

Mara jolted out of bed like she was getting ready for a marathon. She was halfway to the door before she woke up completely. Slowing down, Mara took a few moments to reorient herself to her surroundings: she was back in her dorm room, basically being thrown out of a vision by another person.

Who was this "Terry" girl?

Mara needed to talk to Agent Piper. It couldn't be a coincidence that they were practically twins. Maybe Piper had a sister or cousin that was insanely psychic. But why would she care so much about this particular kidnapping? Did she know Samantha? Was she Samantha's friend?

Mara could still feel the intensity that had buzzed through her when Terry yelled at her. How was Adam faring on his last night in the mental ward? Mara hoped he hadn't woken up like her, running to the door, or worse, screaming. He had been literally called a killer and thrown out of the vision. That must have crushed him.

Glancing at the digital clock by her bedside, Mara noticed it was already six a.m. Taking a deep breath, Mara decided it was time to start her day. There was no way she would be able to get back to sleep anyway. Adam was to be released at noon, and she wanted to be there when he walked out of those doors.

How early could she call Agent Piper?

One thing Mara was certain of: she had to call the FBI agent and ask her if she knew Terry. It was a conversation she dreaded, though she couldn't say why. It was just a feeling.

She also planned to tell Piper about Samantha and Lucy. Maybe the FBI agent could help.

Mara quickly dressed and walked down on campus to the coffee cart that opened at five a.m. She bought a mocha and a breakfast sandwich, consuming them both outside in the brisk morning air. The cold felt good against her skin. Normally, she liked it warm every moment of every second of every day thank you very much, but after last night's events, Mara welcomed the biting wind. It made her feel more awake. The caffeine helped too.

Around seven a.m., it was probably an appropriate time to try calling Agent Piper. She hoped she wasn't going to wake her up. Although Raven wouldn't be that surprised to hear from Mara, she could remember a few times she had called at more unseemly hours when she had a particularly nasty vision. But only the dreams in which she could identify the killer. Mara and the local FBI's sketch artist knew each other quite well. And Mara was proud to say that her dreams had led to two arrests.

Pulling out her cell phone, Mara called Agent Piper.

After the first ring, Raven picked up. "Mara? Is everything

okay?"

A pang of warmth spread through Mara at hearing concern in Raven Piper's voice. It only proved how much the FBI agent cared about her. "I'm fine, but I've had a couple of visions. Well, actually, I had a vision about one girl and Adam had a vision about another and . . . let me just explain . . ."

Mara told Agent Piper everything, from the homecoming dance meeting, to seeing Samantha's face in Kimiko's, to Adam's dream about Samantha—to, finally, their joint dream with Samantha and the girl that forcibly brought them there, Terry. When she told her about Terry, Mara waited to hear how Agent Piper would react, but Raven was silent.

Which told Mara that Raven knew who Terry was.

Mara didn't want to pry, but she was getting yanked into visions by this girl, so she kind of needed to know who she was dealing with. "Do you know who Terry is? Because . . . she looks like you. I thought it was you at first, like a younger version of you . . ." Mara babbled from being uncomfortable.

Finally, Raven cut her off. "Terry is my sister." She paused for a good five seconds, which stretched like an eternity to Mara before Raven continued, "*Was* my sister. Mara, Terry died fifteen years ago."

Dream Entry #4

Back in my dorm and still reeling about what Raven said. Her sister was dead. As in fifteen years dead. It's freaking me out more than a little bit. If Terry is dead, then her ghost is super strong and super pushy when it comes to me. The only thing Raven said about Terry was the fact that she died and that she was psychic, but that was it. I have no idea how she died or why Raven never brought her up until now. Looking back, though, I guess it was kind of obvious that Raven had a personal connection to psychics. She believed me without hesitation and was the reason Detective Nicholson had let me go after bringing me into the police station for Ed Garner's murder.

But this hijacking of my brain? I don't like being pulled and tugged any which way when I'm sleeping. I barely feel like I have any control over my life as it is, especially with my nightmares. But to have a dead person, ghost, whatever, actually be able to pull me into a vision? Or show up in my dreams anytime she wanted was terrifying.

Yes, I realize that I let Adam do it all the time, but he's ALIVE! *And my boyfriend. And he would never pull me out of a dream or out of my head or anything without my permission. From all the movies and television, I should be grateful that some "spirit guide" ghost is trying to tell me something to help this Samantha girl, but the reality feels way different. It's violating. And it's worse when it's a spirit. She could be anywhere. She could be right in front of me and I wouldn't know it! Okay, maybe* I'd *know it, but still. I don't like it.*

It helps slightly that she's Raven's sister. I trust Raven, so that should mean I can trust her sister. It's all I have to hang on to for the moment.

As for Samantha and Lucy, Raven said there wasn't much she could do. She deals mainly with serial killers and this would be classified as a kidnapping. After Raven got off the phone with me, though, she made a few calls. When she called me back, she said that the authorities in Everett had thought Samantha ran away. A couple of her friends had backed that story up, saying that Samantha had said she wanted to move to LA and that she was going to do it with or without her parents' permission. Raven assured me she was going to try to convince the authorities there that it was a kidnapping.

Maybe this kidnapper knew Samantha had plans to run away? Maybe he used it to make sure no one would suspect he took Samantha? I still don't know what Terry has to do with these two girls. Technically, Samantha and Lucy were two years old when Terry died, and Terry and Raven grew up in Mukilteo, not Everett. Raven didn't tell me, but I need to find out how Terry died. Maybe that'll give me some kind of clue as to why her ghost is connected to Samantha and Lucy.

Okay, it's ten a.m. I'm going to go pick up Adam. I'm also going to try not to puke, I'm so nervous.

***

Mara jammed her journal into her bag and left her room in a hurry. She wasn't late, but she wanted to move fast. Like somehow it would make time speed up and she'd be with Adam already.

Flying through the front door of her building, Mara nearly slammed into . . .

. . . her mother: Claire.

"Mara, slow down." Her mother gently touched her arm.

Mara froze, unsure what to say or do. "I gotta go pick up Adam. He's being released today."

Claire's jaw tightened in anger. "Yes. I know. Your father and my petition to the district attorney was denied."

"You petitioned . . . ?" Mara shook her head, rolling her eyes. "Of course you did." But a part of her felt a huge sense of relief. She already knew the DA supported Adam's release by giving permission for Adam to stay with her, but hearing that her parents' petition was officially denied? It meant Adam's release was a certainty.

But thinking of her mother and father actively trying to take away Adam's freedom made her blood boil. "So you'd let Adam rot in a mental institution for the rest of his life thinking that I'd give up on him eventually?"

"I'd rather him rot in jail, but beggars can't be choosers," Claire retorted with just as much anger.

Mara didn't want to hear any more. She shrugged her mother's hand off her arm and started to walk away.

Claire wasn't having it though. She grabbed Mara's arm,

pulling her daughter to face her. "I'll do anything I can to protect you. And yes, I know Adam was abused and manipulated and all the other things you keep shouting at us—but he's still a killer, Mara. He still murdered three human beings. Doesn't that register with you?" Claire stared at Mara like she was some kind of confusing puzzle she couldn't figure out.

"Of course it *registers* with me! I know he killed those men, but Mom, so does Adam. No one is more remorseful than he is. He knows what he did was horrible and wrong. But I'd like to see what you'd do if someone beat the crap out of me, or raped me, or beat me to death! Because that's what those guys did. I'm not saying it's right what Adam did, but there's no question in my mind that those men deserved to die!" Mara shouted.

Seeing the things Mara had seen over the years in her dreams . . .

Though she could never murder anyone herself, she understood it.

And from the look in Claire's eyes, she could see that her mother understood too. She just didn't want her daughter dating the guy who went through with it.

Mara sighed deeply. "Mom, you're going to have to come to terms with me being with Adam."

The struggle in Claire's eyes was obvious, but instead of attacking, she let go of Mara's arm. "I don't know if I can."

"Maybe you should try. Because I don't think you or Dad has even considered trying yet." Mara wished her parents would come around but knew it would take a while if they ever did. The fact that her dad wasn't here indicated that either a) he didn't know Claire was there, or b) he was too upset to come himself. Mara hoped it was "a." At least that way she didn't have to imagine him being disappointed or angry with her.

Whatever battle was going on in Claire's head made her wait a few beats before answering. "If I'm being honest, I don't know if I want to try, Mara. I'd rather Adam was out of your life for good. I keep imagining him . . . what if you made him angry . . . Mara, he could kill you!" There was a note of hysteria in her voice.

Mara self-consciously searched the area for any bystanders, but luckily she didn't see anyone. The last thing she needed was an argument about Adam being recorded and posted to YouTube, especially right before he was about to be released.

But Claire's words hit her hard.

Her parents thought Adam would eventually kill their daughter.

Mara knew there was nothing she could do or say to extinguish their paranoia or fears, but she had to try. "Does Dad feel the same way?" At Claire's nod, Mara continued carefully, "Mom, with what you know about my gifts, do you really think I would be with someone who could hurt me?"

"Yes!" Claire yelled. This time a few heads in the distance turned. Mara pulled her mom to the side of the building where she could keep the two of them out of others' view.

"I watched him kill those people. I was dream-sharing with him. I know him better than any other person on this planet, more than I know you, Mom. I know you believe in my dreams because you've seen the proof of them in the news, but there's more to it than just dreaming about killers and victims." Mara needed her mother to understand the kind of connection she had with Adam. Maybe then she could begin to accept that Adam was in Mara's life to stay. "Adam and I can share dreams, Mom. That's real whether you want to believe it or not. Adam will never hurt anyone ever again. All his doctors agree, the state agrees, and the district attorney agrees, so why can't you?"

"Because you're my daughter! It's different, Mara. And I don't think we can ever see eye to eye on this one." Claire's expression was one of fury and regret.

Mara could work with the regret in time. Right now, however, she was all out of time and she needed to leave. "I'm going to go. I love you, Mom, and I love Dad, but you guys are going to have to come to terms with Adam being in my life. God knows you've tried every legal action you could think of to try and stop me. I'm asking you to please stop."

Claire crossed her arms defensively. "I don't know if I can do that."

"Mom, I'm telling you: if you or Dad ever do anything to sabotage Adam and to get him back in prison, I will never forgive you." And she wouldn't.

"And if he sabotages himself? Will you see who he is then?" Claire's eyebrow rose in defiance.

"I know who Adam is. He's a boy who was tortured by his father, then was told his mother abandoned him by a man who he thought of as his brother. The same man who killed Adam's mother just to keep Adam close to him." Mara figured repetition was the only way to get to her mother. Telling Claire over and over what Adam went through had to sink in at some point.

Claire shook her head. "This isn't over, Mara. I love you, and if it means keeping you safe, I don't care if you never forgive me. You can hate me forever as long as you live a long, safe life."

The seeds of dread grew in Mara's stomach like wildflowers. Her mother was on a mission. So far there was nothing Claire or Ben could do to stop Adam from gaining his freedom, but Mara could see that they were going to be watching him like hawks, waiting for him to fail.

Mara didn't want to argue anymore. Seeing her mother's determination to take down Adam only made her angry. Without saying goodbye, Mara turned her back on Claire and walked toward the parking lot.

Claire didn't follow, didn't call after her. If Claire knew she was losing her daughter, she didn't seem to care. Her obsession with keeping Adam locked up was overriding her ability to give him a chance.

Finding her VW Bug, Mara slid in and drove away from campus.

Stunned emotionally, all Mara could do was drive. Fortunately, she knew the way to the Evergreen Moon's parking structure by heart, so she didn't have to think about where to turn.

The spectrum of everything that Mara had to deal with today overwhelmed her, and it was only ten thirty a.m.! From the highest of highs: anticipating Adam's freedom; to the lowest of lows: her mother confronting her outside her dorm. She didn't know how to handle her parents. It felt like an out-of-control situation that would inevitably lead to some kind of heart-wrenching confrontation. Or, worse, they'd find some way of putting Adam back in jail.

He wasn't even out yet, and Mara was already worried about him going back in.

The last thing she needed was this kind of stress. She never figured that her parents would be the ones to cause it. Parents were supposed to be the people who made you feel safe and secure. Right now, Claire and Ben Johnson were the core of Mara's anxiety. One of the cores anyway. Mara found that lately she had a lot of "cores" of anxiety.

Mara wanted to scream with rage, then huddle into a ball and cry.

And this was the last thing Mara needed to happen right before picking up Adam. It infuriated her that her mother knew this and came to confront her anyway. She did it on purpose. It was manipulative and mean. Mara was certain that her mother wanted to sap out any excitement or happiness Mara had for Adam's release. It was obvious Claire wanted to remind Mara any time she could of the crimes Adam committed.

In a way Mara understood her mother's tactics, but the part of her that was just Mara Johnson, daughter of Claire and Ben Johnson, wanted her parents back. The real ones. The ones that trusted her and trusted her judgment. Because these two acted like Mara was an idiot incapable of seeing right from wrong, incapable of seeing Adam for who they thought he really was . . .

Mara was about twenty minutes away from Evergreen Moon. Trying to push thoughts of her parents aside, Mara didn't look forward to the bus ride up to the facility, seeing as how it would probably be packed with reporters. There was nothing she could do about it though. No one was allowed to park at the facility itself except employees. It was the ride down she was most worried about. If the reporters were excited to see her on the bus, she could only imagine how they were going to react with both her and Adam there as well. The whole thing made Mara sweat with nerves.

The rest of the ride, Mara was officially in what she called coma-mode. It was when she was so far into her anxiety that everything ran on autopilot. Driving the rest of the way to Evergreen Moon took less time than Mara had estimated. Before she knew it, she was pulling into the five-level garage and parking her Bug.

For a moment, Mara thought she might be in the clear since there weren't many people parked in the lot—but then she exited the garage and her heart jumped in her throat. She was officially yanked out of coma-mode. Now she had full-on anxiety and was sure she was about to have a panic attack.

Standing in a tight crowd, over a hundred news crew members waited for the bus to take them up to Evergreen Moon.

Mara suddenly wished she had brought some kind of disguise: a scarf, hat, anything that would hide her very recognizable face. But first her dream of Samantha and then her mom's unexpected visit had flustered her too much to think about it. Now she was stuck having to dive into to the piranha tank of The Press.

Taking a deep breath, Mara decided to be bold and ignore them as best she could. Walking straight up to the bus stop, she waited for the inevitable onslaught of questions.

But . . .

There were none.

Everyone was so focused on getting up to see Adam, no one paid attention to the fact that his girlfriend from the YouTube video stood right next to them. Mara would have laughed, but she didn't want to draw any unnecessary eyes to her. The bus drove up to the spot, and Ron, the security guard, walked down the stairs of the bus but stayed on the last step to address the crowd.

The press members seemed agitated that they couldn't load up into the bus, but Ron appeared to be scanning the crowd.

His eyes met Mara's; he smiled a friendly hello, motioning her forward.

Mara's face turned three shades of pink as all eyes turned toward her. Suddenly light bulbs of recognition went popping off in all the reporters' heads. Before the roar of questions was able to attack her senses, Mara made it safely to the stairs and to Ron. He whistled loudly to quiet the now amped-up crowd.

"Another bus will be coming for you shortly. Ms. Johnson will be taking this one alone, per the district attorney's orders." Ron gave Mara a supportive wink, and for the first time that day, she relaxed. Another gift from the district attorney. The DA had most likely been a bit perturbed by her parents' demand that Adam's release should be reconsidered. All good things.

It was only Mara, Ron and the bus driver that made their way up to Evergreen Moon.

This was it.

This was the last time Mara would ever have to drive up this hill to see Adam. One more ride down the hill and she'd never have to sit in this bus again. That alone made her elated!

With a final screech, the bus came to a stop.

Ron gave her one last smile and nodded to the front doorway. "Looks like someone's waiting for you."

Peering through the window, Adam stood with his doctor and two guards outside the front door.

The door opened to the bus, and right before Mara left, Ron

said, "This bus is taking the two of you back to the parking area. Let's hope those reporters take the bait and get on that second bus: that way they'll all be up here when you two get down to the bottom. I'll try to hold the vultures off you guys as best I can for the ones that stayed down there, but at least you won't have to deal with any of them on the bus or up here."

Not being able to help herself, Mara hugged Ron in gratitude. "Thank you so much."

Ron smiled and patted her awkwardly on the back, not expecting the sudden affection she gave him. "All right, all right, go get your boy and let's get you home."

Mara had never heard better words.

Dream Entry #5

Adam is sleeping soundly in my bed next to me. My bed is a full-size, so it's not exactly roomy, but in this case I'm grateful for that. The closer I am to Adam, the better. Our walk (or I should say run) to my car from the bus was insane. I guess the reporters figured out Ron's ruse of the second bus, because I don't think any of them got on it. I felt like we were movie stars being chased by the paparazzi. We didn't answer any questions, not that we could hear any. It all sounded like one loud buzz of shouting human voices. I thought I was going hit a couple of them as I pulled out of the parking lot. They literally did not move at all.

The ride back to my dorm was amazing because it was so normal, like we'd never been apart. We talked about everything.

Adam said he woke up right after Terry threw him out of the vision, but he wasn't hurt or anything, not physically anyway. The fact that she screamed "killer" at him shook him pretty badly.

And now that he knew she was a ghost? I could tell it made him feel worse for some reason.

But after he had rolled his window down to feel the fresh air on his face, he seemed happy, free, which made my chest swell with emotion and love for him. I really never thought we'd ever be together again in person when he was sent to the mental ward. I figured the rest of our lives would be spent in dreams. Now that we're here together, I can't remember ever being apart.

I'm happy he's sleeping. Despite his surge of adrenaline from gaining his freedom, I could tell he had been exhausted. It didn't help that we started fooling around as soon as I opened my door. I barely was able to shut it before his lips were on mine and he was steering me to my bed. I had let myself go in the moment, in the feelings and sensations of being with the person I love.

As I'm writing this, I'm watching his breath move slowly up and down. He seems so peaceful. I wish my parents could see Adam the way I do. It will just take time. Maybe I can get Josie to help me convince them, or at least to back off from trying to get Adam put away again.

I'm going to check the computer to make sure there's nothing on the internet about us.

***

Mara placed her journal on the bedside table and carefully left the bed without waking up Adam. Sitting down in front of her computer, she plugged in her headphones and fitted them over her ears.

Searching her and Adam's names in Google, two hundred videos popped up. Most of them were copies of the YouTube video of Mara kicking Colt, but there were a couple dozen about

Adam's release.

Some of the headlines made her cringe: "Killer Released," "Serial Killer on the Loose," "Will Mara Johnson Be Adam Layton's Next Victim?"

Apparently, some news outlets had the same imagination as her parents.

Mara watched a few of the videos, but the footage was lame by any standard. It was Mara's and Adam's backs as they ran toward her car. The reports were mixed: some were on Adam's side, some were calling for blood. Mara wasn't sure why she was torturing herself like this. It wasn't exactly making her feel better, but a part of her was intrigued by the fact that other people were fascinated with the two of them. She understood to a certain extent. Their story bordered on a movie or TV show: *Dexter 2: The Adam Layton Story.*

At that moment, her phone buzzed on the desk with a text. Picking it up, Mara read the message.

It was from Kimiko: *You gave me your number, but I bet you never thought I'd text. Just saw the news and that Adam is free. Congrats. You need anything?*

Mara stared at the text for a good five minutes, completely at a loss for what to do. She had a trill of panic when she wondered if Kimiko could tell if she had read the text or not. Mara didn't know enough about technology to know how to check something like that.

Not that it mattered. Kimiko didn't expect Mara to write back right away. She probably didn't expect Mara to write back at all. This was most likely a test to see how Mara would respond.

Finally, Mara typed back: *I need the press to leave us alone. Not sure if that's possible lol.*

After hitting send, Mara's face flushed with embarrassment. It was so casual, as if she were talking to Zia. Maybe she had been "too cool."

Mara had no idea why she cared what Kimiko may or may not have thought about her stupid text. Mara wished she wasn't so neurotic. Her life would be so much easier that way.

But Kimiko's response was almost instant: *Um. I hate to be the bearer of bad news, but I'm pretty sure all three news stations are camped out in front of your dorm.*

Mara leapt to the window, almost giving herself whiplash from the headphones yanking her back. Throwing them onto the desk, Mara peered out the window. With overcast skies, the night was at its darkest, so she had to wait a moment or two for her eyes to adjust. But once they did . . .

Uh-oh.

Kimiko's intel was one hundred percent accurate. It looked like three or four news crews meandering about on the lawn in front of her dorm. She could see their vans parked haphazardly on the loading zone curb close by. Either they had followed them from Evergreen Moon, or somehow the information was leaked that the dean had given permission for Adam to stay in Mara's dorm room.

As if reading Mara's mind (when she came to think of it, maybe she was) Kimiko texted: *They're totally parked illegally. I could call the cops. That way they wouldn't know it came from you.*

Mara still wasn't sure how to handle Kimiko not only being in her life but acting like a friend.

Mara texted: *You would do that? That would be amazing.*

Thank you.

She was going to add a couple of emojis, but their friendship wasn't there yet.

Kimiko's response was quick: *On it. And don't ever thank me. I'll never deserve your thanks. I have a lot of making up to do. If you'll let me.*

A wave of calmness filled Mara. Kimiko seemed to be really trying to make things right. Mara never thought she needed this, but now that it was happening, she found that it was healing her in some way. Going to school every day, avoiding certain hallways, rooms and places, all to avoid Kimiko's wrath, Mara had grown used to it. She never realized until now how much of a toll it had taken or that she carried it with her still. But now, it was slowly being repaired and Mara felt almost weightless. A part of her anxiety was the constant feeling of never knowing where an attack was coming from. She had developed that paranoia from Kimiko's bullying.

Once Kimiko left their senior year, Mara had hoped she'd have some peace, but the students at school and the press were relentless that year. It was Adam's trial followed by Robert's, and since Mara was the only person involved in the crimes that wasn't in jail, she was interrogated by random people every day. She had almost missed Kimiko. At least Kimiko had been a devil she knew how to deal with.

Mara had forgotten about her high school bully and pretty much thought the whole thing had been resolved since she almost never thought about it. But now, having Kimiko apologize to her, Mara realized she'd just shoved those feelings down. She hadn't dealt with them at all really.

Rereading Kimiko's text over and over gave Mara a sense of happiness she couldn't quite describe. A part of her was still afraid Kimiko would take it all back and be cruel to her once again, but Mara was an eternal optimist. She wanted to believe that Kimiko's heart had healed and that she truly wanted to be friends.

Mara texted: *If you manage to get rid of these guys, I'm giving you a big, fat thanks and there's nothing you can do stop me.* Then she added a smiley face.

Wow.

Kimiko had been upgraded to emoji level. It might only be one smiley face, but in Mara's world it meant they were friends.

A yellow heart and a fist bump emoji texted Mara back.

Shaking her head from the bizzaro-world she lived in, a thrill of excitement swept through her when the flashing red-and-blue lights of two police cars pulled up to the parked news vans twenty minutes later. The police quickly wrangled every last one of the news crews and sent them packing.

Mara debated whether or not she should text Kimiko. She wanted to text *thank you*, but she didn't want to start a whole *please don't thank me* rant from Kimiko again.

Instead, Mara laid her phone down, turned off the ringer, and crawled back in bed with Adam. He had slept through the whole ordeal. Snuggling into Adam, then feeling his arms wrap around her, gave Mara instant peace. In that moment, she had never been happier.

***

Where am I?

Dreaming.

Because if this was real, Mara figured she had to be drugged.

She stood against the wall in a small cement room with no windows and no doors. In the center of the room, a single bulb swung on a wire like a pendulum. Mara stepped forward, away from the wall: the bulb changed direction, as if it were repelled by her presence.

Taking another step toward the bulb, resistance prevented her from moving at a normal speed. She looked down.

The entire floor was covered in blood.

So deep that Mara couldn't see her feet or ankles.

As she drew closer to the bulb, it stopped swinging and simply pulled away from Mara, defying gravity by hovering near the ceiling, the wire holding it horizontal with the ceiling now.

Opposite polarity.

Mara and the light bulb were reversed magnets, never to be able to touch each other.

And though she knew it was only a dream, Mara's desire to touch the bulb became almost obsessive.

She jumped up, trying to reach the bulb, but it kept shifting out of reach. With each hop into the air, the blood beneath Mara splashed violently until her entire body was covered in the red, sticky ichor.

Mentally, Mara had to force herself to stop trying to reach the bulb.

It was strange not having control but being fully aware of the dream state. It was as if she were trapped inside her own dream body, which essentially, she was, the more she thought about it.

But Mara managed to stop jumping for the bulb, then leaned back against the wall, so that was progress.

The bulb dropped back to its original spot in the center of the cement room, swinging like a pendulum once more.

A young man materialized in the cement room. He stood across from Mara on the opposite wall, staring at the bulb like a cat following a toy with its eyes. He had dark hair and dark eyes and looked like he could be no more than fourteen years old.

"Hello?" Mara said aloud.

The boy didn't appear to see or hear her. If he did, he wasn't acknowledging her existence.

Sounds of splashing liquid grew louder, and Mara looked down at her feet. The blood was rising and appeared to have a current of its own, choppy like the ocean in a storm.

In a matter of moments, the blood was up to her knees and flooding fast, the rough waves splashing all the way up to her face. As Mara wiped her eyes clean, the young man walked toward the swinging light bulb.

Unlike Mara, as soon as he approached the bulb, it swung directly into the palm of his hand.

He held it lovingly, looking at it as if it were the most precious thing in the world.

Like static, Raven's dead sister Terry popped into the room next to the boy, glitchy like before. Mara wished she could adjust the dream world's antenna to get Terry in focus.

Staring at Mara as if she needed her to understand, Terry touched the shoulder of the young man as he held the bulb in his hand lovingly.

The blood grew more and more violent the higher it rose.

Just as the blood was about to cover the boy's hand and the bulb, his eyes met Mara's, and they were full of rage.

He crushed the bulb with his hand.

Light exploded and shards of glass flew directly at Mara, her arm flying up to protect her face . . .

When nothing struck her body, Mara pulled her arm away. She was in the basement with Samantha again. Chained to the wall, Samantha was exactly as Mara had seen her before. She looked like a caged animal, her clothing torn, her skin cut and bruised and dirty hair, matted and greasy.

Normally, Mara would have been relieved that she was no longer in the strange cement room with creepy-boy and Terry anymore, because it hadn't been real, only a dream. Seeing Samantha in front of her was actually happening at this very moment and there was nothing she could do about it.

Her thoughts kept drifting back to the first dream though. Who was that boy? Why did Terry have her hand on his shoulder? Was that a dream from Mara's subconscious? Or was it Terry trying to send her some kind of message?

Too many questions.

And none of them helping find Samantha at the moment.

Even though Samantha had only been there a few days, it looked like she'd been there for months. What this guy had been doing to her made Mara's skin crawl. Samantha was awake, though, and whimpering quietly. It looked as if she was making the noises to remind herself that she was still alive.

Looking around for Adam or even Terry, Mara realized she was alone—on the astral plane anyway.

If Terry had truly been with Mara in the bloody cement room, she hadn't followed her here.

The locks on the door clicked open one by one.

Mara whirled around to see who was coming down the stairs. Maybe this was it. Maybe she'd be able to identify the man who took Samantha. But as he carefully walked down the steps, Mara noticed that he wore a ski mask. He looked as if he were about to rob a bank. Along with the ski mask, he wore all black from head to toe. Apparently, he didn't want Samantha knowing who he was either. Did that mean she knew him?

Finally reaching Samantha, the man took a small matchbox out of his pants pocket.

Opening the box, the man pulled out a match and lit it, watching it burn. When the flame was its largest, the man threw it at Samantha's face. Samantha screeched in pain as the fire burned her skin.

Through the ski mask, Mara could see the tugging of a smile from the man. He was enjoying himself immensely. And so began his entertainment for the night: lighting matches and throwing them at a seventeen-year-old girl.

Then a horrid thought hit her.

What if he was going to kill Samantha tonight? What if he was about to kill her *now*? If Mara was going by her dream life's track record, then witnessing a murder "live" was number one in her playbook.

Mara decided to be proactive in this vision.

She stared directly at the kidnapper's eyes and mouth, since they were the only things showing through the ski mask. The only things distinguishable about them was that his skin was white (shocker, most serial killer/psychos were), his eyes were dark brown (or at least Mara thought they were, it was hard to tell from the darkness of the room), and his lips were thin and looked young. Mara couldn't tell if he was a teenager or in his twenties, but at least she could rule out anyone over the age of thirty. Or if he was older, he was one of those people that didn't show their age.

Wanting to look away, Mara made herself watch as the man began forcing Samantha's mouth open and shoving lit matches down her throat.

Not wanting to see anymore, Mara closed her eyes within the dream, hoping she could escape this vision and move on to something more normal like flying or having superpowers—just no more basements with kidnapped, tortured girls or weird light bulbs that were repulsed by her.

Bracing herself, Mara opened her eyes.

Relief spread through her. She was no longer in the kidnapper's basement or the room full of blood; she was in a small bedroom. The one thing she was sure of, though, was that she was still in a vision. Mara felt grounded, real, as if she were standing in a real place, feet firmly on the ground.

Glancing around, Mara's eyes finally rested on . . .

Lucy Tildon, lying in her twin bed, stared at a ceiling filled with stick-on glow-in-the-dark stars.

Groaning internally, Mara figured she'd make the most of her visit.

What was it about Lucy Tildon that drew Mara in? Was it because Lucy was like Mara, a victim of bullying? Did that connect them somehow? But Mara was connecting with Samantha too. So why would she connect with both the bully and their prey?

The room itself was easily relatable to Mara: posters of Doctor Who, Benedict Cumberbatch as both Sherlock and Dr. Strange, and a bookshelf full of Mara's favorites: *Mortal Instruments*, *Broken Earth* trilogy, *Vampire Academy*, and a ton of other goodies. One thing Mara knew was that she'd get along great with Lucy. At least about pop culture anyway.

Mara wasn't exactly sure what she was supposed to do. Was this going to be her whole night, being forced to witness a teenager's insomnia play out before her? Mara would rather be . . . sleeping! Visions took a toll. It was energy spent, unlike regular dreams where she could still wake up feeling rested.

Come to think about it, that was one of the things Mara had wanted to ask her neuroscience teacher. Stupid jerk.

Welcome to Mara's life. Being told she was a fraud, and yet she was literally standing in some stranger's room watching the girl count plastic stars. Mara wanted to plop on Lucy's office chair at her small desk, but it wasn't as if she'd actually be able to relax.

It was all a waste of time.

Frustration began to build inside of her.

Maybe she could try to jump into Adam's dreams. She wasn't as good at it as he was, but she'd done it from time to time. Concentrating solely on Adam, Mara desperately tried to jump out of this vision and into Adam's dream space.

Nothing.

After a few more attempts, it was apparent to Mara that there had to be a reason she was here in the dark with Lucy Tildon.

A noise from outside Lucy's window made Mara jump despite the fact that she was essentially a ghost in the room.

Lucy leapt from her bed and quietly opened the window.

The boy from Mara's first vision crawled through, Barry, if she remembered correctly.

Okay, this was starting to get interesting. Or really awkward. Mara didn't want to watch a make-out session with two high schoolers. Why would the Universe want her here for that?

But when Barry was finally inside, he whispered to Lucy, "It's totally true. Sam didn't run away, she was kidnapped."

It was hard to read Lucy, but she appeared to be taken aback by the news and whispered back, "Who would kidnap Samantha Perkins? You're sure your cousin isn't BSing you?"

"He has a friend in the FBI, and he's positive. Apparently, they got some phone call, a tip or something, and now they're looking into it as a kidnapping." Barry sat down on the office chair, while Lucy sat on the edge of her bed.

Lucy shook her head. "Do you think she's okay?"

Barry smiled. "Do you care?"

Shrugging, Lucy looked thoughtful. "I was glad she was gone, but what if some psycho serial killer took her? I wouldn't wish that on my worst enemy, and Sam *is* my worst enemy."

"Serial killer? That's a leap. It's probably her dad. Sam's mom has full custody of her and Brian and pretty much banned their dad from ever seeing his kids. There's some crazy statistic like ninety percent of kidnappings are parents. Anyway, that's what my cousin told me," Barry whispered.

"That makes sense, I guess." Lucy shook her head. "I don't know why I jumped to serial killer. Too much TV."

Mara could see that Lucy still looked conflicted. Whether Lucy just had good instincts or some kind of psychic ability, or she was involved in the kidnapping itself, Mara couldn't tell.

Barry turned serious. "We'll find out tomorrow. They're going to bring Sam's dad into the FBI and question him." He paused.

"Do you really think she was taken by a serial killer?"

Lucy didn't laugh it off like Mara thought she would. Instead, she nodded slowly. "I have a bad feeling, Barry. I haven't been able to shake it since we heard Sam was missing." Sighing, she continued, "I feel like if it had been her dad that took her, I wouldn't be feeling this constant state of dread."

Barry looked scared and whispered, "Should we look for her?"

Lucy forced a small smile. "Weird, right? That somehow I'd be the one who wants to help Samantha Perkins?" Then Lucy set her jaw, determined. "Yeah. I think we should try. I don't know how to explain it, but I feel like she's in real trouble."

"Well, you've never been wrong, not since I've known you. I've learned to trust your instincts," Barry responded. He was trying to be encouraging, that was obvious, but Mara could see that Lucy's words scared him.

Mara wished she could tell them that Lucy was right, that Samantha was indeed in trouble, that currently a crazy man was throwing lit matches down her throat . . .

Shuddering at remembering that image, Mara shifted her attention back to Lucy and Barry.

YANK!

Pulled backward, Mara flew out of Lucy's room . . .

***

Mara's eyes opened. She was surprised she hadn't jolted out of bed, but she was somehow getting used to all the pulling and yanking that was going on in her dreams. Mara had no idea if she was pulled out by someone like Terry, or if she had pulled herself out subconsciously. Unfortunately, Mara didn't have enough control over her dreams and sleep to know. She hoped it had been her and not Terry. Everything that was happening to her was weird enough; she really didn't need ghost-girl taking over.

Looking over at her clock, it was four a.m. Adam was still fast asleep and luckily looked quite peaceful. Grabbing her cell phone, Mara, as quietly as she could, tiptoed out of the dorm, down the hallway to the dorm floor's shared private study. At first glance, the large room looked like a chaotic whirlwind of chairs and couches with a three-person vinyl plush couch, six matching vinyl plush chairs, and a dozen plain wooden chairs all placed sporadically around the room. A few desks and a handful of full bookshelves lined the walls. The design was for privacy and studying, but Mara had seen students moving chairs around for a more social gathering. Right now, to Mara's relief, the room was empty of people.

Sitting down in a vinyl chair, the air escaped from the plastic fabric, causing Mara to sink in deep. She chose the chair farthest from the door in the back corner for maximum privacy, but she also faced it outward so she could see if anyone walked in.

It was Zia time.

Four a.m. on a Wednesday meant seven a.m. on the East Coast and an hour before Zia's philosophy class. Mara had Zia's schedule memorized due to the three-hour time difference. Any pocket of time they could grab to talk to each other Mara was going to take. Besides, Zia was probably dying to hear how everything went with Adam.

Hitting the FaceTime button for Zia on her phone, Mara waited with anticipation for her best friend to answer.

Sure enough, with a small buzz, Zia's beautiful face filled

Mara's screen. Her dark skin, full lips, button nose, and large brown eyes were a welcome sight that instantly made Mara feel better.

Zia started before Mara could speak. "Your exit is all over the internet. Are you guys okay?"

Mara turned the volume down a smidge to ensure she didn't wake anyone up in the dorm, then she spoke quietly. "We're fine. Adam's here with me."

"Thank goodness! I got so worried those vultures were going to circle you everywhere you went. How's campus security? Have they assigned you some guards? I can call the dean if you want. Trust me, I can make a stink." Zia was in full protective mode. It made Mara wish her best friend was here with her now. No one could make Mara feel safer than Zia. But she wasn't here. She was in New York.

And Mara was stuck with . . .

Kimiko.

Which, weirdly, wasn't a bad substitute.

"What's that face?" Zia asked suddenly. "You have that worried face going on. Are you sure you're okay?"

"Really, I'm fine. Just a lot of stuff happening all at once. Some insanely weird stuff." Mara wasn't sure where to start.

Zia's interest was obviously piqued, because she moved closer to the camera. "Mara, spill."

Mara told Zia everything. From Kimiko, to the dreams with Samantha and Lucy, to Terry the ghost hijacking her visions.

After Mara finished, Zia let out a huge breath. "Man, that's freaking crazy. I don't know what to respond to first."

Mara laughed. "I know, right? I think the Kimiko thing

weirds me out more than this kidnapper dude."

Zia nodded. "It's nice to see her try though. Kimiko used to treat me and her friends the way she's treating you now. That's why it took watching how horrible she was to you on that YouTube video to even see her evil side. I'm glad she finally pulled that stick out of her butt and is genuinely trying to make it up to you."

Then Zia paused, shaking her head. "But this ghost person . . . that's terrifying! Can't you find someone to exorcise her out of your head or something? Is that possible?"

"I have no idea. I doubt it, though, since I never know when she's going to take over my brain." Mara let that sentence sink in. "Okay, saying that out loud made the whole situation a million times more freaky."

"Well, at least you know who she is. That's gotta mean something, right? And we know Raven is good people, so Terry can't be that bad. And she doesn't seem to be trying to hurt you. It sounds like she's trying to warn you of something," Zia mused.

"Yeah, she's so protective of Lucy. I just wonder why." Mara couldn't figure out why a fifteen-years-dead girl would come back to haunt Mara's dreams to protect a teenager Mara was positive she'd never met.

"Well, you know what you have to do, right?" Zia asked as if Mara was supposed to know exactly what she was about to say.

But Mara had no clue.

"I'm kind of at a loss. I'm not even sure what I'm going to do today, let alone what I'm supposed to do about all of this dream crap."

Zia shook her head as if Mara's ignorance was cute.

“What?” Mara couldn’t help but smile, which in turn made Zia smile.

“You have to go meet Lucy.” Zia refrained from saying “duh,” but her expression said it just fine.

And with sudden clarity that only a best friend could provide, Mara knew Zia was right.

She had a mission for the day.

Mara and Adam were going to Everett High.

Dream Entry #6

I'm still waiting for Adam to wake up. That boy can sleep! He looks so peaceful, though, so I don't have the heart to wake him, and there's really no hurry. I got up so freaking early that it feels like it's midday even though it's only eight a.m. I want to grab us something from the coffee cart and bring it back up here, but I'm afraid he'll wake up and panic that he's alone, so I'm sitting at my desk writing in my dream journal.

Last night's dream . . . dreams . . . so many insane visions last night! The Lucy one especially got me thinking. It was interesting hearing Barry tell Lucy that she's always had good instincts. That may be code for being someone like me. I'm definitely going to have to be careful how I bring that up with her, assuming I'll get to talk to her at all.

Also, I'm still not sure how I was pulled out of each vision? I mean, the weird cement-light-bulb-pendulum-blood-room dream was something unto itself. It obviously isn't a memory, but it has to mean something significant, whether it was my own brain trying to work something out or a message from Terry? I wasn't sure. I'll have to percolate on that one.

As for the last two dreams, I didn't see Terry in either of those. She had no problem showing herself in the first dream, so why would she disappear for Samantha and then Lucy?

It sucks not being able to ask Terry anything. But Terry is dead and I have no idea how to reach her, and when she's in my dreams she's fuzzy, not quite there. I've never had much luck with Ouija boards and I wouldn't have the first clue how to perform a séance, so what am I supposed to do? If I'm being honest, I don't want her in my brain if she's going to pull me around to places I don't want to go like weird rooms full of blood and creepy kids smashing light bulbs with their hand. Just me? Ugh.

But maybe she won't be as angry at me because I'm going out to meet Lucy today, which means hopefully I can find a way to protect her like Terry wants.

This is so frustrating. I don't know what to do. And after watching that evil man throw lit matches into Samantha's mouth and on her face . . . ? That image is seared in my head. I can't help shuddering every five seconds at the mere thought of having to go through that. My mouth hurts thinking about it.

But what I'm avoiding completely is the fact that Samantha might be dead.

I really don't want to think that way, but I'm not sure that when I dream-jumped away from Samantha and over to Lucy . . . that Samantha's kidnapper didn't turn into Samantha's killer. I hope not.

Oh, Adam's waking up!

***

Mara placed her journal down on her desk and playfully jumped onto the bed as Adam slowly sat up. He laughed and pulled her close to him, kissing her gently.

"I have the worst morning breath." Adam cringed at himself, pulling away.

Mara kissed him again, then said, "I ate half that tin of Altoids. I'll be tasting only mint for the next hour, so I'm good for the both of us."

"In that case . . ." Adam placed his hands on the small of Mara's back and drew her closer, pressing his lips to hers.

Mara's body tingled from the sensation, and the rest of the world melted away around them. It was as if she floated on a cloud, while every pleasure center in her body filled with joy. Being with Adam was like connecting to a part of her deepest self. She couldn't describe the intensity she experienced when he touched her. It was almost like her skin was made of electricity.

"Whoa," Adam said, slightly out of breath. Drawing away just far enough so he could talk, his lips were still agonizingly close.

"Yeah, pretty much." Mara found she was out of breath too, and she suddenly understood where the saying "take my breath away" came from.

Adam leaned back onto the pillow, entwining his hand into Mara's. He stared at her as if he were seeing an angel on Earth. Mara could feel her face burning what was probably a fuchsia pink and smiled. "Stop looking at me like that."

"I can't help it. I keep thinking we're dreaming, that none of this is real. I can't believe I have a second chance." Adam's voice was thick with gratitude, and it gave Mara a slight pang of guilt that she knew her parents were secretly plotting to rob Adam of his freedom. But she didn't want to ruin the mood, so she kept her mouth shut.

Mara nodded toward the window. "Last night a bunch of reporters were camped outside, but believe it or not, Kimiko called the cops on them, and now they're gone."

Adam shook his head in disbelief as he played with Mara's fingers still clasped in his. "Kimiko. So weird."

"Any dreams last night?" Mara asked. She hoped he'd had a vision of Samantha as well after she had left the poor girl. Mara really wanted to know if she was still alive.

But Adam shook his head in the negative. "Just the *normal* ones. Although I did have a weird one about a frog that ended up being my biology teacher." He smiled, then turned thoughtful at Mara's expression. "From the look on your face, I'd say you had a doozy. Did you see Samantha again? Is she . . . ?"

Mara finished Adam's thought. "No. She isn't dead. At least she wasn't when I left her. But, Adam, it was so horrible. He was throwing lit matches in her mouth and smiling the whole time."

Adam drew her down to him so that she rested on his chest, his arms wrapped around her protectively. "I'm so sorry." Then he made sure Mara's eyes met his. "We have to find this girl before it's too late."

"Which leads me to another vision," Mara groaned.

"Geez, two in one night?" Adam's voice tinged with worry.

"Three," Mara corrected and proceeded to describe the details of each vision.

Adam took it all in, then said, "It's strange that the bulb kept moving away from you but not from the boy. And then he crushed it?"

Mara nodded, interested that he was focused on that dream more than the others.

"In my therapy we talked a lot about dreams and light bulbs or the sun or anything with light. Light *usually* represents the soul." Adam tilted his head to the side, thoughtful.

"But who is the boy? He seemed to love the light bulb, then he crushed it," Mara puzzled aloud. "You think it was his soul?"

"Or someone else's?" Adam shrugged.

Mara sighed. "Maybe Terry will show me more later."

"Not sure if that's good either." Adam squeezed Mara's hand supportively. "How long you been up, by the way?"

"Since four, but it ended up being a good thing because I was able to FaceTime with Zia in New York."

Adam kissed the top of Mara's head. "How is she?"

"Honestly, I'm a horrible friend and I don't know: we only talked about me. I should call her back." Mara hit her palm to her head. How could she have not asked Zia how she was doing? She knew her friend understood, especially since Adam got out only yesterday, but Mara promised herself she'd call Zia back later and only talk about All Things Zia.

"You are the opposite of horrible. Zia cares about you, and she understands you're dealing with a lot right now."

Mara kissed Adam gently on the lips. "I'll make it up to her." She pulled away. "I wish I knew for certain that I was the one who woke myself up."

"You're worried that Terry pulled you out? And you didn't see her in the last two dreams?" Adam asked carefully.

"Yeah. She didn't show herself, so it's entirely possible it was me who did it." Mara paused, thinking. "I really hope it's me, because I don't think I can handle having a ghost control my sleeping life. I already feel exhausted from lack of sleep last night. Zia thinks we should go to Everett High today and meet Lucy. Maybe tell her about Samantha?" Mara wasn't sure what Adam's reaction was going to be.

But he nodded. "I think that's a great idea. Do you think Agent Piper will want to meet us there?"

"Maybe. I think she normally only works on serial killer cases, but she said she would try to be a part of the investigation as much as she could." Mara still didn't like the fact that Raven wouldn't be the agent in charge. "But we can do the preliminary work. You know, be two stalker creeps that pin down a seventeen-year-old and tell her I've been dreaming about her and that we've both been dreaming about Samantha and she's being tortured. I'm starting to rethink this plan." Rambling only brought clarity to how crazy the idea of going up to Everett was.

Adam kissed her gently to calm her down. "You're seriously stressing. We're going to go up there. She's not going to think we're *stalker creeps*, and we'll tell her about Samantha. Maybe we can pool our resources and find her before that guy *does* turn into a killer."

Mara took a deep breath and started to relax. "You're right. Okay, let's do this."

"Can I get dressed first?" Adam smiled.

"I like you much better in your jammies." Mara smiled back.

"A T-shirt and boxers hardly count as jammies. I'm pretty sure

I need to get some jam-jams with pictures of sushi or something cool like that." Adam pulled Mara in for another kiss.

She could get used to this life.

After another mind-blowing kiss, Mara finally drew away. "I'm taking you to breakfast. I've been up for four freaking hours already, and I'm starving."

Giving her one last kiss, Adam jumped up out of bed, pulling on his jeans.

"I just realized, you totally don't have any other clothes, do you?" First not asking Zia how she was, and now this. More proof for Mara that she was a horrible friend/girlfriend. She should have bought some extra shirts and pants for him before he was released.

Adam walked over to her, cupping his hands around her face. "Do not stress about this. I can wash these. Clothes are so not important."

"I should have thought of it." Mara wasn't ready to let herself off the hook.

But Adam could obviously not care less. He laughed a little and kissed her again. "This is why I love you. You're upset about clothes. I'm fine. Now can we get some food? I'm starving too."

Mara smiled back, then took a quick peek out the window. "Just making sure we're still clear . . ." Looking down at the lawn, there were no signs of news crews anywhere. "Okay, we're good."

Walking through the dorm hallway, then taking the stairs to the bottom floor, the halls were empty. No doubt everyone was already in class, but still, it made her paranoid. It was hard to shake the feeling that she was some kind of prey noticing that the forest was suddenly quiet.

There was nothing she could do about it either way, so the only move was forward. Holding Adam's hand a little bit tighter, Mara opened the front door to her dorm building.

Expecting an onslaught of reporters, Mara encountered—no one.

Adam searched the area when he asked, "Is it always this empty?"

"No, not at all. I think we should get ready to be ambushed."

His hand tightened in hers, then he responded, "I got you. They'll be after me more than you, so let me take the brunt."

"In no universe is that happening." Mara wasn't about to let Adam's first day be a living nightmare.

Mara's body tensed like a soldier preparing for battle. No one was in sight, yet both she and Adam were on high alert instead of enjoying the fact that they were alone. Mara knew better though. When an environment was the opposite of its normalcy, something was about to go down.

"Is there some kind of back way we can go?" Adam asked, thinking strategically as well.

Mara shook her head. "There's only a courtyard around that corner, then straight to the coffee cart."

"That corner there?" Adam nodded to the side of her dorm building.

A total blind corner because of the large trees next to it.

"Yup," Mara said.

"Let's get it over with."

Corner coming.

Mara almost wanted to close her eyes, afraid of what she expected to find.

They rounded the corner.

Mara really hated being right.

Like a flood of human-sized ants, reporters, YouTubers, bloggers, vloggers, all came rushing at the two of them. In a matter of seconds, Mara and Adam were an island in the middle of chaos. The shouting alone made Mara want to crawl up in a ball, but hands tugged on her shirt, people shoved up against them, and there was a moment when she got smacked in the head by someone's elbow.

Adam surrounded her with his arms, trying to act as a human shield, which immediately made Mara want to do the same for him. She should be protecting him, not the other way around.

Inching forward, only Adam spoke, trying to shout over the shouting. "If you want to talk to someone, talk to me! Leave Mara Johnson out of it!"

No one heard him, which made Mara think, *Why are they here if they won't be quiet enough to hear what me or Adam has to say? What's the freaking point?*

Only seconds had passed, but it felt like hours. Mara's breath caught in her throat. She couldn't get out. She was stuck in this crowd that wouldn't let her go. Only Adam's arms gave her any comfort, but even that became claustrophobic after a while. Mara needed air. She needed to breathe out in the open with arms flailing. She needed space. Her short, quick breaths spun her head. Mara's brain knew she was having a panic attack, but her body would not calm down no matter how hard she tried.

Stumbling forward, Mara stared up at Adam. "I'm going to pass out." She honestly didn't know how he could fix it, but she had to tell someone.

Adam's body tensed, determined. "Ready to become bulldozers?"

Mara nodded. Anything to get out.

"'Cause we may get sued." Adam appeared just as scared of the prospect of shoving these people as he did being surrounded by them.

Because . . .

Mara filled with dread.

Because if he did anything to violate his parole, he'd be sent back!

Just as Adam was about to use his arm as a plowing machine, Mara grabbed him and shook her head. "No. Your parole!"

Shaking his head, he answered, "I have to get you out of here."

Mara's panic dissolved, replaced by what she called her "crisis mode." Even with high anxiety, Mara could be surprisingly level-headed in an emergency. When it was happening to her: sheer panic. When it came to someone she loved: pure adrenaline-induced protector.

"Don't worry about me. I'm good. We'll get out of here. It may take us all day, but eventually these people will realize they're not getting anything out of us." Mara spoke as calmly as she could to try to steady Adam (and herself).

Adam's grip tightened as he nodded.

Random questions hurled over the blanket of shouting. How on earth did they expect Mara to answer such insanity?

"MARA, ARE YOU IN LOVE WITH ROBERT GARNER?"

"ADAM! ARE YOU JEALOUS OF ROBERT?"

"IS IT ROBERT'S BABY?"

Adam apparently started to hear some of these idiotic questions as well, and his expression was one of confusion rather than anger. "What's going on?"

Mara had to admit: the line of questioning wasn't one she'd been expecting. She had expected some curiosity about Robert—but babies? Love? Jealousy? Something had happened that neither Mara nor Adam knew about.

They had to get the heck out of this donut of shouting people.

"NOW!" a voice screamed.

And a path suddenly opened before them. Twenty UW football players moved the press aside like paper dolls, until they reached Mara and Adam. Forming two lines, the giant athletes created a perfect hallway for Mara and Adam to walk through to freedom.

Not able to help herself, Mara smiled. Kimiko stood at the end of the man-made corridor with a grin of her own.

"Are you coming or what?" Kimiko said.

With a run, Mara and Adam waved their thanks at the football players and dashed to safety.

"We're not out of the clear yet," Kimiko said as she saluted the football players who, to a man, nodded in unison as if she were their queen or something.

Some things never changed. Kimiko had a beauty and charm about her that automatically made people (especially guys) do things for her.

This made the third time Kimiko had come to Mara's rescue, and she had to admit, she was boarding the trust train. Kimiko was coming through for Mara like a true friend, and though a part of her was conflicted because of all the grief Kimiko had given her over the years, the bigger part of Mara was happy that someone like Kimiko could potentially change.

Mara and Adam followed Kimiko at a slight jog. Looking over her shoulder, Mara noticed that the football players now formed a line, holding back the vultures, and the distance between them was growing larger and larger.

"We'll have to take my car since yours is being staked out," Kimiko informed them.

Mara's hand never left Adam's as they followed Kimiko through campus, dodging anyone and everyone that remotely appeared interested in them. Mara was sure ninety percent of the people they passed were students or professors, but not wanting to be cornered again, she wasn't taking any chances.

Finally, they reached Kimiko's VW Jetta and piled inside. Adam jumped in the back, giving Mara the shotgun seat.

Once they were on the road, Mara finally found her voice. "Thank you so much, Kimiko. I don't know what we would have done without you."

"Yeah, thanks," Adam said, and Mara could tell he was genuinely touched by Kimiko's heroic effort to rescue them from the mob.

Kimiko shrugged. "I told you, you don't ever have to thank me for anything. I'm just making up for all the crappy things I did and said to you. Trust me: we are in no way even."

"I'm not keeping track, and neither should you. You've more than proved that you're trying to be a better person." Mara said the words, but the years of being bullied still lingered in her subconscious. It was more that Mara *wanted* to believe what she was saying. Anyway, it felt right.

Kimiko didn't respond right away, obviously taken aback by Mara's blanket forgiveness, but after a moment of silence, she said carefully, "I didn't want to tell you this because I didn't want to ruin the progress we've made so far, but I know why all those crazies were there waiting for you."

Adam leaned forward, interested. "Weren't they there because they knew I stayed the night?"

Kimiko leaned her head to the side as if she didn't want to continue, but she did anyway. "That was why the first midnight gang came, but when the police dispatched them, it looked like you guys were in the clear." She paused as if unsure she should continue.

A knot twisted in Mara's stomach, sensing where this was headed. "Just tell us, Kimiko."

"As soon as Adam's release date was announced in the news, I put out my feelers for any and every bit of information I could get. I have a lot of friends and a lot of sources on campus." Kimiko took a deep breath, then continued, "This morning, my friend in the admissions office said she saw your mom organizing that particular group. I guess she told them that crap about Robert to make sure they'd follow you."

"How did she know who Mara's mom was?" Adam's lips tightened as if he didn't remotely believe Kimiko's source.

But Mara did.

She knew it was true the moment Kimiko had said it.

Kimiko answered Adam, "People know who Mara's parents are. Pretty much everyone you knew was in the news in one way or another. Besides, after the blow-out argument Mara had with her mom yesterday, everyone was kind of on watch for Claire."

Mara blushed. "People saw that? I didn't see anyone." She was suddenly extremely embarrassed.

"They don't have to be outside to see you. There were a lot of people staring out their windows . . . with cameras." Kimiko sounded like it pained her to say these things, which was a huge improvement from the past, when she would have enjoyed it thoroughly. Then she added quickly, "She did kind of threaten to sabotage Adam's parole."

"What?" Adam choked out.

It hurt to see him so upset. Mara didn't want him to know the extent her parents were willing to go to keep them apart.

Kimiko bit her bottom lip, as if she wanted to cry. "I'm sorry. I thought you knew that."

"I knew Mara's parents tried to get a restraining order, but I didn't know they were trying to get me sent back to the psych ward." Adam sat back, shoulders slumped.

Mara turned her body around to see him. "I really thought they were just trying to scare me. I didn't think they'd do anything like this."

"So your parents were betting on the fact that I'd hurt someone to get us out of there and break my parole." Adam sighed. "I almost did. They were right about me."

"They are not right about you. You *didn't* hurt anyone. You chose not to." The taste of rage bubbled up like bile in her mouth. She never wanted to see or talk to her parents ever again. It wasn't just the horrendous fact that they wanted Adam to go back to incarceration, it was the fact that they were willing to put their daughter in a position where a mob of media could have hurt her. They were so hell-bent on taking down Adam, they didn't stop to think that Mara could have been seriously injured. She wasn't, of course, but if Kimiko hadn't come to save them, Mara wasn't so sure she'd have made it out unscathed.

Hate.

That was what pumped through her veins right now.

Pure hate.

Kimiko glanced over at Mara, her shoulders tightened. "I'm so sorry. I thought you should know."

Mara could barely hear Kimiko, her anger boiled so fiercely. Picking up her phone, Mara dialed her mother.

"Hello? Mara, are you okay?" Claire's voice sounded scared, but that only intensified Mara's fury.

"No thanks to you!" Mara screamed.

"Mara, I had no idea—" Claire didn't try to deny it.

Mara interrupted, "No idea that a mob of media crazies would pin your daughter down and trap her, especially after making up insane accusations about Robert Garner! A *real* psychopath! Knowing that your *daughter* has severe anxiety and almost passed out from the biggest panic attack she's ever had!"

Claire was full-out crying. "Mara, I didn't . . ."

"I don't want to hear anything from you or Dad ever again as long as I live! Which probably won't be long thanks to you!" Mara hung up before her mother could say anything. And just to shut them out completely, Mara blocked both her mother and father from her phone. She was still on their phone plan, so it wouldn't last long, but it felt good to do anyway.

Adam leaned forward, placing his hand on Mara's shoulder. "I'm not worth this. Your parents are way more important to your life than I am."

Now Mara was mad at Adam. "Don't you say that. Don't you ever say that! What my mom did today was reckless and irresponsible and put us both in danger. That's not what moms should do! Not my mom anyway. She's going freaking nuts!"

"She's going nuts because I'm a convicted murderer and we're together. I can understand where she's coming from," Adam responded, his voice laced with shame.

But it was Kimiko who spoke before Mara. "You may have killed those lowlifes, but it doesn't make you one. I saw what Robert did to Colt, manipulating him, twisting him into someone else. If he hadn't killed himself . . ." Kimiko stopped, a catch in her throat, then she plunged forward. "If Colt hadn't killed himself, he would have been right there beside you, getting rid of the garbage in this world. I don't care what anyone says about you. Those men did despicable things, and they deserved to die. If Mara's parents can't see you for who you are, then they should be the ones who are ashamed, not you."

Mara and Adam both stared at Kimiko in shock. It was like invasion of the body snatchers. Was this really the girl who had tortured Mara in school?

The answer was no, no she wasn't. She had evolved.

It gave Mara a surging hope she couldn't explain. It made her believe even more than she had before that Adam was truly going to be okay. That he would recover fully from everything that had happened to him and be able to come to terms with everything he had done. If Kimiko could be a new person, then anyone could.

Everyone was silent for a good minute.

Then Mara started to laugh.

Adam and Kimiko looked worried that Mara had lost it.

Mara let them in on what she found funny. "I sounded like a four-year-old: 'I don't want to hear anything from you or Dad ever again as long as I live!'"

Kimiko smiled. "Don't forget, you also said, 'which probably won't be long thanks to you.' That was dramatic."

Mara laughed harder. It felt good. Like she was releasing all the tense emotions she'd been building up the last couple of days.

Adam obviously didn't feel like laughing, but he picked up her hand and kissed it with a smile. It was the sadness behind the smile that caused Mara to stop laughing.

That and the obvious fact that no one else found it as funny as she did.

Because it really wasn't funny.

Mara shook off her feelings of depression and anger and turned to Kimiko. "You want to join us in meeting a girl I dreamt about who can help us with another girl who's been kidnapped?" Not convoluted-sounding at all. Then Mara told Kimiko everything, from the dreams, to Terry, to Zia's advice on paying a visit to Lucy.

After Mara finished, Kimiko raised an eyebrow, surprised. "The one who was kidnapped is still alive?" Kimiko was aware that most of the people Mara dreamt about ended up dead the same night she had a dream about them.

"Alive for now. We hope anyway. We need to know more," Mara admitted honestly.

"I'm in. Give me the address." Kimiko didn't flinch.

Mara took a deep breath of satisfaction. She felt as if she was assembling some kind of ragtag psychic squad, and it would be useful to have someone who could possibly read other people's minds. Mara wasn't sure how reliable Kimiko's gift was for her. Mara knew she couldn't control her own abilities very well. Either way, Kimiko would be a huge help.

And who knows, maybe Kimiko could find the killer on sight.

Dream Entry #7

I'm writing in Kimiko's car because I need to vent for a bit. We're parked at Dick's, and I am sitting here alone while Adam and Kimiko are getting us lunch. I'm in a comfort-food kind of mood, so I asked them to get me eight sides of tartar sauce and an extra order of fries. Grease and tartar sounds really good right now.

I still can't believe my mom would do that to me. I guess there were a lot of "I still can't believes" for me in the last week. Maybe I'm dreaming and I'll wake up at any minute. Waiting . . . "Wake up!" Yeah, that's what I thought. Stuck in the real world where the two people I'm supposed to feel the safest with have resorted to putting my life in danger just to break up me and my boyfriend. What's funny is the fact that they're so worried about me being with Adam because he killed those men, but I feel way more safe with him than I do with them. They're my parents, they're supposed to protect me, not throw me to the wolves to prove their point.

Heck, I feel safer with Kimiko at this point, and that's saying something.

We're about fifteen minutes away from Everett High according to the GPS, and I'm still not sure what we're going to do when we get there. I guess we'll make a request to see Lucy Tildon at the office? Yeah, that doesn't sound stalkery or weird. I'd suggest we park across the street from the school and wait until we see her, but that sounds even more creepy. There really isn't a winning way to do this. And with all the news and internet fame, it's more than likely that people will recognize me and Adam. Most people know what he did, and the teachers and principal presumably don't want a convicted murderer talking to one of their students.

Now that I think of it, maybe Adam should wait in the car.

I don't know.

My impulsiveness is now competing with my anxiety at this point. I'm not sure which one will win.

I see them coming back. Time to eat.

***

Mara gratefully took the white paper bag from Adam and began to devour her burger and fries.

Crawling into the back seat, Adam laughed. "They looked at us like we were insane when we ordered all those tartars."

Mara practically used up a whole container of tartar sauce on one fry. But the entire eating experience took the edge off of a horrible day so far. She stopped enough to smile back. "I swear they put crack into this stuff," she said, dipping her burger into the tartar sauce as well.

Kimiko simply nodded as she, too, ravaged her burger and fries.

Running from press and social media pariahs obviously stirred up an appetite.

In less than five minutes, all traces of food had been consumed. Even Adam ended up wolfing down his meal. Not the healthiest of breakfasts, but to Mara it hit the spot.

Not needing any prompting, Kimiko started up her car and continued to follow the GPS's directions to Everett High.

No one spoke as the last fifteen minutes to their destination loomed ahead of them.

Finally, the large concrete sign "Everett High School" came into view on the flat lawn of the school. Her palms began to sweat.

Kimiko pulled over to the curb across the street and parked her car, then she turned to Mara. "This is your rodeo. How you want to handle this?"

Mara glanced over at Adam for advice, his expression just as perplexed.

Peering over at the school, Mara shrugged. "I hadn't really thought this through. I just know I need to talk to Lucy."

"Lucy-who-is-in-class-right-now." Kimiko didn't bother to hide her judgmental tone, a little bit of the old version of her popping out.

But Mara had to agree with her attitude. What *had* Mara been thinking?

Kimiko stared at the school as if it would somehow give her the answers. After a moment, she raised an eyebrow in thought. "I think I have an idea. But you two have to stay here. I don't want anyone recognizing you and throwing us out."

Without another word, Kimiko exited her car, then hurried

across the street and into the school.

Mara turned to Adam. "What do you think she's going to do?"

Adam shook his head. "I have no idea, but I'm learning not to underestimate her."

"Yeah, seriously," Mara agreed.

Adam brushed the hair out of her face lovingly, then asked, "You doing okay? You were pretty angry."

Mara sighed. "I still am, but now I'm more sad than angry."

There was no other way to describe the grimace on Adam's face except "guilty," and that was the last thing Mara wanted. "Don't," she said. "Please don't blame yourself for what happened. That was all on my mom."

"Mara, even if your mom hadn't called all those people there, you know that at some point eventually we'd end up being surrounded by them. You said yourself that they'd been camped outside the window last night. Did you really think calling the cops and having them evacuated would solve the problem?" Adam replied gently.

"What's your point?"

"My point is that, by being with me, you're going to get mobbed, for a while anyway." Adam leaned back in his seat, obviously ashamed.

Which only made Mara want to hug him. "You do get that the press would be following me whether we stay together or not. If we stay together, it's 'How could she stay with a convicted killer?' If we break up, it's 'Mara Johnson fears for her life and escapes serial killer.'"

Adam sighed, obviously not sure what to say.

"My point is: we're going to be the center of attention right now no matter what, and I have no intention of leaving you."

Adam leaned forward and kissed her. When he pulled away, he said, "I love you."

Mara kissed him back, then answered, "I love you, too."

After a few more minutes, Kimiko ran back to the car, sliding inside. "Okay. Lucy is going to meet us after school at a coffeehouse down the road called Clutch."

Adam looked more curious than surprised. "How did you pull that off?"

Kimiko smiled. "I told the front desk that I was Lucy's cousin and that there was an emergency I needed to tell her about. She told me what room Lucy was in, I grabbed her from class, asked her if she knew who Mara was—she did—and told her that Mara had been dreaming about her and that Samantha was being tortured. And she agreed to meet."

Mara's eyes went wide. "You told her all that?"

Kimiko's expression was one of righteousness. "Sometimes telling the truth is the quickest way to get what you want." Then she shrugged. "To be honest, she didn't seem all that surprised that you dreamed about her. She looked kind of excited by it."

Mara wasn't sure how to process this information. The fact that Lucy knew about Mara wasn't a surprise, since everything that had been happening to her and Adam was a local story. But excited? What was Mara getting herself into?

Finally, she said to Kimiko, "Let's go to Clutch then."

Kimiko typed the address into her GPS and they were off, headed toward the coffeehouse. It only took a couple of minutes, and Mara figured this place was a regular hangout for most of the high school students. Walking inside, Mara felt instantly at home. The décor was cozy and warm, with soft, plushy chairs and reclaimed wood tables. Viewing the artwork on the walls, small placards displayed that the art came from local artists. It was very homey, and from the wafting smell of deliciousness, Mara could bet that their menu items would be tasty as well.

Ordering three mochas, the trio sat down in the corner. Mara and Adam took the love seat, and Kimiko sat on an armchair across from them. Adam leapt to his feet when their order was called, to bring back three piping hot mochas. As far as food and drinks went, Mara was having a pretty good day. Taking the first sip was as good as Mara had hoped it would be: rich, creamy, and full of chocolatey goodness. If she hadn't been waiting for a girl she'd been dreaming about to show up, Mara could almost pretend this was a normal day.

Except for the fact that Kimiko Thompson sat across from her.

Yeah.

"It'll be a couple of hours until she gets here. Are you sure you want to stick around?" Mara asked Kimiko, suddenly worried she had ruined Kimiko's plans for the day.

"This is the only place I want to be. If I can help this Samantha girl in any way, I want to," Kimiko said earnestly.

So this was Kimiko's "Redemption Tour," with Mara as her first stop and helping people the ultimate destination. Mara could respect that. Looking over at Adam, from the expression on his face she could tell he had similar goals. Well, if she could help them find a better way in life, then Mara was just fine with that.

The hours passed, and Mara found herself enjoying the moment. This was her first real day with Adam. Even though they had spent almost every night together in their dreams, it was so much different in real life. The way his hand always wanted to be wrapped in hers and how he looked at her with such appreciation it almost made her blush every time.

Kimiko was *actually funny*. The way she told Mara and Adam stories about the last two years of her life, a couple of them almost made Mara cry with laughter. Then Mara told a few stories of her own, usually involving something horribly embarrassing, and they made everyone laugh as well.

It was nice. Truly nice. Mara wished she could capture this one afternoon and bottle it up, saving it to go back to anytime she felt crappy.

A little after three o'clock, Lucy and her friend Barry walked through the front doors of Clutch. With an excited whisper to Lucy, Barry's eyes sparkled in excitement when he spotted both Mara *and* Adam sitting on the couch waiting for them, (or waiting for Lucy, but Mara had assumed the girl would bring backup and that was obviously Barry). They quickly ordered their own coffees and had them in hand when Kimiko waved Lucy over.

Sitting on the love seat facing Mara and Adam, Lucy met Mara's eyes.

"You're the dreamer, right?" Lucy asked, forehead crinkled with curiosity.

Mara felt like she was under a microscope; she hadn't expected to feel this way. She had wanted to be the interrogator, not the other way around. Still, she answered, "I dream stuff and it happens, yes."

Nodding as if this answered everything, Lucy replied, "Samantha is really being tortured?"

Suddenly, confronting Lucy seemed almost silly. Why was Mara here? Lucy didn't know where Samantha was. Lucy was more in the dark than Mara. At the least, Mara knew Samantha had been abducted and was currently being tortured by her kidnapper. Lucy was just someone Mara dreamt about, someone connected to Samantha . . .

Lucy interrupted her thoughts by asking, "Am I next? Is that why you're dreaming about me?"

Mara wasn't sure how to answer. *Was* that why she was dreaming of Lucy? It definitely was a fear. Terry seemed so adamant about protecting her. So, was Lucy truly the next victim on this kidnapper's list? And if he did take her, what did that mean for Samantha? Would he kill Samantha first, then take Lucy?

Mara was spinning, but she found herself saying, "I don't know why I'm dreaming about you. Adam dreamt about Samantha the same night I dreamt about you, so the two of you are connected. Probably because Samantha bullies you? I really don't know yet."

Both Lucy's and Barry's eyes stared at Adam as if he was some kind of exotic animal they were scared to interact with. They immediately focused back on Mara, obviously too intimidated to talk to Adam.

Then Barry suddenly blurted, "I'm Barry Ford, by the way."

Mara decided not to mince words and responded, "I know. I dreamt about you at the homecoming dance meeting and last night when you snuck into Lucy's room."

If two people could've gulped, Lucy and Barry would have in that instant.

"Whoa," Lucy said with slightly widened eyes. "Can you read my mind too?"

Mara nodded toward Kimiko. "No. That's her department. I just keep dreaming about you and Samantha. Maybe that means the kidnapper knows you both?"

It was almost amusing, Lucy and Barry swinging their heads over to Kimiko.

Kimiko shook her head. "Relax, I'm not going to read your minds. It doesn't work like that anyway. I can't exactly control it."

Adam sat forward to grab the two teenagers' attention. "Is there anything you can tell us that might help locate Samantha? She's running out of time."

"Is she hurt badly?" Barry asked, since Lucy's still form indicated she might be a little shell-shocked from Adam's "running out of time" bomb.

Mara decided to step in. "Yes. This man is torturing her severely. We need to find her before . . ." She couldn't find the right words to finish the sentence.

But Lucy did it for her. "Before he kills her."

Mara nodded.

Lucy sat back onto the couch, her expression genuinely puzzled. "I asked around today, since I'm sure you saw last night . . . or maybe you didn't . . . I . . . this is weird."

Mara tried to encourage Lucy to continue as best she could. "I saw that you two were going to try to find out what happened to Samantha."

"Right . . . Barry is in better with Sam's friends, so he talked to them while I tried to figure out who spoke to her last, what time and where. I know the police already did that, but some of the kids that saw her don't like the police, so we thought we might get something more out of them." Lucy started to relax a little. "So Mike seems to be the last one to see her. He was outside in the quad doing homework when he saw Samantha hurrying toward Hall B, which is weird because she was supposed to be at the homecoming dance meeting . . . or . . . well . . . you know, you were there I guess . . . but anyway, the meeting was in Hall A, so no one knows why she was headed to Hall B."

Mara could see Adam's wheels turning as he asked, "What's in Hall B? Any of her classes or teachers?"

Lucy shook her head. "That's the thing: Sam doesn't have any classes in Hall B. So we were thinking that whoever she met in there was the person that took her?" She eyed Mara, Adam, and Kimiko for approval.

Mara shrugged. "Maybe. But she could have left Hall B entirely. Is it on the way to the parking lot, or a shortcut to anywhere?"

Barry answered thoughtfully, "Sometimes students cut through there to get to the cafeteria, but this was after school; the lunchroom was closed."

Lucy added, "What we're talking about now is more in-depth than what the cops did. No one thinks Sam is kidnapped, they all think she ran away 'cause there's no evidence of a struggle or anything. They're saying your friend Agent Piper is kind of into things . . . well, into psychics and stuff . . . and no one around here really believes in that . . . sorry." Lucy lowered her head slightly at the last admission.

But Mara was used to it, and she was sure Raven was too.

So, the authorities weren't taking this case seriously.

Barry interjected, "Sam's mom is always out of town on business or taking sabbaticals without Sam or her brother. Her dad hasn't seen her in weeks because of the whole custody thing. Honestly, neither parent seems all that upset. I think they want to believe she ran away."

Lucy added, "Samantha's car is gone. That's kind of the whole reason they think she took off. I think the cops put out an APB for the car, but I really don't know for sure."

Mara sat forward, thinking aloud. "It means the kidnapper did something with the car. Maybe it's parked at his house in his garage or something. Maybe if we find the car, we can find Samantha?"

Adam turned to Mara. "Raven has to get involved in this. We need FBI resources to look for a car. They have access to cameras and things that the police don't have access to."

Mara agreed. "Yeah, maybe if we tell her no one is taking this seriously, she'll be able to do something." Then she focused on Barry. "What do the popular girls say? Anything that might help?"

Barry appeared as if he was really starting to get into this whole investigation thing. He leaned forward and spoke in a conspiratorial tone. "They're absolutely convinced that Samantha ran away. They said she's been talking about it for a while and hasn't exactly made it secret. I guess she just broke it off with Todd, and her friends figured leaving was the reason for that."

Kimiko asked Barry, "How long have Samantha and Todd been going out?"

"Since junior high. Everyone thought they'd get married and pop a few kids out after college. They're both going to go to the UW," Barry answered.

Kimiko addressed Mara. "If she just broke up with her longtime boyfriend, something was wrong. Or she was doing some serious soul searching. If I were in her friends' position, I'd think she ran away too."

Mara began to feel like the unofficial leader of this little detective agency. She nodded. "What about Todd? Could it be him?"

Lucy shook her head. "Todd was at football practice all afternoon when she supposedly ran away . . . or was taken. Then he was at the game that night. And for one of the popular kids, he's surprisingly a nice guy."

Mara wasn't as convinced, but she'd deal with researching Todd later. Her mind turned to other possibilities. "So, if not Todd, then the kidnapper must have known all about the break-up and their history together. He definitely goes to your school. There's no way he'd have access to all this info as an outsider."

"Unless he was a really good stalker," Lucy volunteered.

"True," Mara conceded. "But let's go on the assumption that it's someone at your school."

Lucy took a sip of her coffee. "Well, there are plenty of people who both love and hate Samantha."

"Let's start with the haters first," Mara suggested, and everyone mumbled their agreement.

"I'm going to be suspect number one if the cops ever take this seriously," Lucy announced with a slight shake in her voice.

Mara wanted to be honest, so she said bluntly, "Yes, you are.

But if we can find Samantha before that, then you won't have to worry about it getting that far. Can you make me a list of all the people you can think of that might hold a grudge against Samantha?"

Lucy nodded. "It's a long one."

"We'll try to get through them as fast as possible," Mara said.

Adam asked, "What do you suggest? Going by their houses?"

"Yeah, see if we can recognize anything, or sense anything. I don't know. We don't have much to go on, but at least it's something. Between the five of us, we have to be able to discover something. And in the meantime, maybe Agent Piper can track down Samantha's car."

Everyone's energy shifted to anticipation, making Mara believe they were all eager to participate, even Kimiko, who had only come along for the ride initially. Or, point in fact, she *was* the ride.

Mara and Lucy exchanged phones and typed in their contact information on each other's phone. Mara made sure she gave Lucy her email address as well as her number.

"Email me that list of people and keep me updated by text. Good?" Mara directed her focus on Lucy.

"List, texts, got it." Lucy stood up to leave.

Barry quickly followed suit, standing up with his friend. Before leaving, Barry shyly glanced over at Adam. "Congrats on your release, dude."

"Uh, thanks." Adam shifted uncomfortably.

As Lucy and Barry left Clutch, Kimiko turned to Adam. "Feels weird to be congratulated for being released from a mental ward?"

Adam leaned back on the couch. "Absolutely."

Kimiko continued, "You think that kid was a *fan*?"

Mara hadn't thought of that. She hadn't picked up any dastardly vibes from Barry, but then, she had thought Robert was a good guy for a moment too. "We'll keep an eye on him. He technically should be one of our number one suspects. I know they trust this Todd guy, but we should check him out as well, see if he's psycho. But Barry does know both girls and is close to Lucy, so if it were him, he may want some kind of revenge?"

"Definitely a start," Kimiko agreed.

At least they had a direction to go in now.

"Let's head back. Hopefully, campus police will have the mob cleared out by now." Mara finished the last of her mocha, and the three of them left Clutch and piled into Kimiko's car.

The ride back was spent going over the list of people Lucy emailed to Mara. She was surprised at how fast Lucy had compiled it. Then again, Mara knew every person Kimiko bullied when they'd been in high school together. There were fifteen people on the list with addresses. They were able to throw out five of them right off the bat because they were girls; Mara and Adam were positive the assailant was a man. Then they narrowed it down to eight because the others on the list were too young. Mara remembered through the ski mask that the kidnapper was young, but not that young. He'd have to be a junior or senior to be considered.

It was nice having a goal and purpose. It allowed Mara not to think about all the other stuff going on in her life. She made a quick phone call to Raven and asked her if she could run a search for Samantha's car, and Raven told her she started that search the day Mara had called. Feeling stupid, Mara thanked the agent and hung up.

Once they reached campus, the three of them grabbed a bite at a restaurant across from the parking lot. They talked more about what their next steps were going to be until Mara couldn't keep her eyes open anymore.

Kimiko walked them both back to Mara's dorm, just to make sure there were no surprise news gangs waiting to spring on them. It appeared as if campus police had indeed done their job by clearing out anyone who wasn't a student or faculty member.

Waving their goodbyes, Mara and Adam walked up the stairs and down the hall to Mara's dorm room. Mara was grateful for not having a roommate. It would have been an extra element of stress if she'd had to deal with another person when coming home with Adam in tow.

With waking up at four a.m. that morning, even though it was only eight p.m. now, Mara was exhausted.

Flopping onto her bed, Mara closed her eyes and fell instantly asleep.

Dream Entry #8

I can't believe I slept for twelve hours! It's eight a.m. and I'm writing in bed. Adam is still sleeping but, honestly, I'm not sure when he went to sleep, so he might be out for a while.

I had another doozy last night, and I have no idea what it means. Shocker. It was of Terry and Raven. I'm sure it's because now I know they're sisters . . .

Actually, I have no idea why I dreamt it. Terry scares me, and this dream only made it worse.

Terry stood on an island the size of a small car. It was surrounded by an ocean of blood, choppy, as if there was some kind of storm coming, though there were no clouds in the sky. The island itself was not like one of those cartoon islands with a single palm tree. It was made of rocks, sharp and ragged, with Terry's feet resting on spiked points.

I couldn't see myself like I normally do in dreams like this one. I was only a witness this time, an invisible witness.

Terry began screaming and, though no sound came out of her mouth, I could read her lips. One word: Raven.

As if calling her into existence, Raven appeared in the ocean of blood, swimming, panicked, blindfolded. No matter how hard Raven tried to swim forward, she stayed in the exact same spot. And the harder she tried to swim, the more she started to sink.

Terry tried to reach for Raven, all the while screaming her name again and again, but still no sound would come out. Terry grabbed at her throat, trying to force some kind of noise to come out.

But nothing.

Stepping one foot off the jagged rocks and into the ocean, Terry was stopped by an invisible barrier. Pounding on it with her hands and arms, Terry hammered against the solid clear wall until the bones in her arms snapped and broke through the skin. Terry didn't notice. She kept battering her broken, bloody arms against the wall that separated her from her sister.

Raven kept swimming, but she was sinking fast now, choking on the blood, drowning without even knowing where she was.

Finally, in a last desperate attempt to reach Raven, Terry backed up and ran toward the invisible wall, the sharp rocks tearing at her feet. She hit it full force, and her entire body collapsed on the pointed rocks, impaling every surface of her body as if she had fallen on a bed of nails.

Then my astral self or whatever went to Samantha after that insane-o nightmare. She looked like she was in a coma. At first I thought she was dead, but then her chest moved up and down, so at least I knew she was breathing. This is insane. I've never experienced anything like this before. Normally, I'll see a person the night of their death and that's it. Horrific, yes, but then it's over. I can wake up and recover, or help, or anything! But this? This is making my whole body and mind ache with sympathy. I've never seen anyone be tortured like this before, and I never want to again. This poor girl may have been horribly cruel to people, but no one deserves this, no one.

As I write this, my mind wanders to Kimiko. She was just like Samantha: a true, real-life mean-girl. But she's changed. She's like a whole new person. Or, maybe for the first time, Kimiko is able to be herself. The mean girl was a façade covering up how miserable she was. I had a big, long text conversation with Zia about it before I started writing in my journal. Zia is thrilled that Kimiko is finally becoming a decent human being. I think it makes Zia feel better about the fact that she used to not believe me when I told her Kimiko was horrible. I'm encouraging Zia to reach out to Kimiko. They always had some kind of connection. It would be nice for them to be friends again.

I sound like a therapist!

I'm trying very hard to erase the images of Samantha out of my head. I feel so helpless. I searched everywhere in that room for any clue or sign of where she might be. I did notice something new this time though. When I had searched the room before, I was positive there weren't any windows, but this time I noticed that there are two small ones painted over in black paint.

My only shred of hope at this point is that we find any house with paint on its basement windows. That's it. That's the only clue I have, that and the weird bloody-ocean-spiky-rock-island.

So yeah.

I got nothing.

***

Mara put her pen down and stuffed her journal in her bag for later. They needed to go to those houses on the list Lucy gave them as soon as humanly possible. Samantha was going to die if they didn't find her, of that, Mara was certain. And since they were possibly the only people looking for her, they had to try.

Since Adam was still asleep, Mara went out into the hallway to call Lucy.

After a few rings, Lucy picked up. "Hello?"

"Hey, Lucy, it's Mara. I'm thinking we need to get a move on with the house hunt. I saw some windows in a vision last night. They were painted black in the kidnapper's basement. I figured it's a start anyway," Mara confided.

A disappointed sigh from the other end. "Barry and I searched every house on the list at the crack of dawn this morning. We couldn't wait, too antsy. But Mara, none of them had basements."

A sinking sensation in Mara's chest threatened to take her breath away.

"I should check again. Maybe you and Barry weren't searching carefully because you didn't know about the painted windows." Her hope seeped away with each word. "And did you check Todd's house? I know you didn't think he was a suspect, but . . ."

Lucy cut Mara off. "We did. He was the first house we

went to. And, Mara, we searched those houses like we were inspecting for termites." Lucy's voice sounded small and sad. "There were no basements. It was the first thing we looked for." After a small, tense silence, Lucy said quietly, "I just want to find her."

"Yeah, me too." Mara didn't know what else to say.

They really did have nothing.

A house that could be anywhere in all of Seattle or Everett? Or it could be somewhere in a fifty-mile radius, or hundred-mile radius, if Mara was being honest with herself.

She felt completely helpless.

"Barry and I will keep wandering around the area, and if we find anything, I'll call you." Lucy tried to sound optimistic.

"Text me updates," Mara conceded.

"Will do. Bye, Mara," Lucy said shyly, then hung up.

Mara stood in the hallway alone for a long while, paralyzed with an overwhelming feeling of debilitation.

The small list of people who might have grudges against Samantha had been their only lead.

Glancing up at the clock in the dorm hallway, reality sank in.

Mara remembered she had her neuroscience class in a half hour. She had planned to skip it, to go on the hunt for painted basement windows, but seeing as that wasn't going to happen, she decided to try to live a normal life today. She hadn't had any real quality time with Adam, so maybe today could be the day for that.

But if she was going to class, she needed to get ready. Walking back into her dorm room, Mara quickly got dressed.

Feeling a knot of dread in her stomach, Mara wasn't sure if she'd be welcome at class after the last session. Dr. Laurence had been shocked and embarrassed by Kimiko's outburst last session. And since it was in defense of Mara, he might have them both escorted out. Mara really wasn't sure. She was tempted to skip again, but after everything that was happening with Samantha, and their only leads being dashed, there was a part of her that wanted to see if she could get Dr. Laurence to help her figure out what her brain was doing and how it worked during her sleep.

Maybe Kimiko's confrontation had humbled him? Mara seriously doubted it. Usually when people got embarrassed like that, in front of so many others, they fought back at the person who had done the deed. Mara just hoped Kimiko wasn't going to flake; otherwise, she'd have to face Dr. Laurence by herself, and at the moment that was a terrifying prospect.

Right on cue, Kimiko texted Mara: *Are you going to class or are we house hunting?*

Mara smiled and wondered if Kimiko had read her mind. She texted back: *Lucy and Barry already checked the houses. No go. Class it is?* Mara phrased it as a question to give Kimiko the option of skipping if she wanted.

Kimiko responded: *Let's do it. We should walk in together.*

Mara texted: *Where do you want to meet? We should sit together too.*

Kimiko texted: *Agreed. I'll meet you at the coffee cart in five.*

Mara texted: *On my way.*

Mara leaned down and kissed Adam's forehead. He stirred lazily awake.

"Go back to bed. The list of houses was a bust, so I'm going to class, but I'll be back in a couple of hours," Mara said quietly.

"You searched the houses without me?" Adam was already trying to get out of bed, but Mara gently pushed him back down.

"No, Lucy and Barry did. No luck. They even checked Todd's." Mara couldn't hide the disappointment from her voice. "You relax. I'll be back soon."

"You want me to walk you there?"

But Mara gently tucked him back in. "I'm fine. Kimiko and I are going together."

Adam smiled. "I never thought you saying that would bring me comfort."

"Tell me about it." Mara laughed a little and shrugged. She couldn't either.

Mara raced out the door and hurried to the coffee cart, where Kimiko was waiting with two coffees and two bagels.

She handed a pair to Mara. "I wasn't sure if you wanted cream or sugar, so I figured you could put it in yourself."

"Thank you, this is so nice." Mara's stomach growled, and the bagel was going to really hit the spot.

Kimiko smiled. "Sure, my pleasure." Then she gave Mara a withering look. "Are you ready for this? We may get kicked out as soon as we enter."

"At least we'll be together." A tiny part of Mara's brain froze at that sentence, but she mentally shrugged. Like it or not, the Universe had made it abundantly clear: Kimiko Thompson was her friend.

Wolfing down her bagel, Mara hurried to keep up with Kimiko, who moved a little faster than Mara had expected. Normally, a death march took some time. At least that was the pace Mara had wanted to go.

"We should just drop the class," Mara found herself saying to Kimiko.

Kimiko stopped Mara right before they were about to go in and stared her in the eyes, determined. "We're not going to let some blow-hard determine our college career. We have every right to take this class. No fear, okay?"

Mara nodded in agreement, but her insides flip-flopped.

Side by side, Mara and Kimiko walked into the half-full class and sat near the back, just in case they had to make a speedy exit.

Mara's heart stopped when Dr. Laurence's eyes met hers, then he glanced over at Kimiko.

Here it comes.

But nothing. He went back to skimming over his lesson plan as if two ordinary students had sat down in his class.

As for the other students, they all kept glancing from Dr. Laurence to Mara and Kimiko, waiting for an all-out brawl, or something exciting. But after a few minutes of a whole lot of nothing, it seemed like everyone gave up on the idea of anything happening, which for most of the kids in the class was disappointing since the subject of neuroscience wasn't exactly high on their "entertainment" list.

When the bell buzzed, Mara kept waiting for the proverbial shoe to drop, but it never did. For the entire lecture Dr. Laurence kept it civil, he kept it informative, and surprisingly, he kept it cool. Mara almost didn't know what to do with herself when he finished up the class with a promise to explore more theoretical aspects of neuroscience.

The bell buzzed and class was over. Did they dodge a bullet?

As the class began to file out of the room, Mara really thought they had until . . .

The fateful words came out of Dr. Laurence's mouth. "Ms. Johnson, Ms. Thompson, may I see the two of you up here please?"

Gulp.

Mara and Kimiko gave each other a nod of support as they walked up to Dr. Laurence at the front of the class. Some of the students lingered, obviously wondering if they were finally going to get that confrontation they had been hoping for.

But Dr. Laurence squashed it by addressing the remaining students. "It's time to leave."

The students tried to hide their disappointment as they left the room.

After the class was empty, Dr. Laurence sighed as he looked at Mara and Kimiko. "So . . ." he said.

So? Mara found it difficult to breathe.

Kimiko took the lead though. "*So?* Let me guess, you're wondering how I was able to tell you about your dream that you had told no one about?"

Dr. Laurence raised his eyebrow at Kimiko's attitude, but then visibly calmed himself. "I figured that part out on my own."

Mara didn't like the sound of that. It sounded like a nonbeliever who had come up with a "theory" that would debunk their gifts.

But Dr. Laurence surprised them both again when he said, "You read my mind."

Kimiko reared her head back slightly at his honesty. "Yes, I did. You were thinking about that god-awful dream the entire class, then when you ridiculed Mara, I had to say something."

"I wasn't trying to ridicule anyone." Dr. Laurence sounded like he meant that, but still, what he had said . . .

Kimiko wasn't letting him off the hook. "How else would one interpret: 'I would guess that your dreams come from the cortex since that's where we invent monsters and imaginary events'?" Another surge of friendship toward Kimiko filled Mara.

Dr. Laurence slowly started to nod. "You're right. That was unnecessarily cruel and uncalled for. I've had to deal with a lot of crazies and . . ." He stopped himself, seemed to think better of what he was about to say, then continued, ". . . people who claimed to be psychic, and in my experience, I've never believed any of them. It wasn't until you shared my dream with the class that I realized I may have been hasty in my presumptions."

He turned to Mara. "I contacted the FBI and asked for the case files on you and Adam Layton. I told them it was for research for my class since you had claimed that you dreamt of the murders that had taken place. They refused at first until I was able to talk to an Agent Piper. When she heard I was your professor, she sent me the Cliffs Notes version, then expressed to me that she never would have broken the case without you, nor would she be alive."

A pang of love filled Mara for Raven. She had unknowingly put Mara's professor in his place, thinking he genuinely was doing research for his class. Mara suddenly found her voice.

"So what are you saying? You believe me?"

"I'm saying: I'm keeping an open mind, but yes, I'm inclined to believe you. Not that it should matter what I think," Dr. Laurence clarified.

"That's the truth." Kimiko wasn't done with her attitude yet, and Mara appreciated it.

Dr. Laurence ignored Kimiko's brashness and said, "I'm also inclined to help you. I've never truly explored the neuroscience behind what people call psychic dreams, but if you agree, I'd love to observe you while you're asleep."

"Like watch me?" Mara thought that sounded a bit vampire-creepy.

Dr. Laurence chuckled. "No. With equipment. A real study. So you can find answers as well."

A thrill of excitement filled her chest with a sudden hope that she might be able to find Samantha. "I'm in," she said without conferring with Kimiko.

But Kimiko appeared genuinely pleased by the notion.

From the deep breath, slightly widened eyes, and raised eyebrows, Mara could only conclude that her teacher was a bit shocked that his request had been accepted. "Good. That's excellent news." Dr. Laurence nodded his appreciation. "The campus has a Sleep Lab in Building 20. I can meet you there tonight at nine p.m. if you want to get started?"

"Yes, that would be wonderful. Thank you so much, Dr. Laurence." Mara was genuinely grateful and genuinely happy. This was what she had wanted from the start. She just wanted to learn the science behind her dreams if that was possible, and if there was a chance that these machines might be able to find Samantha . . . She didn't know how, but Mara held on to any hope that she could.

Then a thought hit her. "Can I bring my boyfriend? He dreams too." And he had a stronger connection to Samantha since he'd dreamt about her first.

Dr. Laurence couldn't hide the surprise from his face. "Adam Layton? Do you think he'd agree to that?"

"I'm not sure, but I can ask him," Mara answered. She didn't want to volunteer Adam for sure without getting his permission first, but she was pretty sure he'd do anything that might help find Samantha.

"That would be great for my research, thank you, but even if he doesn't make it, I'll see you at nine?" Dr. Laurence asked, hopeful.

"Yes, I'll see you at nine."

Kimiko had to get the last word in when she warned him, "I'm coming too, to keep an eye on you."

Dr. Laurence didn't seem fazed at all by this. "Of course. I'd expect nothing less. Mara is lucky to have a guardian like you. Good day, Ms. Thompson, Ms. Johnson. I'll see you tonight."

And with that he left the classroom without another glance back.

Mara and Kimiko stared at one another, not sure what to make of what had just happened.

Finally Kimiko spoke. "Well, that was weird."

"Yeah, but am I crazy? Maybe we could figure out a way to find out where Samantha is?" Mara confessed her secret hope, and besides that, Mara liked the idea of finding out something scientific about her gift, that it would somehow give her legitimacy from previous doubters like Dr. Laurence in the future.

"I don't know how it'll help, but it's worth a shot," Kimiko conceded, then nodded toward the door. "We better get back to your boy and tell him what you volunteered him for."

"I didn't promise Dr. Laurence anything." Mara was suddenly

panicked at the thought of volunteering Adam for something that he might be adamantly against.

"Yeah, yeah." Kimiko rolled her eyes playfully. "That boy is crazy about you. If you told him to eat a slug, he'd do it in a heartbeat."

"That's not true," Mara disagreed.

"Uh-huh," Kimiko laughed knowingly. "You keep telling yourself that." Then she said thoughtfully, "Adam will want to help. Now, let's get out of here."

Mara agreed with that, and the two of them left the classroom.

Kimiko said her goodbyes at Mara's dorm building, and Mara went upstairs to find Adam eating a donut with a cup of coffee at her desk. He was scrolling through the internet.

When Mara walked in, Adam smiled. "These donuts are amazing."

Mara walked over to him and sat on his lap, his arms wrapped around her. "My professor is finally taking my dreams seriously-ish."

Adam perked up at that. "That's good news, right?"

"He wants to do a sleep study on me," Mara explained. "Of course this will be the first night I don't have one of my visions. I've never wanted to have one more, now that Lucy and Barry couldn't find the house. This may be our only hope of finding Samantha. I have no idea what Dr. Laurence's probe-y things will say though."

"Could I do it too?" Adam asked with interest. "Maybe it'll up our chances of finding her."

"I'm so glad you said that . . ." Mara started, then finished quickly, "because I kind of volunteered you, but then I told him

I'd have to ask you first. But it would be perfect because you know how to dream jump on command and—"

Adam silenced her with a kiss, then said with a smile, "This is a good thing."

Mara had been so afraid she had overstepped her bounds, but was now relieved Adam was on the same page for trying anything to rescue Samantha.

He kissed her again. "And I'll make sure I dream jump into your head, instead of bringing you into mine, so we can get the best results from your scan. Hopefully, we can jump to Samantha's location and see what the machines tell us." Then he asked, "Are you sure we can trust this guy? I would think dream scans from a convicted killer and the girl whose dreams brought him down would be worth something to the press or at least a bestselling book from a tenured science professor."

Mara shrugged. "It's kind of worth the risk, don't you think?"

"For potentially finding a girl who's being systematically tortured? Uh, yeah. But also, long-term here, if he does find definitive proof, then people will stop looking at us like we're lying freaks," Adam said with some emotion.

Mara nodded and was glad Adam knew what she was thinking. The chances were low that these machines would help them find Samantha, but they had to try. And Adam was right about the long-term. Mara hated uttering the word "psychic" out loud for constant fear of judgment, but if there was some way to prove what she could do scientifically, then maybe people would view her differently.

"Well, we have all day to kill. What on earth should we do?" Adam's arms wrapped around her a little tighter.

“I guess we’re staying in.” Mara smiled and leaned down, kissing Adam with all the passion she felt for him. His lips moved with hers, and her brain melted into the sensation.

Adam lifted Mara up into his arms and brought her to the bed, his hands clasping her waist as he laid her down gently onto the covers.

His gentle touch made Mara’s head explode with a love she couldn’t put into words; it was so powerful.

Mara let her mind meld into the moment as she and Adam made love.

***

The whole day was the “Mara and Adam” reunion Mara had imagined for their first day together. She hated that it was at the expense of not finding Samantha but, as there was nothing either of them could do, Mara decided to just enjoy the moment. She could barely come up for air as they lost themselves in each other.

And pizza. Lots of pizza.

Ordering in, watching Netflix, and being intimate with each other.

Mara couldn’t remember having a more perfect day.

That was why when Mara glanced over at the clock and it said 8:43 p.m., she leapt out of bed. “Holy crap. We have to get to the Sleep Lab!”

“Oops! Little distracted.” Adam laughed.

Tearing out the door, the two of them hurried over to the building where the Sleep Lab was and waved when they saw Kimiko waiting outside with a cup of coffee in her hands.

“I would have brought you guys a couple of cups, but I figured the caffeine wouldn’t be good for a Sleep Lab,” Kimiko greeted them.

"Good call," Adam acknowledged jovially.

The three of them walked into the building and made their way to the third floor, where the Sleep Lab resided.

Dr. Laurence was already there setting up his equipment.

There were several rooms with open doors along the east wall. Mara could see beds in each of them.

At the center of the lab was Dr. Laurence's station, which gave Mara a modicum of relief. Part of her had been worried her professor was going to hover over them the entire night. It was nice to see that she and Adam would be in a separate room.

Dr. Laurence's face brightened when he saw the trio enter. "Please, come in." He ushered them over to his station. It was a brown desk with eight monitors placed on a shelf above. Four computer towers rested underneath the desk, with a stack of notepads being the only thing on the desk itself. Dr. Laurence held his hand out for Adam to take, which Adam did heartily. "Very nice to meet you, Mr. Layton. I'm so glad you decided to volunteer."

"Call me Adam, and I'm just as curious as you are on what the machines will pick up." Adam was super polite as usual.

Dr. Laurence appeared extra excited at Adam's enthusiasm.

Mara had never seen her teacher have this much energy for anything. It wasn't that his lectures were boring, it was that he was so much more animated now. Like someone had flipped a switch in his brain.

Dr. Laurence continued, "I managed to reschedule all the students coming in for a sleep study tonight, so we'll have the place to ourselves. I figure you two will want as much privacy as possible, considering the mob that accosted you yesterday."

"Uh, thanks." Mara was still shy around teachers, especially outside of a classroom setting. It was too . . . personal.

But Dr. Laurence didn't seem to mind a bit. Or, at least, he appeared used to this kind of behavior from students. He motioned to the two bedrooms directly in front of them. "You'll have to be in two separate rooms so we can have an accurate reading."

Debating whether or not she should tell Dr. Laurence of her and Adam's true intentions of trying to find Samantha, Mara decided she'd wait to see what happened first. Why stir the pot if Mara couldn't jump into Samantha's location?

"Let's get you guys hooked up." Dr. Laurence motioned toward the rooms with his head, and he was smiling.

Mara had never seen him smile, let alone a smile directed at her, and she decided she liked it. It was far better than having him belittle her in front of all her classmates. She'd take happy-professor over angry-professor any day.

Adam pushed slightly forward so that he could go first, since he knew Mara was a little nervous. He kissed her forehead before he went with Dr. Laurence into one of the bedrooms.

From afar, Mara could see her professor suction cup what looked like endless leads on Adam's head, face, and chest.

Kimiko watched as well. "I swear if Dr. Laurence does anything wonky, or thinks anything wonky, I'll wake the two of you up and we're out of here."

Mara gave her a smile of thanks, then motioned to the monitors. "Try to figure out what he's recording. I want to know if you see anything different. I kind of don't trust that he'll tell us everything." Mara couldn't help but suspect that Dr. Laurence would try to use the results as proof that Mara was a fake, rather than the other way around, considering her history with the professor.

After a few moments, Dr. Laurence motioned for Mara to follow him into the bedroom next to Adam's. As she gave Adam a little wave as she passed by, Adam looked like he had electric insects crawling over his body. She knew she'd soon be joining him, but it gave her a jolt of panic. What if she couldn't fall asleep? What if Adam couldn't reach her? What if this whole thing was a mistake?

Before Mara could run in terror, Dr. Laurence plopped the sensors on her. They were cold and sticky as he situated each one individually in the proper place. And just as quickly as he started, the professor was finished. "I know it's going to be hard, but the sooner you fall asleep, the sooner we can see what's going on in that brain of yours."

No pressure.

"I'll try," was all Mara could say.

Dang. She was more nervous than she thought. There was way more than a sleep study at stake here. A girl's life depended on Mara to help find her somehow.

Dr. Laurence smiled and left the room.

Peering toward her teacher's desk, Kimiko gave her a thumbs-up before Dr. Laurence shut the door, leaving her in darkness.

Invoking her meditation for sleeping, Mara breathed in while repeating the word *relax*, then breathed out repeating the word *sleep*.

Clearing all thoughts from her head was difficult, but the day's events had left her physically exhausted at least. That would help for sleeping . . .

***

Mara was with Samantha.

Wow.

She thought for sure she'd be floating in dreamland for a while before she ended up here. Mara had begun to doubt that she'd end up here or at Lucy's at all! Visions weren't something she could control, especially when Mara desperately wanted to be here. But from the bruises, cuts, and burns on Samantha's body, Mara figured whatever was drawing her to Samantha was coming to a head.

"Is she even alive?" Adam's voice came from beside her.

His hand entwined with hers, and she held on to it tightly. Mara was tired of seeing Samantha being tortured more and more every day. It weighed on her soul. Her helplessness at its peak.

"I can see her chest move," Mara said, using the same tactics as before to know if Samantha was alive or not.

"Barely," Adam observed somberly.

"She may die of her wounds." There was a catch in her voice.

Adam's hand squeezed tighter in support. "What can we do?"

Mara stared at Samantha at a loss. "I don't know."

Piper's sister, Terry, materialized in front of them.

And she was in total focus.

No sizzle. No static.

Perfectly solid.

Seeing Terry there, feeling her presence, sent shivers down Mara's spine.

"Please," Mara pleaded, "tell us where Samantha is! You're a ghost. You can see things we can't! Tell us!"

But Terry shook her head, no longer half there, no longer yelling or angry. Mara would have thought Terry was real, like Adam or herself. Then Terry said very clearly, very coherently, "I can't see where she is. I'm drawn here the same as you." Then her mood shifted, her expression angry like before in the earlier visions. "I see more important things! Things you need to do!"

After a quick moment, Terry appeared to calm herself again, explaining, "Samantha and Lucy are completing a circle for the man that lives here, but you have to protect her."

"We're trying!" Mara was upset herself.

Adam tried to intervene. "How do you want us to protect Lucy?"

This seemed to spark Terry's temper again. She screamed, "You understand nothing! Protect her from *him*! I can't see him, but I know him! My mind is confused, it's not all here!" She began to pace, frustrated. "I was sleeping for a long time, then I was awake. I don't remember much about myself, about what happened to me. Pieces of my life come in brief flashes. It's . . . confusing. He hides from me! But he's going to take her! It's what woke me up! He's going to take her to where I am! I can't have her here! It's not her time! Don't let him take her to me! It's all up to you!" Every word was directed at Mara, as if Adam hadn't spoken or was even in the room.

"I will." Mara made the promise out of desperation. Each screaming word sent chills through her bones to the point where

Mara shivered in the vision.

Adam turned to her. "Mara, your lips and skin . . ."

Mara's arms were blue. She grew colder by the second.

Adam went into protection mode. "You're killing Mara!" He took his free hand and shoved Terry as hard as he could. Surprisingly, his hand made contact even though she was a ghost, and Terry flew back against the wall.

This amped up her rage even more. Leaping to her feet, Terry charged toward Adam.

Mara couldn't stop her teeth from chattering. She knew she was in a dream, but she felt like she was freezing to death.

Adam wrapped his arms around her as tightly as he could. "Hold on."

Right before Terry could make contact with the two of them, Adam yanked them out of the vision.

***

Mara woke up, but she was dazed and disoriented.

Distant, urgent voices echoed in the background.

She barely made out Kimiko screaming, "*You son of a bitch! You did this to her!*"

Then Dr. Laurence's panicked response: "I don't know what's happening! I swear I was just monitoring their brain waves!"

"I got it, I got it. Move over." Adam's voice was soothing in the tunnel Mara was in.

Feeling his arms wrap around her, Mara's heart rate began to slow down to a normal pace, but she was still . . .

Freezing.

Adam's voice grew louder as Mara started to come out of her daze. "We need heaters and blankets!"

Dr. Laurence answered, "I've got an electric blanket in the other room. I'll be right back."

Finally, Mara's eyes were able to focus, her teeth chattered, but she managed to say, "I'm okay. I'm just so cold."

Kimiko's face leaned close to Mara's, her eyes saucers of concern. "Your temperature dropped suddenly, and then you turned all blue. I thought Professor A-hole did something to you, but he was more surprised than I was."

Dr. Laurence rushed in, plugged in the blanket, then handed it to Adam to wrap around Mara. It took a few minutes, but then the heat kicked in and Mara's body began to relax.

Once she was coherent and warm enough to talk, she addressed her teacher, whose face was pale. "What did the scans show? Could you find her? Was there anything?"

Dr. Laurence shook his head in confusion. "Find who? Were you looking for someone?"

Mara's teeth chattered, though she was rapidly warming up. "The missing girl in the news: Samantha Perkins. We were there. Can the scans show us . . . anything?" It sounded stupid as soon as Mara gave words to the theory. What would computer readings show about locations? It would just be showing what was happening in Mara's brain.

Shaking his head, Dr. Laurence said, "I haven't examined the scans. We need to make sure you're all right first. I've . . . I've never seen anything like this. I wouldn't have believed you if you told me. Of course you know that already. I'm an arrogant fool . . ."

Mara cut her teacher off before he rambled any further. "I'm going to tell you what happened, and you're not going to want to believe me, but it's the truth, okay?" When Dr. Laurence nodded, Mara continued, "I was in a vision. Samantha: she's not doing too well. I don't think she's going to make it much longer. A ghost—Terry Piper, she's FBI Agent Raven Piper's dead sister—keeps telling me to protect another student, Lucy Tildon. For some reason Terry seemed to be angrier this time. I think she was frustrated with me, and the angrier she got, the colder I got. If Adam hadn't pulled us out of there . . ."

Kimiko placed a grateful hand on Adam's shoulder.

Dr. Laurence nodded. Mara could see the conflict inside him. He didn't want to believe, but he also couldn't explain what had happened.

"As a scientist, I do find it hard to comprehend what you're telling me. But I saw it . . . I *saw* it." He shook his head as if trying to convince himself, almost like he wondered if Mara had set up the lab before she came and was playing a hoax on him.

Mara knew she needed to back off on explaining what happened in her vision. Visions were one thing, visiting ghosts were something else entirely. So she decided to appeal to his scientific nature. "Let's look at those scans."

Dream Entry #9

We're at home now. Even Kimiko is staying the night on the extra dorm bed of my imaginary roommate. After going over some of the results from the sleep study, it was clear that Dr. Laurence needs to go over them himself. They meant nothing to any of us, except that it looked pretty cool. When I got hit with the cold attack from Terry, my heart rate skyrocketed and the heat sensors immediately showed my whole body as a blue cartoony blob, whereas before it was all red and orange. I'm still freaking out about what Terry did to me. I'm terrified to go to sleep. I thought I was scared before, but now?

Could she kill me? Is that possible? It certainly felt that way. I'm going to call Raven in the morning, see what she can tell me about her sister that might help with the attacks.

I'm curious what Dr. Laurence is going to find. He seemed amped up when we left him. I think his doubts are gone now, seeing everything he saw firsthand, which is both good and bad. I'm afraid he's going to want to use me as his lab rat, but I'm okay with that if it means we might be able to locate Samantha. I still don't know how, but I'm weirdly hopeful. He already asked when I was free again for another study. He stopped midsentence, though, when Kimiko looked at him like she was going to punch all his teeth in. I gotta say, I'm so glad she's on my side as opposed to being my enemy. She's already asleep. I can hear her snoring softly. And Adam is beside me zonked out as well. I pretended to go to sleep first (he wouldn't shut his eyes until I did), but I was too wired and I wanted him to get some rest.

Out of all this, my biggest concern is Samantha. Once I had the electric blanket, I was fine, but she was still out there in some deranged lunatic's basement covered in wounds that she may die from. It was difficult to believe Terry that she couldn't tell me where Samantha was. How could a ghost not be able to . . . I don't know, float up and see where the darn house is? You'd think being a ghost would have some perks! Adam, Kimiko, and I all vowed that tomorrow we are going on our own house search. We're going to drive and drive until we find those black-painted basement windows and get Samantha out of there.

In all likelihood stupid and pointless, but we have to try. Maybe Kimiko's mind reading will help? We just don't have any answers.

And if we do miraculously find Samantha, I'm praying we won't be too late.

***

Mara wasn't sure how she was going to sleep.

When she had finally recovered fully from the freeze-attack, her first instinct was to call her mother. Claire had always been the one Mara turned to when she'd have a particularly bad vision or experience. The hard reality was, her parents weren't there for her anymore. They cared more about Mara breaking up with Adam and sending him back to the psych ward than they did about their daughter. Whether they saw it that way or not, the proof came from their actions. *They* stuck the press on Mara, and *they* weren't here for her tonight.

It strangely helped Mara to think about all the horrible decisions her parents had made the last week or so. She'd rather be angry than sad. It was just too painful otherwise.

Mara tucked her journal under her pillow and laid her head down. If she fell asleep, she fell asleep. She didn't think it was going to happen though.

***

Okay.

If Mara didn't know she wasn't in a dream, she'd be seriously freaking out right now. Her body was crammed in a small metal box. Trying to adjust herself, Mara found that she couldn't move much in any direction.

Where was she?

Three slits that looked like air vents stood at eye level and were her only source of light. Peering through, she could see people walking at a leisurely pace. From their age, they were high school students.

At that point the mystery was over: Mara was inside a locker.

It made her appreciate the fact that at least Kimiko had never shoved her into a locker. Of course, if Kimiko *had* ever done that, Zia would have raised holy hell, which was no doubt why Kimiko had stuck to the mental torture variety.

Mara tried to push her hand through the metal door to see if she could control this dream. It hit solid metal. This was someone else's vision or memory. She'd just have to live through it.

"Adam?" she called out.

Maybe this was a memory of his? Mara knew Colt had done some horrible things to Adam before they became secret friends with Robert, though Adam never mentioned being shoved inside a locker.

After a moment and no answer, Mara knew this couldn't be Adam's dream. He would have heard her and let her out by now.

So, no Adam—and still stuck in a metal rectangle.

Knowing it was a dream didn't stop Mara from cramping. When was she going to wake up? More importantly: Why was she here?

A figure approached the locker at a fast pace as the students thinned out and headed to their next class. Through the slats, Mara recognized Terry instantly, her face worried as she dialed the combination to open the door.

Please don't freeze me. Please don't freeze me.

But like a sweet breath of relief, the door swung open and Mara spilled out onto the linoleum floor.

"Terry, what are we doing here?" Mara asked, still afraid Terry might attack her again.

But this Terry wasn't ghost-Terry. This Terry's eyes were round with concern, and she was immediately helping Mara to her feet . . . acting as if she hadn't heard Mara at all. "I can't believe he did this to you."

Mara started to answer but found other words spilling out of her mouth without her control. "How did you find me? You don't even go to this school."

Whoa.

Mara was in some kind of memory vision. She looked down at her arms, legs, and body . . . a boy, definitely a boy. From the lankiness and size, probably around fourteen?

Like the young man from the cement room full of blood who Terry had stood next to.

Was this the same person?

If this was Terry's memory, why was Mara seeing through the boy's eyes?

And being shoved into a locker? Bullied?

Was this the kidnapper as an adolescent?

If it was, then Terry knew him.

If Mara was in the kidnapper's body—right now, in this memory—she needed to try to get Terry to say his name. Identify him.

Find Samantha.

Supporting Mara by the arm, Terry led her toward doors that were labeled as the exit. "I was sitting in Biology, and I saw a vision of you stuffed inside your locker. I came as soon as the bell rang, but I had to take my bike so I'm sorry it took me so long."

Answering words poured out of Mara's mouth without her control. "Are you kidding? Don't apologize. I would have been in there all night if you hadn't had a . . . vision . . . or whatever. How did you know my locker combination?"

As Terry and Mara stepped outside, Terry turned to her and smiled. "That came to me too."

So Terry had visions of this guy and tried to help him.

But if Mara was truly inside the body of the kidnapper, which she was positive she was, what turned him into an abusive psychopath who kidnapped bullies and tortured them? And what had happened to Terry? Had this guy's bully killed her and *that* was why he took bullies, to somehow punish them for Terry's death?

Before Mara could think more on the subject, words were forced out of her. "Thank you, Terry. I don't know what I'd do without you." A surge of affection flooded through Mara as the words came out of her mouth.

The kidnapper loved Terry, and from the sparkle in Terry's eyes as she looked into Mara's, Mara could tell that Terry loved him back.

Still feeling the warmth of the feeling between Terry and the kidnapper, Mara drifted into another dream. As in a real, honest to goodness, normal dream.

Well, almost normal. What set it apart from a truly normal dream was the fact that Mara was still aware. But she'd been aware in dreams before and had really enjoyed them. These were the kind of dreams that she could control. Not the kind where she was stuck in lockers and couldn't speak her own words!

And no name.

Mara hadn't heard Terry use his name.

She was still in the dark as to the kidnapper's identity.

Needing to relax and distance herself from all her anxiety and stress, Mara decided she would fly because . . . flying. No real explanation required.

And Mara needed that right now, especially after being stuffed into a metal box.

Imagining the ground to be the greenest of green and the sky to be the bluest of blue, Mara created a serene setting. Then she jumped and was instantly airborne. Feeling the air against her face, soaring across the green landscape, Mara let go of everything and just allowed herself to truly be free.

No more violent images, no more anguish about her parents, and no more stressing about anything.

Just Mara and the sky.

A tugging almost dropped her from the air.

Her stomach sank. Was this ghost-Terry grabbing at her? Memory-dream-Terry seemed okay, but ghost-Terry had almost killed her!

But the tugging was gentle, more a nudging than the yanking ghost-Terry had exhibited before.

Mara decided to allow herself to flow with the slight pulling. It somehow felt right. Familiar.

As she glided closer to the ground, Mara saw her destination and it made her heart soar with longing and happiness.

A field of sunflowers.

Where, in a small grove in the middle of the field, Mara could make out Great-Uncle John waving at her with a smile, as he had when he'd been alive.

As she landed in front of him, his arms wrapped tightly around her. Feeling his warmth gave Mara a comfort she desperately needed. She knew in that moment that this was real.

The spirit of Great-Uncle John was here, in front of her, hugging her . . .

Because he knew she needed him.

It filled her eyes with tears of gratefulness and intense love.

No more Terry, just Uncle John please.

Pulling away, John scruffed Mara's hair with affection like he used to. "Been pretty rough for you, huh, kid?"

Mara couldn't find words, so she simply nodded.

Her great-uncle brushed his hand against her cheek, his eyes full of concern and affection. "Terry has loosened her grip a bit, but when she's angry . . . let's just say angry ghosts are hard to reason with."

"She tried to kill me." Mara voiced her fears.

"She didn't mean to. She doesn't know how powerful she is. I helped her, though. The next time you confront her, she'll be more willing to talk . . . or more capable anyway, at least I hope so."

"That body I was in. It was the kidnapper, wasn't it?"

Uncle John nodded. "I can't see him though, and Terry can't seem to say his name or show who he is. Her mind isn't all here yet."

Mara knew she should dig for more information, to help save Samantha, but she wanted to be here, in the present, with John. "I haven't seen you in a while . . . I thought you were gone." Looking at their surroundings and then up at his face, she said, "This feels like you're alive and here with me." Mara didn't want it to end. When everything happened with Adam and Robert, her great-uncle had found ways to communicate with her, warn her, but it was never this open, this easy.

"I think it's because of Terry. She was like you when she was alive, and I think she somehow opened a part of your brain that let me in fully. I don't know if it'll stay that way." John looked hopeful though. "I can already feel myself fading, so we'd best be quick."

A knot in Mara's stomach wrenched at the thought of leaving.

But she knew she had to focus on Samantha. She asked, "I

know you can't see the kidnapper, but do you know where the missing girl is? Can you see her?"

Great-Uncle John shook his head. "I can't. I'm tethered to you, Mara. I can only see what you see. Terry is the same. It's the only reason I was able to help."

"Terry is tethered to me? How? I never knew her." Mara didn't mind the word *tether* in regards to her great-uncle, but hearing it in reference to Terry? Was she stuck with this ghost for the rest of her life?

"It's because of your connection to Raven that Terry came to you. And because of your gifts. It seems like she knew this creep before she died. But I'm only guessing, Mara." His eyes filled with tears as he looked at Mara. "I'm just a spirit that can't let go of his grandniece."

Wrapping his hands around hers, he squeezed tightly. "You must be careful, Mara. I can't see everything, but I can see you're in real trouble again. But you can trust Adam and Kimiko. They'll help you through this." John's hands began to fade. "I have to go."

"No, please stay. I need you," Mara pleaded desperately.

Leaning down, John kissed the top of her head. "I'm always with you."

***

Mara woke with a start.

No! She desperately wanted to go back to Uncle John, but her phone buzzed and beeped to the point where she was forced to wake up fully. Not remembering setting it, Mara reached over to her table and shut off the alarm.

Kimiko groaned from the bed across the room, while Adam

was . . .

Gone.

Mara jolted out of bed. "Where's Adam?"

Kimiko groggily sat up in bed, searching the room. "You know as much as I do."

A jab of panic. Her first thoughts were that he'd been taken by the kidnapper somehow. She knew it was irrational, but her brain still wasn't working properly without coffee.

Kimiko got out of bed and walked over to Mara. "You okay? I'm sure he just needed some air or something."

Mara nodded, trying to shake her fears.

The doorknob rattled, and Adam walked through it with two paper bags and a tray of coffee.

Kimiko gave Mara a knowing nod. "See?" Then she stood up and helped Adam with the coffee and one of the bags. "You're a saint."

Adam visibly cringed at the compliment, which broke Mara's heart, but she echoed Kimiko's sentiment. "That smells amazing. You're amazing." Mara walked over to Adam and kissed him her thanks.

Placing the food down on a desk, the three of them chowed down on fast-food breakfast sandwiches and black coffee. It hit the spot.

Through full bites, Mara admitted, "I was worried about you."

Adam's chest fell, and Mara wished she hadn't said anything, but he replied, "I wanted to surprise you. I honestly didn't think you'd be awake. You were out cold, which made me very happy."

"I had a flying dream, so that was awesome." Then Mara

turned serious. "I also dreamt of Terry . . ."

"What?" Adam and Kimiko said in unison, fear and worry in both their expressions.

"Relax. It was a memory, the kidnapper's I think. Ghost-Terry wasn't even there. It was just memory-Terry, so she couldn't hurt me." Mara told them all the details of the memory, then she added, "My great-uncle John's ghost visited me too."

"You had a busy night. His spirit was actually there?" Kimiko asked. "I'd give anything to see my grandmother again."

Mara felt for her, especially since Mara had witnessed Kimiko's grandmother's murder in her dreams. The fact that her great-uncle (who was really her grandfather in her eyes) was also murdered only made Mara realize how much more the two of them had in common.

Mara told them everything John had said in the dream.

"So neither ghost can help us find Samantha." Kimiko sighed in disappointment. "But we now know that Terry knew the kidnapper before she died." She shrugged. "Progress." Then she smiled. "But I'm weirdly giddy that your uncle told you that you can trust us. Because you can." Her expression was tinged with insecurity.

Nodding, Mara said, "I know I can."

Mara's phone rang, and she reached over to pick it up. "Hello?"

"Mara, it's Raven." Agent Piper's voice sounded concerned.

"I was going to call you. Something big happened with your sister last night, and I don't think Samantha has much time," Mara thundered forward.

Agent Piper replied, "You'll have to tell me the details later, but Mara, Samantha Perkins has been released. The police found her naked in her car. It was parked in an alley in downtown Seattle. She's at the hospital, and they're not sure she's going to make it. Do you think you can meet me there?"

Mara's stomach dropped at the news. Responding quickly, Mara said, "Of course. I'm going to bring Adam and Kimiko too."

"The more help the better. The police still thought Samantha had run away. We lost so much time, and I'm not sure she'll be much help. The trauma is so great, Samantha hasn't spoken yet. The doctors say it could be from the severe burns she has in her mouth and throat, but it could also be that she's in shock."

Mara remembered those burns. It was horrible thinking about what Samantha had gone through. "Which hospital?"

"Seattle Memorial, room 238."

"We're on our way." After exchanging goodbyes, Mara hung up the phone.

Mara filled in Adam and Kimiko on everything Raven had told her.

"I noticed Agent Piper glossed right over the part where you told her about her sister acting wonky," Kimiko pointed out.

"Yeah, I noticed that too," Mara agreed. "Maybe when we get to the hospital we can talk to her about it. Let's just get over there."

They all agreed and headed out the door. This time Mara decided she wanted to drive, so they all piled into her VW Bug and drove to Seattle Memorial. Parking was a pain due to the excessive amount of news trucks. Mara was getting the feeling that she'd never be able to shake these guys. They weren't after her and Adam this time, though, they were after Samantha. Of course, as soon as the two of them were spotted, the reporters would have a field day, wondering why Mara Johnson and Adam Layton were visiting FBI Agent Raven Piper and the victim, Samantha Perkins. Mara hoped they could avoid most of the media if at all possible.

After they signed in as visitors, an attendant motioned them toward a side hall. "Agent Piper said I'm to take you up the service elevator. She doesn't want you with the press and other visitors."

Always thinking ahead, Mara was relieved to be led by the attendant up the service elevator and down an almost empty back hallway until they reached Agent Piper.

When Raven saw Mara, she immediately embraced her. Sometimes Mara forgot how beautiful Raven was, with her long black hair tied in a loose bun, big dark brown eyes, and perfect bone structure that accentuated her Native American heritage. Dressed in a dark blue pantsuit, Agent Piper was as professional as ever.

"Mara, so good to see you." Raven's eyes wandered over to Adam and Kimiko. "Adam, Kimiko." She nodded a respectful hello to each of them.

"Are they letting anyone see Samantha?" Mara asked, not sure if they'd be able to meet the girl.

"I made special arrangements for you to see her—but only you, Mara." She eyed Adam and Kimiko. They didn't seem to mind. Though technically Adam had dreamt about Samantha first, Mara was sure Raven only trusted *her* with seeing Samantha. Raven believed in Adam and understood what had happened to him. Heck, she even testified to get him out of the mental ward.

Still, ultimately, as an FBI Agent, she always had to worry whether or not Adam would kill again. An occupational prejudice.

Mara nodded her agreement, and Raven led her to Samantha's room. The hallway had been roped off from the press to give Samantha and her family some privacy. Mara couldn't see the press from her vantage point. She wondered how far back they really were. The room had been cleared out. Not even Samantha's family was there, and Mara figured that was Raven's doing, to give Mara the freedom to try to communicate with Samantha without fear of judgment.

Samantha was as Mara had left her, although the bruises and cuts were far more vivid in person than in the dank basement of her vision. The hundreds of welts stood out to her more than any of the other wounds she remembered when the lit matches hit Samantha's skin. She was hooked up to machines and an IV.

"Go to her. See if you can get her to talk." Raven's tone was full of hope. Agent Piper must have convinced Samantha's parents that Mara had a good chance of breaking through to their daughter in order to let Mara be alone in the room with Samantha.

Mara didn't want to get Raven's hopes up, but she genuinely wanted to try to communicate with Samantha as well, so she said nothing and went to Samantha's bedside.

Samantha's eyes were open, though she might as well be asleep, since there was nothing going on inside. She stared at the ceiling as if in a trance.

Sitting down next to her, Mara gently held Samantha's hand and tried to concentrate on sending waves of calm toward the poor, tortured girl. After a few minutes with nothing happening, her hopes dashed. This girl was too far gone.

When Mara began to take her hand away and give up, Samantha's fingers suddenly clenched down onto hers, desperately. She stared at Mara with wide, terrified eyes.

Samantha began whimpering, "You were there. You tried to help me." She repeated it over and over, and it brought Mara to tears. Her voice was raspy from the burns, but she was able to speak clearly despite the amount of damage that was done to her mouth and throat.

Shock ran through Mara. Samantha had been able to see her. Or at least that was how it sounded. But Mara wasn't sure if Samantha was truly comprehending what was happening, so she wanted to try to soothe her somehow. "I was there, and I would have busted you out if I could have found you. I'm so sorry."

Samantha calmed down enough to look at Mara, and Mara could see sanity slowly starting to creep back into Samantha's demeanor. "How were you there? I thought you were my guardian angel. I wasn't alone."

Mara had never been called a guardian angel before. She also didn't know if anyone had ever seen her—because usually if she dreamt about someone, they were . . . well, they were dead. If the victims she had dreamt about in the past had been able to see her, then maybe they didn't feel alone in their last moments of life.

Samantha pulled Mara's hand in closer, now hugging it with both her hands. "Now that you're here, I don't want you to leave. You were like a mirage, my only hope that I'd be rescued. And then he let me go. I couldn't move, or think, or talk, but inside my mind, I was free. I knew once I saw you, I'd come back to myself. And I did. I'm myself again." Samantha cried and smiled and laughed.

Mara worried that Samantha was still in shock, her voice laced with a shred of insanity. But as far as tortured victims went, at least Samantha spoke coherently.

Raven stepped in at this point. "Samantha, would you like to see your parents?"

Samantha didn't let go of Mara's hand, and Mara was pretty sure she was losing all circulation in it, but she didn't want to pull it away either.

Looking over at Agent Piper as if seeing her for the first time, Samantha nodded, then she said, "I would like to see them, thank you. Is Lucy Tildon here? I want to see her, too." Then Samantha turned to Mara. "I was terrible to Lucy. I need her forgiveness. I need to show her I'm a better person now."

It was like déjà vu with Kimiko, but Kimiko hadn't needed to be tortured to figure out the error of her ways.

But something in the way Samantha asked seemed off to her. It wasn't that her motivations were ill-intended, they just felt . . . rehearsed. Mara knew she was being paranoid, but it hit her in the gut.

Raven glanced at Mara before she left to retrieve Samantha's parents. It was an expression that screamed her thanks.

As soon as Raven left the room, Samantha clasped tighter to Mara's hand, and she didn't think that was possible. Mara held back a yelp of "ouch" as Samantha's panicked eyes met hers. "He's watching. He's always watching. We can't escape him. He'll grab you too when he gets the chance. He hates the mean ones like me. He taught me to be good. You understand, right? You *do* understand. I know you do. You were with me."

Mara wasn't sure how to respond to Samantha's crazy rant. What disturbed her most was the whole "we" part. *We* can't escape him. That rang a little too true for Mara.

Walking in at that exact moment, Samantha's parents rushed in at the sight of their fully awake daughter, Raven close behind. Mara observed that they were typical upper middle-class parents, nice clothes, coifed hair, and faces too groomed for the plebes. Before this kidnapping, Samantha wasn't exactly a nice person, and usually that stemmed from the parental units, so Mara had no doubt that these people wouldn't be the cream of the crop when it came to kindness. Maybe it was their divorce that made Samantha mean? Or maybe just plain neglect. They hadn't really been too concerned that their daughter was missing in the first place.

So Mara wasn't surprised when Samantha's father pried his daughter's hands away from hers so he could give her a hug. Samantha fought back slightly but eventually let Mara go of her own volition.

Physically relieved, Mara proceeded to massage the circulation back into her hand.

"You're awake. Thank God!" Samantha's mom gasped as she shoved her ex-husband aside to hug her daughter as well.

"Mom, that hurts," Samantha said, sounding muffled through her mother's jacket.

Her mother jumped back as if she'd touched fire. "I'm so sorry, sweetie."

Samantha's dad accused his ex-wife sarcastically, "Surprise, surprise, only thinking of yourself when your daughter has been kidnapped and tortured for the last week."

She eyed her ex-husband with hate. "You're lucky I'm letting you see her."

Samantha screamed. "Shut up!"

That stopped the two of them cold.

After a moment of awkward silence, Samantha's dad said, "We talked to the doctor, and your wounds aren't as severe as they previously thought, so you're going to make a full recovery, kiddo." He sounded like he was trying to be positive, but it was clear that it was not in his nature.

Mara suddenly felt very uncomfortable in this family reunion. And Mara didn't really want to be around if Samantha went on another warning-of-doom tirade. Standing up, Mara announced, "I'll let you guys talk."

Samantha's eyes darted in terror. "NO! Don't leave!"

Both Samantha's parents turned to Mara, their eyes full of judgment, but eventually her mom reluctantly held her hand out for Mara to take.

Awkwardly, Mara took the woman's perfectly manicured hand as Samantha's mom said, "Agent Piper told us you helped wake our daughter up. That's quite a talent. Thank you."

It was the most forced thank-you Mara had ever experienced, and it made her feel dirty somehow. She pulled her hand away gently so as not to offend the woman.

Samantha acted like she couldn't care less about her parents; she only appeared to want Mara to stay. And then she searched the room again. "I asked for Lucy. Is she here?"

Raven shook her head. "Lucy Tildon is in school."

"School, right. I should go to school. I must have missed so much while I was gone." With a loud grunt of pain, Samantha pulled herself out of bed before anyone could stop her.

Mara was so surprised by the action, she didn't know how to respond.

It was Raven who acted first, though, by gently pushing Samantha back down on the bed. A couple of Samantha's leads had fallen off when she stood up, and now her machines began beeping and making obnoxious noises. A nurse ran in for fear of something happening to Samantha.

The nurse quickly placed the fallen leads back onto Samantha's chest, then checked the machines to make sure they worked. "No more shenanigans. Stay in bed. You need to heal and rest. You're not out of the woods yet."

"I'm fine, really," Samantha pleaded. "I need to see Lucy. I need to apologize to her. It's vital." She said it as if her life depended on it.

Samantha tried to leave the bed again, but the nurse was not having it. She forcefully placed Samantha back in the bed, much harsher than Agent Piper had. "I mean it. If you can't stay in bed on your own, we'll have to put restraints on you."

Samantha immediately recoiled and whimpered.

The nurse gasped, realizing the impact of her threat to a survivor who had been chained to a wall. "I'm so sorry. We would never restrain you. I don't know what I was thinking . . . Just stay in bed, please. It's for your own good."

To calm things down further, Raven added, "I'll go pick up Lucy from school and bring her here. How does that sound?"

Samantha slowly stopped whimpering, and her eyes cleared once more. She whispered, "Yes, thank you. I would greatly appreciate that."

Her politeness appeared to surprise both her parents. They shared a look that said something was very wrong with their daughter, but they kept any comments to themselves.

"I want to be alone with the angel now please," Samantha said matter-of-factly.

Her mother's eyes widened. "The angel? Is she delirious?"

"She means me." Mara shifted uncomfortably owning up to that title. "I don't think she knows my name." Turning to Samantha, she said, "I'm Mara."

Samantha smiled as if remembering something only she could see. "Mara," she repeated.

Mara didn't want to be alone with Samantha again, but she wanted her to be better, and if she could help, then she would.

Samantha's parents appeared a bit miffed that their daughter would rather be with a stranger than them, but Mara didn't blame Samantha; they didn't seem like good people or that they could get along for longer than three minutes. After a forced goodbye, her parents left the room.

Raven eyed Mara in a way that asked: *Are you going to be okay?*

Mara nodded. "Tell Adam and Kimiko they can go if they want." Mara didn't want them having to hang around if they weren't allowed inside the room with her. Handing Raven her car keys for Adam, Mara smiled her thanks.

But Samantha blurted, "You have friends here?"

Mara turned back to Samantha. "Yeah, they came with me."

"Are they the ones that were next to you?" Samantha asked.

Mara kept getting shivers every time Samantha referred to seeing the dream versions of herself and, apparently, Adam. But it wasn't Kimiko she had seen. It was Terry.

Maybe this was a good time . . . "Yes, that was Adam, but the girl was Agent Piper's sister, Terry."

Raven immediately stiffened at the mention of Terry.

Mara regretted saying it out loud, but she needed Raven to hear her because . . . hello? Almost froze to death!

Samantha glanced at Raven curiously. "She did look a lot like you, but younger. She wasn't very nice to Mara last night. She hurt her, then made her go away. I don't think I like your sister."

Mara noticed that Samantha's tone ranged from completely coherent and sane, to crazy lunatic, to somewhere in between. At least she confessed that last part while bordering on the sane, so maybe Raven would listen.

Raven's eyebrows crinkled in instant concern at Mara. "She hurt you? What did she do?"

Mara plowed forward before she could talk herself out of it. "Terry yelled at me to protect Lucy. The more she yelled, the colder I got. When I woke up, my body was blue and they were throwing an electric blanket on me to warm me up. They think I almost died." She threw that last bit in for good measure. It felt good to confess to Raven, as if somehow she could do something about her sister. Mara knew this was illogical, but maybe Terry would stop attacking her if Raven could communicate with her somehow.

Raven was silent for a moment before she spoke, then she said, "I'm sorry."

Mara's face flushed with embarrassment. "It's not your fault."

Samantha viewed the exchange with rapt attention, as if watching a television show.

Finally Raven spoke again, "I haven't thought about my sister in years. She's the reason I'm in the FBI. Her death, anyway." Then she straightened her pantsuit as if she'd shared too much. "I'm going to go get Lucy. We'll talk more about this later. In private."

Samantha chimed in, "Bring in Mara's friends."

Raven nodded and left the room.

Mara's belly knotted for causing Raven to feel the pain of her sister's passing all over again. And even though her great-uncle John thought Terry might be calmer the next time Mara saw her, Mara wasn't quite as sure. The bottom line was that Terry was erratic and dangerous.

And next time they met, Mara was afraid she wouldn't wake up.

Dream Entry #10

Samantha's asleep, and Adam and Kimiko are playing cards. They're playing something called Euchre, which I'm pretty sure the only people who play that are grandparents. But they seem to be having a good time, and I need a moment to myself to write down my thoughts.

Okay, thoughts . . . What in the flippin' flip is happening right now? I feel like I'm living some kind of supernatural sci-fi movie. I always thought dreaming of murderers was bad, but this psychic-ghost-Samantha-seeing-us thing really freaks me out. She saw us! All three of us! Like we were ghosts or angels or something (okay, one of us was a ghost, but still!) How in the heck did she do that? Is she psychic? Is she . . . What? I'm so confused. And she's still doing the whole "I'm coherent one minute, then crazy the next" bit. I'm shocked she can be sane at all given the amount of abuse she's been through. Maybe that's why she was able to see us. She had been beaten so badly that she was able to see through . . . what do they call it? The "veil" or something? You see? I'm a terrible psychic, I completely suck at it. I don't know any of the terms or how anything works. I just randomly get attacked by ghosts and see horrible crimes.

Yeah, my life is fantastic.

Raven's been gone for a couple of hours. She has to drive up to Everett and back, so it could take a while. I'm curious how Lucy is going to be when she sees Samantha—and vice versa. They were mortal enemies. Now what are they? And now that Samantha is free, does that mean Lucy is next? And who the heck was this guy that took her? He left her alive! That's good, right? Then why do I feel more doom than I did before?

We have to find this guy before he takes someone else. Before he takes Lucy. Criminal Minds *is coming back to me in spades. Maybe Samantha was his first, so he didn't kill her, but his second is when his sickness escalates and then he* will *kill. I hate not knowing. I'd say I should try to dream something, to maybe learn anything about this guy, but I'm terrified of ghost-girl. I've only slept once since the incident without her showing up. To be fair, Uncle John did kind of say she'd be more tolerable. Maybe the fact that Terry hasn't come to haunt me or do something else to me means he's right?*

I really know nothing, and it's driving me nuts.

Write more later.

***

Mara couldn't believe how late it was getting. Samantha's parents had come in several times throughout the day, giving all three of them side-eye, but they didn't kick them out. At this point, Mara wasn't sure *why* they were still there—except that anytime Mara tried to hint that they should leave, Samantha started freaking out and whimpering. She even liked Kimiko right off the bat. Shocker.

Eventually, Samantha drifted off, and Mara thought that was a good thing. The nurse kept saying Samantha needed rest, then gave Mara the side-eye. There was a lot of side-eyeing going on, and Mara was tired of it.

A knock on the door.

Nearly falling out of her seat, Mara turned to see a young man who looked to be in his late twenties/early thirties walk through the door with a bouquet of spring flowers. His face was friendly as his eyes met Mara's.

"Hi. I'm Jack Franklin. I'm Samantha's English teacher. I came down as soon as I could. How's she doing?" he asked Mara as if she were the one in charge.

And Mara answered like she was: "She seems to be doing better. The doctor thinks she'll make a full recovery."

Letting out a huge breath, Jack smiled. "That's great news."

Mara could tell that this smile had made many a girl have a crush on Jack Franklin. And in all probability, she would have been one of them.

Jack placed the flowers down on Samantha's side table as carefully as he could so as not to wake her, then he gave the three of them a once-over. "Are you three students at Everett High?"

"Oh, no," Mara answered. "We're just . . . friends of Samantha's."

He pressed his palm to his chest. "Oh good, I was afraid I just didn't remember you, and then I'd feel like a jerk."

"I'm Adam." Adam placed his hand out, and Jack took it heartily.

"Pleased to meet you," Jack responded in a friendly tone.

Kimiko put her hand forward. "Kimiko."

Jack took it as well, then turned to Mara. "And you are?"

Mara suddenly felt stupid. She had been the one talking to him the whole time and had forgotten to introduce herself. "I'm Mara."

At hearing her name, Jack quickly turned back to Adam, and Mara saw him make the connection that everyone these days inevitably did. "You two are . . ."

Adam finished Jack's thought. "I'm Adam Layton, and this is Mara Johnson."

"Right." Jack appeared to be pondering why a convicted murderer and the girl who dreamt about said murderer were sitting around Samantha's bed, but then he shook his head. "I'm glad Samantha has good friends."

That was generic. But to be fair, what could he say?

After a moment, Jack asked Mara, "So you dream about murderers?"

Mara didn't want to get into it with a complete stranger, but the situation was becoming awkward enough without her shutting him down, so she decided to make it brief. "Usually of the victim. It's why I'm here." She nodded toward Samantha.

Jack's eyes widened. "You dreamt about her? Is that why they were able to find her?"

"No. I wish. I really tried to see who did this, but he kept hidden, even from me. And there was no way to find out where he lives," Mara vented her frustration.

"He? So you're sure it's a *he*?" Jack leaned forward, obviously fascinated.

"Yeah." Mara didn't feel like elaborating.

And luckily, Jack got the hint. "Anyway, I wanted to give her the flowers and see how she's doing. They're from the whole staff. She's one of my best students, and everyone was very worried about her. I'm just glad she made it out."

Before Mara could respond, Raven walked in with Lucy and Barry in tow. It seemed the two students were inseparable. It reminded Mara of how her and Zia used to be.

Lucy's arms were wrapped around her body tightly until she saw Jack and let them fall to her side. "Mr. Franklin? What are you doing here?"

Barry's face broke into a large smile. "Hiya, Mr. Franklin."

Jack smiled back at the two of them, then motioned to Samantha with his head. "I'm here to check on Samantha. I volunteered to be the representative for the school." Then he eyed Lucy carefully. "I'm surprised you're here though. I thought you and Samantha weren't . . . close."

In that instant, Mara knew Jack was completely aware of Samantha's bullying of Lucy.

Lucy shrugged. "I guess Samantha asked for me."

Jack's mouth slightly opened at that statement. "That was not something I expected to hear."

Raven put her hand out. "I'm FBI Agent Raven Piper, and you are?"

"Jack Franklin. Samantha's English teacher. I came on behalf of the staff to make sure Samantha was okay," Jack said, slightly shy, repeating yet again that he was here for the school and not just for himself.

But the way he looked at Raven . . .

Mara and Adam exchanged glances. Jack definitely had a thing for Agent Piper. And to Mara's surprise, the way Raven gazed back at him, the FBI agent might just return the attraction. Mara never imagined Raven dating anyone ever, so it was both weird and kind of nice seeing her look at a guy with interest.

"Lucy?"

Everyone's heads turned at the sound of Samantha's voice.

Samantha's bruised and battered face sought out Lucy until their eyes met. Then Samantha began to cry, really cry.

Lucy stood there shifting from foot to foot, uncomfortable.

Mara felt exactly the same way. Should someone comfort her? It was surreal, with seven people in a room, doing nothing, and a battered girl crying.

Kimiko was the first to respond, which made Mara feel terrible about herself but relieved that someone was comforting Samantha. Kimiko placed her hand on Samantha's, and it seemed to be enough to calm her down.

"Lucy, I'm so sorry. I'm so sorry for everything that I've ever done to you. I know words will never be enough, but I plan on proving to you that I'm a better person," Samantha rambled through choked tears.

Lucy moved closer to the bed, eyes slightly bulging. "Are you okay?"

Samantha finally stopped crying after a few moments and motioned Lucy to her.

Mara's shoulders tensed. Samantha was unpredictable because of what happened to her, and Mara wasn't sure she wouldn't grab Lucy and attack her or something.

But Samantha reached out and gently took Lucy's hand.

Through swollen and bruised eyes, she looked up at Lucy and said in her rough voice, "I really am sorry. I had a lot of time to think when I was taken, and all I thought about was how I treated you."

Lucy's face flushed, and she quickly said, "Sam, you may have been mean at times, but you never did anything like what happened to you."

Samantha shook her head. "Don't make excuses for me, Lucy. I got what I deserved. You see, I've come to realize that what happened to me was justice. I was being punished for how I treated you."

"*No one* deserves what happened to you," Lucy said with finality, and Mara agreed wholeheartedly.

"*No one* deserves what happened to *you.*"

Mara's stomach twisted in knots. They were both right. Sure, Samantha's torture was extensive and its effects right in front of everyone's faces, but that didn't mean Lucy hadn't gone through psychological torture from Samantha for weeks and months and years. Which was worse? Mara's eyes flickered over to Kimiko, who could barely make eye contact to anyone in the room. Samantha's apology must be bringing up a lot of old wounds for Kimiko—and a lot of regret.

Two couples in that room with same relationship: bully and victim. And both were trying to find their footing in a new, healthier possible friendship.

It was no wonder Mara had connected to these two.

Lucy didn't respond right away, then she finally nodded. "To new beginnings?"

Samantha smiled, and Kimiko flashed a concerned look at

Mara. Mara had no idea why. She desperately wanted to talk to Kimiko privately.

Mr. Franklin took it upon himself to address the room. "That was . . . really beautiful. I hope you girls can resolve your differences and be friends."

It was as if Samantha had just now noticed Jack in the room. "Mr. Franklin. I didn't see you. Thank you so much for coming." She gawked at him like an adoring fan, or at least that was what it seemed like to Mara.

Jack had an aww-shucks quality about him that Mara liked. He smiled back and said, "Everyone at Everett High wanted to make sure you were okay. I volunteered to come see you myself." Again. Reiterating how he didn't come of his own volition. It was logical, especially for a teacher who was young and handsome. He presumably didn't want to give students any wrong ideas. But something about it felt off somehow.

Feeling strangely conflicted, Mara glanced at Kimiko's face again. Another flash of concern came Mara's way.

What was Kimiko seeing that Mara wasn't? Or was she mind reading? Mara wished she had that skill because she'd use it right now on *Kimiko*!

Adam's hand intertwined with Mara's, and she calmed down. His hope-filled eyes and small smile matched how she had initially felt, that what they were witnessing was a truly great moment. But now, seeing Kimiko, brows furrowed, Mara overanalyzed every single detail of every single person in that room. Aside from Mr. Franklin being repeat-o-guy, Mara came up with nothing, but that didn't mean there wasn't something there.

At that moment, Samantha's parents barged into the packed

room with the doctor. They did not look pleased.

Samantha's mom glared at Raven. "I think all these people should leave, and you can come back to finish your questioning later."

The doctor echoed the sentiment. "Family only." Then to Raven, "Tomorrow—and you only. Samantha needs her rest."

Relief rushed through Mara. She really wanted to leave. And she really needed to talk to Kimiko and Adam. And Lucy. And . . . Mara's mind raced. Too many thoughts, too many worries, and too many moments happening around her that she couldn't control or comprehend.

Raven didn't argue. She must know that she had already overstepped her bounds, but Raven never did anything without a purpose. Mara's guess was that she wanted to see the interaction between Samantha and Lucy, presumably because she had a suspicion about Lucy's involvement in the kidnapping. It didn't matter that Mara was sure Lucy was innocent.

Or was she sure?

To be honest, Mara wasn't sure of anything anymore. She decided to let Raven do her thing, and hopefully the FBI agent would share. In the meantime, Mara would keep an eye on Lucy. Now that Samantha had been returned, it was hard to shake the feeling that Lucy could be next.

Walking down the isolated back hallways to avoid the press, Mara and the others made their way to the service elevator. No one spoke, and it was beyond awkward. Mara could tell that Lucy and Barry wanted to talk to her, Adam, and Kimiko, but she wasn't sure how they'd be able to separate themselves from Raven and Jack without being obvious about it.

As the elevator doors opened to the garage, Mara didn't have to worry for long when Jack turned to Raven. "Do you mind if I speak with you in private?"

Mara took that as her cue and waved to Raven. "I'll call you later when I learn more about the dream tests." Then she turned to Lucy and Barry. "You guys need a lift?"

Lucy took the hint quickly. "Yeah, that'll be great, thanks."

And Raven was pinned into the situation with Jack whether she liked it or not. However, by the expression on her face when glancing at Jack, she seemed content with it. "Text me when you get back to your dorm. Let me know you got home okay."

"Will do." Mara waved and began to walk toward her car with the others. To Kimiko she asked, "What was that look—"

Kimiko cut her off with a small shake of the head. Mara got the hint. Kimiko didn't want to talk about it in front of Lucy and Barry.

Lucy didn't seem to notice the exchange as she plowed forward. "Like I told you, Barry and I went to every one of those houses on the list, including Todd's place, and we found nothing. I don't think any student took her, or if they did, their hatred of her is secret."

Barry added, "I went to all her friends, thinking one of them might be jealous enough, or have a boyfriend that . . . I dunno . . . anything . . . but nada. And we really searched. So unless the kidnapper is one of those guys and they happen to own another house, we have to assume it's someone we haven't thought of."

"Well, we were just guessing anyway." Mara sighed.

Lucy's mood was lighter. "At least we don't have to worry

about it much anymore. Sam is back, so danger gone, right?"

Mara didn't feel that way at all. If anything, she felt as if things were about to get far worse. She didn't want to worry Lucy or Barry, though, so she answered, "Yeah, of course. Let's let Raven catch this guy. Hopefully, he got what he wanted out of Samantha . . . revenge . . . whatever it was . . . out of his system."

Kimiko added, "You guys did great. I know the last thing you wanted to do is spend time with Samantha, but it sounded like she's genuinely trying to make amends."

Lucy nodded. "I'll come visit. That's not the Sam I know, which is a good thing. I just wish she hadn't had to be tortured to get there."

"We all do," Adam agreed, lowering his head.

Oof.

Mara imagined that seeing a victim of a horrendous crime must have reminded Adam of what he had done.

Right now Mara wanted to talk to Kimiko alone and Adam alone. The situation must be killing them both. Mara didn't know what she could do or say to help either one of them.

Mara drove Lucy and Barry home, and they all got to know each other a little better.

Lucy was an only child, Barry her only friend. She was really into drawing and art and had already been accepted into an art school in Rhode Island called RISD, and she couldn't wait to leave Everett and go. Mara asked to see some of her artwork, and Lucy joked that she could show her the next time Mara fell asleep.

Barry, on the other hand, appeared to be an anomaly. He had all the makings of a guy that would be bullied or teased in high school—tall, skinny, bad acne, into computers and gaming—but on the contrary, everyone loved the guy, even the popular kids. Even Samantha. It reminded Mara of the kind of relationship she had with Zia. Everyone loved Zia, too, but Kimiko hated Mara, so everyone else steered clear of her.

Lucy and Mara were so much alike. Mara really hoped that was the reason Mara dreamt of Lucy. She wanted to believe this whole thing was over, at least when it came to Samantha and Lucy.

Dropping both Lucy and Barry off at Lucy's, Mara drove Adam and Kimiko back to the dorm. Kimiko decided to stay the night again at Mara's, and Mara was tempted to ask if Kimiko wanted to be her permanent roommate. A thought that was mind-blowing, but now quite a comforting idea. Mara figured she'd put a cork in it for the moment and see how things went before she asked.

Plopping down on the bed after ordering pizza, Mara turned to Kimiko, who sat at Mara's desk. "So, can we . . . ?"

Kimiko nodded. "It might be nothing."

Adam flopped next to Mara, but his interest was piqued by their tones. "What might be nothing?"

Mara explained the two "looks" Kimiko had given her. The first one after Lucy said "to new beginnings," and the second when Samantha gaped at Mr. Franklin adoringly.

Adam asked Kimiko, "What did you sense?"

Kimiko leaned back in the chair, thinking, as if trying to figure out the best way to proceed forward. "It wasn't a direct mind read or anything, it was just a weird feeling." After another moment of processing, she continued, "When Samantha smiled at Lucy's toast 'to new beginnings,' it was a smile of relief."

"But that makes sense. She wants Lucy's forgiveness, right?" Adam said.

"That's what I thought at first, but it was different. She wasn't relieved that Lucy had potentially forgiven her, it was that she was relieved because she had gotten Lucy to say the words. Like that had been the goal, not the forgiveness itself. Does that make any sense?" Kimiko didn't seem like she was entirely convinced herself. Before Mara could respond, Kimiko finished her thought. "And the second was the same. When Jack said he was happy she was okay and she smiled back, it wasn't a smile of *I love this guy* like she wanted everyone to think, it was more of *thank God I pleased this guy.* I don't know. It makes no sense."

A chill ran down Mara's spine.

It made total sense.

In that second, Mara knew: Jack Franklin was the kidnapper.

Mara stood up like she had been hit with a crowbar in the back.

Adam jumped up quickly after, obviously scared by her reaction.

Kimiko's eyes stayed on Mara, wide and searching. "What is it?"

"I know who the kidnapper is," Mara announced.

Kimiko leapt to her feet, realization hitting her as well. "Mr. Franklin."

"Yes." Mara and Kimiko stared at each other, shocked.

A pang of doubt from Mara. "But how did Samantha know who he was? He was always wearing a mask."

Kimiko shook her head, eyes certain. "No. She *knew* who

he was. And remember she was taken from the school. I would think someone would have noticed a guy in a mask that day."

Mara nodded. "You're right. He must have offered her a ride home or something. But why wear the mask later then?"

Kimiko responded, "I don't know. Psychos always have some weird rituals. Maybe that's one of them? Like how executioners wear a hood? Honestly, we can't worry about that right now. We have to tell Raven."

Adam didn't question their conclusion of who the kidnapper was. "Should you call Raven now? It looked like she was going to start dating the guy."

Mara's heart practically beat out of her chest. "It did look like that, didn't it?"

"It makes sense. He wants to know what she knows, so he takes her out on a date . . ." Kimiko rationalized.

"Okay, I'll text her. She wanted me to text when I got home anyway." Mara grabbed her phone and was about to type when she said, "What do I say? *Hi Raven. Just an FYI: Jack Franklin is the guy who took Samantha*?"

Adam shook his head. "No. Don't tell her over text. Jack might still be with her, and if he sees, he may hurt her."

"Great. I've somehow put her in another position where she's alone with a lunatic. At least she suspected Robert when she agreed to meet with him. With Jack, she has no idea. And I think she likes him!" Mara was guilt-panicking.

Kimiko spoke calmly and levelheaded. "Just text her that you made it home okay like she wanted. Tomorrow you can tell her you had a dream or something and that you know it's Jack Franklin."

"Right." Mara liked that idea. She texted Raven and quickly received a response back: *Take it easy and I'll talk to you in the morning.* "Okay. You don't think he'll do anything to her?"

"Technically, he didn't kill Samantha, and we know who he is, so we can track him down this time and save Raven if he tries anything," Kimiko answered in a soothing tone.

Mara began to relax and sat back down on her bed. "Are we sure it's Jack Franklin?" Even though Mara felt it to the core of her being, she needed reassurance.

Kimiko sat down on the chair, confident. "Never been more sure in my life. But if you want proof before you tell Raven, let's get it. It won't hurt to go to his house tomorrow while everyone is at school."

"Do you think I should warn Lucy?" Mara asked, suddenly worried that Mr. Franklin would snatch everyone he came in contact with right away.

"Yes, but not tomorrow morning. We don't want him to get suspicious," Kimiko offered strategically.

Mara agreed, and once they came up with a plan, they ate their pizza, stayed up talking a bit more, then finally decided to go to sleep.

Dream Entry #11

It's morning and I didn't sleep at all. I can't. I'm too scared for Raven and Lucy. And, honestly, of Terry. Great-Uncle John said she'd be "capable" of calming down, but I couldn't trust it. Not that I can't trust him, but I just don't trust Terry. I'm afraid she's going to scream at me that I'm not protecting Lucy enough now that I know who the kidnapper is, and her screaming means turning me into a popsicle, so I chose the warmth of three cups of coffee. I pretended to go to sleep for Adam and Kimiko.

I hope I can stay awake all day and, truthfully, for the next couple of days. Just until Raven puts this guy behind bars.

I thought I'd feel better when I knew who the kidnapper was, but now everything is so much worse. How do I prove it? The guy has everyone wrapped around his finger, even Raven, even me! I had thought he was cute! Maybe Raven suspects the guy, but from the look on her face, the girl was crushing. But she's an FBI agent! Shouldn't she . . . I don't know . . . know? I guess people think the same thing of psychics, like how many people asked me after Adam was convicted, how didn't I know? And again, how I should have known the moment I laid eyes on Robert.

The truth is: I did kind of know. My dreams were screaming it at me. I just didn't want to see it. I didn't think to suspect it. Adam was the first guy I'd ever been with, the first guy I ever loved. Why on earth would I think he was capable of killing anyone? And Robert? My gut warned me instantly about him, but I talked myself down, telling myself I was jealous of his close relationship with Adam. I rationalized everything!

But this was different. I didn't have a close connection to Jack Franklin. So when Kimiko told me about her weird telepathic moments, I knew right away, like I normally do when I see a bad guy. But dang! Jack Franklin hides it so well! He is good. When he walked into that hospital room, I didn't think a single horrible thought! Why is my radar so on in some moments and so utterly off in others? I'm just glad I have Kimiko and Adam with me. Kimiko is like a ninja mind reader, and without her I might be in the dark about Jack still. My instinct is to trust people despite my instincts! Talk about living life in a backwards, dangerous way. I have to be smarter. I have to be more aware of my surroundings. I have to "open both sets of eyes" as Great-Uncle John would say.

So, as dangerous as it sounds, we plan on going to Mr. Franklin's house, make sure he's the kidnapper, then call it in to Raven. Simple. While he's at school. They'll arrest him, and I can tell Lucy. Then everyone is safe. No more Terry, and I can sleep again!

Kimiko is waking up. Hopefully, next time I write, Jack Franklin will be behind bars.

***

Mara dropped her journal on the desk, yawned, and stretched as if she had just woken up as well. "I could really use some coffee. What about you guys?"

"Oh, definitely," Kimiko muttered through a large yawn.

"Make that three," Adam grumbled from the pillow beside Mara.

"I'll get it," Kimiko volunteered. "I've cut into your two-sies time way too much by staying the night here. Don't go porno nuts, though, I'll be back in ten." With that Kimiko threw on her jeans and dashed out the door.

"Porno nuts?" Adam laughed. "I'm sorry we missed out on being her friend in high school. The girl is witty."

"She was too busy torturing me for me to notice that wit, but Zia always told me she was funny."

Adam pulled Mara in and kissed her passionately. She forgot everything horrible in her life just to experience this one moment of pure joy.

Finally pulling away, Mara smiled. "Good morning."

Adam smiled back. "Good morning."

"IT'S YOUR FAULT!" Terry's voice screamed from behind Mara.

Mara whirled around to see a flickering image of Terry pointing at Mara, fury in her eyes.

"YOU LET IT HAPPEN!" Terry yelled.

Then she disappeared.

"Holy!" Adam exclaimed. His arms wrapped around Mara

from behind, and his hands shook. "You saw that, right?"

So much for her great-uncle's prediction that Terry would be calmer the next time Mara saw her.

And to manifest outside of a dream?

It was nothing Mara had ever experienced before, and her body trembled from the shock of it.

"What do we do?" Mara asked, clasping her hands together to stop them from shaking.

"Call Lucy."

Mara fumbled for her phone. She'd waited too long! She should have told Raven last night! Jack must have known that Mara would figure him out! He knew about her from the news. He knew about Adam. Maybe he picked up on Kimiko's expressions. Mara didn't know, but if Terry was making house calls outside of the dream world, then Mara had screwed up big-time.

Dialing Lucy's number, Mara's heart thumped out of her chest. But to her shocked relief, Lucy's voice answered, "Mara? Is everything okay?"

"Uh, yeah, hi. Are *you* okay?" Mara had no idea what to think at hearing Lucy fine and dandy. Relief? Confusion? Both.

"I'm fine. I'm on my way to school now. Did you have another dream?" There was a shake to Lucy's voice. Why else would Mara Johnson be calling her at this time of day?

Mara made a command decision. She had no idea why Terry did what she did, but maybe in ghost world, time was off somehow, and maybe Terry saw Lucy being taken in the future and thought it was now. Mara wasn't going to let that happen, so she said, "I did have a dream last night, Lucy," Mara lied so Lucy would believe her. "Your teacher Mr. Franklin is the kidnapper."

"Wait. What? You've got to be joking."

"I wish I was, but there is zero doubt, you hear me? Zero doubt. Stay away from him, okay?" Mara needed to make herself clear.

"I have two classes with him, English and free period. Do I skip? Do I stay home?"

"Yes. Don't go to school today. Let me call Raven and see if we can find the proof we need to get this guy arrested. Until then, play sick, I don't care, but do not step one foot in front of that man, you got me?" Mara said as forcefully as she could.

"I got you. I'm not leaving my room."

Mara had been afraid of Lucy going off on a tirade of how wonderful Mr. Franklin was and that Mara must have gotten things wrong. But it seemed Lucy trusted Mara's dreams more than she wanted her favorite teacher to be innocent.

"Perfect. I'll call you when I know more," Mara said.

"Should I tell Barry?" Lucy asked.

"Yes, definitely. The more of you who know, the better," Mara answered.

"Okay, I'll call him." There was a pause, then Lucy said, "And, Mara?"

"Yeah?"

"Thanks. For everything."

"Don't thank me yet. Just cross your fingers we can nail this guy." Mara wished psychic knowledge and dreams were enough to have someone arrested, but this was sadly not the case.

Mara hung up the phone and turned to Adam. "As you heard, she's fine. So what was Terry's surface attack about?"

Adam shook his head. "I don't know. She screamed like it was a done deal."

"Yeah." A horrible thought began to gnaw at Mara. She dialed Raven on her phone. It rang and rang until it finally went to voice mail.

"What is it?"

"Hang on." Mara didn't want to speak her suspicions for fear of making them true. She dialed Raven's field office.

After the second ring, the receptionist picked up. "FBI Seattle Headquarters, how may I direct your call?"

"Agent Raven Piper please," Mara answered, trying to hide the quake in her voice.

"Hold, please." The receptionist took a few more moments, then came back and said, "I'm sorry, Agent Piper has taken personal leave as of this morning."

"Personal leave? Do you know when she'll be back?" Mara's chest tightened to the point where she wasn't sure if she'd be able to breathe much longer.

"I can't give you that information, I'm sorry." The receptionist didn't sound sorry at all.

"Please, my name is Mara Johnson. I have very important information to give Agent Piper about a case. Is there any way you can reach her?"

A long pause, then a sigh. "Give me your name again and number, and I'll have the agent assigned to her cases call you back."

“You have another agent assigned to her cases?” Mara swallowed.

“That’s what happens when you leave for any given amount of time.” The receptionist had an attitude.

Mara knew she was going nowhere with this lady, so she gave her name and number, hung up, and didn’t expect an answer anytime soon.

“Raven went on personal leave.” Mara’s eyes suddenly filled with tears. She called Raven’s cell phone over and over, but it kept going to voice mail.

Adam embraced her, letting her head fall on his chest, tears streaming down her face.

“Terry wasn’t talking about Lucy, she was talking about Raven. She was trying to protect her sister. I’m so stupid!” Mara wanted to stop crying, but lack of sleep and the possibility of Raven being in danger overwhelmed her to her breaking point.

Kimiko walked in with a smile, holding coffee and pastries, until she saw Mara in tears. “Oh God, what happened?”

“We got a visit from Terry, and Raven is gone. We think she’s been taken,” Adam answered for Mara.

Kimiko clenched her fists onto the side of the coffee holder. “Well, we know who did it. Let’s go get her!”

“If Jack was so suspicious of us finding him out that he kidnapped an FBI agent, do you really think he’d keep her at his house?” Mara wanted to be gung-ho like Kimiko, but she couldn’t imagine Jack Franklin being that careless.

But Kimiko wasn’t backing down. She pulled Mara up out of Adam’s arms, jammed a coffee and a donut into Mara’s hands, and said, “He may not have Raven at his house, but we know he had Samantha. In all likelihood he tried to cover all the evidence, but you and Adam had a firsthand look at that place, so if we can find anything that incriminates him, we can at least get him arrested. Now, drink and eat up. We're on a mission. There's no crying in detective work."

Mara nodded, downed the coffee, and practically stuffed the entire donut in her mouth. The sugar and caffeine would kick in soon. She needed every ounce of strength she could get.

Adam was right beside her, drinking his own coffee and puffed pastry that Kimiko handed him. Mara caught him giving Kimiko a nod of thanks and Kimiko shooing it away like it was nothing.

Kimiko drove. They took the long way to the parking lot since news had gotten out that they were at the hospital with Samantha. Even though Raven had kept them hidden as much as possible, they had still been spotted. Barely managing to escape the mob of YouTubers and news crews, the trio hopped in Kimiko's car and headed toward Everett. Since it wasn't as simple as Googling Jack's home, Mara paid the forty bucks to access a website that tracked down people for you. She wasn't sure how legit it was, but it did produce an address.

Considering that Lucy was at her own house, they couldn't be sure Jack was at school either. Scarily, he might be at his house, but at this point, they had to risk it.

As they pulled near to what they hoped was Jack's home, Mara's palms began to sweat. Kimiko parked five houses away, just in case Jack walked out suddenly and they needed to hit the gas and leave.

Adam exited the car before Mara could stop him. "I'm going

to check his mail. Make sure this is the right place."

Walking down to the house, Adam discreetly opened the mailbox, pulled out a couple of envelopes, then waved for Mara and Kimiko to come over.

Exiting the car, Mara couldn't help but shake. Definitely too much caffeine, no sleep, and soul-crushing worry. But she swallowed it down and joined Adam.

"This is the place." Adam nodded toward the abode.

It was a small two- or three-bedroom house in craftsman-style architecture, with yellow paint and white trim. Not exactly the house of a deranged torturer, but that was almost always the case in Mara's experience. Freaks like Mr. Franklin blended in better than healthy, normal people. It was the nature of a sociopath.

Mara's eyes immediately went to the basement windows.

No paint. All clean.

"No," Mara exclaimed and ran toward the house to peer inside the basement windows. Inside was a cozy den with carpet, a television, a recliner, and a plushy leather couch. Nothing like what Mara saw in her dream.

Adam leaned in next to her, his thoughts the same since he'd been there too.

"Let me guess, not the same place?" Kimiko sighed in defeat.

Mara plopped on the grassy ground and shook her head, feeling defeated herself. "No. Not even an 'I just cleaned this place up' vibe."

"Damn it," Kimiko grunted. "He obviously owns someplace else. We just have to find it."

"Can I help you?"

Mara's blood froze.

Jack Franklin walked out of his front door dressed in a suit and tie. Upon seeing the three of them, he feigned his surprise. "Oh, hello. Mara was it? And you're Adam and . . . Kimiko, right?"

Mara jumped to her feet, defensive. Instead of playing it coy, like she thought she was going to, she went straight for the jugular. "Where's Raven?"

"Agent Piper?" Jack appeared genuinely perplexed. "I don't know. We were going to have dinner, but she got a phone call from her mother. Apparently, there was a family emergency."

A stab of doubt. Maybe Raven *was* on personal leave. Maybe Mara's imagination was going haywire and she was seeing a villain inside a nice guy.

Adam looked like he might be feeling the same way as he attempted an awkward smile at Jack. "Did she say what the emergency was?"

Jack shook his head. "I barely know her. I hardly expect her to confide in a complete stranger."

Mara's instincts were to retreat, find Raven's parents' number, see if they could reach her . . .

As if sensing Mara's doubts, Terry materialized next to Jack.

Mara tried to hide her surprise and pretended that she couldn't see Terry.

The ghost stared up at Jack with pure hatred, then turned back to Mara and said, "He has her. I can't find her. You have to make him tell you." Terry disappeared, as if staying on this plane of existence was difficult for her.

Mara could tell that Adam and Kimiko hadn't seen Terry. She only showed herself to Mara.

"Interesting that you haven't asked us what we're doing here." Mara cocked her head to the side.

In that second, Mara saw a flicker of annoyance from Jack. She had caught him, just for a second, in his good-guy guise.

He didn't bother trying to come up with an excuse or proceed to ask what in fact they were doing there, he simply stood there, staring at Mara.

And it was terrifying.

So much so that Adam stepped in front of Mara to their break eye contact, then said, "Where is Raven?"

It took Jack a few seconds, then he smiled larger. "I told you, kids, I have no idea. Now, I'd like things to remain friendly, but you are trespassing. I really don't want to call the cops."

Kimiko guffawed. "I bet you don't."

His eyes whipped to her with a flash of anger.

They were definitely pressing his buttons.

"Please leave," Jack said through clenched teeth.

"Not until you tell us where Raven is." Mara stood her ground, though it was a bit difficult with Adam standing in front of her.

Jack didn't answer. It was as if he were trying to rein in his temper. He simply walked back into his house and shut the door behind him calmly.

Kimiko stomped toward the door to undoubtedly begin pounding on its surface, but Mara gently touched her arm. "He's just going to call the cops, and they'll side with him."

"We can't just sit here. He practically confessed!" Kimiko seethed. "I was even starting to believe him until you pointed out that he hadn't asked why we were here. His lying skills are mad good. How did *you* know?"

"Terry popped in and told me he has Raven."

"I didn't see her," Adam confessed.

"She only showed herself to me. I think she's calmed down enough to help us." At least, Mara hoped so.

Kimiko nodded toward the sidewalk. "Let's get out of here. I don't want him hearing us." The three walked back to Kimiko's car, Kimiko unlocking the doors. "We're not honestly leaving, are we?"

"No way," Mara confirmed. "We'll stake him out from your car and follow him wherever he goes."

"Good plan," Kimiko agreed.

Adam volunteered, "I'll search for anything having to do with Raven while we wait. I can look up her parents' number, see if we can get them to call the FBI and ask where their daughter is."

With a plan in action, they all piled into the car and stared at Jack's house like it was about to soar away carried by flying monkeys.

Mara scooched in and got comfortable.

This was going to be a long day.

Dream Entry #12

We've been watching this lunatic all day, and he hasn't left the house. He must have called in sick to work. Kimiko parked so we could see his back door as well as any windows in case he tried to make a break for it hoping we wouldn't see. It's nine p.m. already, and I can't believe I'm still awake. It's been thirty-four hours since I slept, and my brain isn't functioning properly.

Adam Google-searched the crap out of anything and everything Raven Piper. He did end up finding her parents' number, but when he called, it was disconnected. We weren't giving up though. Jack had to leave some kind of trail. He somehow forged a personal leave letter from Raven, or forced her to write one, perhaps the latter, which makes me sick to my stomach.

No more visits from Terry, which I have to say I'm a little disappointed by. I know, weird, right? After she almost Mr. Freezed me to death, I never thought I'd ever want to see her again. Heck, the whole reason I'm sleep-deprived is because I'm trying to avoid her. And a lot of good that did, since she showed up twice while I was awake anyway! But I could tell that, while she was still panicked, Terry wasn't angry anymore. She had obviously seen this coming and had tried everything she could to stop it (except for being freaking specific! Why couldn't she have said, 'Hey my sister Raven is going to be taken by Jack Franklin.' No? Too easy?). I know, I'm being so hard on Terry. She could barely manifest herself at first, so her ghost-brain was most likely muddled and confused, but still, it's frustrating. Now that Raven is actually taken though, it's clear that Terry had just wanted to see her sister safe.

Adam ended up finding out Terry's story at least. It took him a while, and a lot of digging deep, but he found an article about her death in the Seattle Times. *She was murdered, bludgeoned to death. To this day, no one knows who did it, which means they're still on the loose. It made sense that Terry's murder was the reason Raven became an FBI agent, and why she has a soft spot for people like me with psychic abilities.*

Now, Terry's sister has been taken by a sociopath. Sure, Jack hadn't killed anyone . . . yet. But that was a big yet! My gut tells me it's only a matter of time! And why would he ever release Raven? She'd just arrest him! She's a liability to him! But maybe he took her because he knew her? The vision I had when I was stuffed in that locker, Terry and Jack knew each other, but did that mean Jack knew Raven? If Raven did recognize him, she had shown no signs of it, so maybe Terry had kept her friendship with Jack a secret? Ugh. I know absolutely nothing, and it's making me nauseous.

Thinking of what we are currently doing by stalking him, we're a liability too. But the more people that are onto him, the less likely he'll kill. At least, that's what I keep repeating over and over in my head. Because if anything happens to Raven, I'll never forgive myself. I should have known Terry wouldn't be talking about Lucy. She didn't know her. But it was such a stretch to think that she'd be talking about Raven! My mind is jumbled. With no sleep, every emotion feels heightened.

***

"Did you text Lucy?" Kimiko asked, interrupting Mara's journaling.

Placing the diary back into her bag, she picked up her phone. "I did an hour ago. She must think we're nuts." Mara had been texting Lucy all day, making sure she was okay. Even though she knew Jack was physically in his house, her paranoia was much stronger than her logic.

Mara texted Lucy: *You still good?*

Lucy's response was immediate: *Yup. All good here. Still stalking Mr. F?*

Mara texted: *He hasn't left the house, so not much stalking to do, but if he leaves, we're on it.*

Lucy texted back: *Keep me posted.*

Mara responded: *Will do.*

"She's fine," Mara informed Adam and Kimiko.

"This guy isn't going anywhere. He knows we're out here." Kimiko couldn't hide the frustration in her voice. She had made five food runs on foot today, saying she needed to "eat her stress." Mara had three cheeseburgers still uneaten in the fast-food bag next to her feet.

Mara nearly dropped her phone from the sudden sound of it ringing. Examining who was calling, she announced, "It's Barry. I texted him to go keep Lucy company." Swiping right and putting him on speaker, Mara answered, "Hello?"

"Mara? Is Lucy with you?" Barry's voice sounded worried.

Mara's breath caught in her throat. "What? No. Where are you?"

"I'm at Lucy's. I tried knocking on her window, but there was no answer. So I went the front door, and her parents let me in. Mara, she's gone." Barry sounded like he was about to start hyperventilating.

"I literally just texted her, and she said she was fine," Mara said breathlessly.

Barry choked. "She's not here."

Adam was out the door so quickly Mara hardly knew what to do. Kimiko followed, and Mara fumbled to do the same. "Barry, I'll call you back. We're going to make sure Jack is still in his house. Maybe Lucy needed some air." She said it, but she knew it wasn't true.

Somehow, some way, Jack Franklin had escaped his house and taken Lucy. Mara knew it in her soul.

Running with the others, Adam pounded on Jack's door, but predictably there was no answer. Kimiko headed to the backyard, and they both followed.

Kimiko was angry. "We had eyes on both exits! He must have snuck out while I was getting food. You guys must have looked down or something!"

"Don't blame us! We kept our eyes on this house the entire time!" Frustration boiled inside of Mara too, and she let her anger slip.

Adam ignored the both of them and searched the area with

his phone's flashlight since it was quite dark in Jack's backyard. Mara and Kimiko followed suit, and the three of them looked like they were on the hunt for a missing pet as they combed Jack's rather large backyard. It was at least half an acre of perfectly shorn grass.

Then Mara saw it: two wooden doors built flat onto the ground. A storm shelter. Adam and Kimiko hurried to her side, and Adam swung open one of the doors, flashing his phone inside, to reveal a set of rickety stairs.

"Do you think they're down there?" Mara asked, though she already knew the answer was no.

Adam walked down the stairs. "I don't think so; otherwise, why would he leave? But we should check it out."

Nodding, Mara and Kimiko followed Adam through the long hallway that led to a door. It was open. Jack couldn't care less if they went inside. He had fooled them. He had escaped right under their noses and kidnapped Lucy.

Just to make sure, Adam opened the door, and sure enough, the furnished basement Mara had seen through the windows outside stood before them.

"But Lucy texted me all day. She texted me two minutes before Barry called!"

"It wasn't Lucy who was texting." Kimiko shut the door to the basement and led the way back down the long hallway.

Mara decided to test that theory and texted to Lucy: *We will find you, and we will take you down.*

Lucy's phone texted back: *So angry. I told you I was fine. You're the one stalking Mr. F.*

Mara wanted to throw her phone. Jack had been playing

them all day, and probably laughing the whole time, texting them as Lucy, knowing it would keep them there.

Exiting the shelter, Adam shut the wooden door. "We need to find this guy."

Mara was at a loss. "I know, but how?"

"We have to try to find him in our dreams or something. You're connected to Lucy—and to Raven too. If you can find them, I can find you, then maybe we can figure out where they are," Adam suggested desperately.

They had tried the same thing with Samantha, but with no luck. But they were out of choices.

Mara nodded. "Let's get back to the dorm and go to bed."

It took them a good half hour to finally reach Mara's dorm. Kimiko distracted the handful of news crews that had staked out near the parking lot, then doubled back and met Mara and Adam in Mara's room.

"I'm going to need some tea or something to try to sleep," Adam said.

Mara handed him a box of chamomile tea and dropped on the bed. "I'll meet you in there."

Closing her eyes, exhausted, Mara instantly fell asleep.

***

Mara could hear screams. She was in a black tunnel, and somewhere, someone she knew was crying in pain.

Concentrate.

Mara tried to focus on the voice itself.

It was Lucy's.

Like Samantha, it seemed Mr. Franklin was torturing his other student as well.

Colors and details swirled around her until she found herself in Jack's basement. Or more precisely, his *other* basement. Mara wished she knew someone at the FBI who would take her seriously, then they could have them search for any other properties under Jack Franklin's name. Although Mara knew he was probably smarter than that. The odds were slim that he put this property in his name.

Mara saw Raven first, chained in the same place Samantha had been. She rushed over to the FBI agent and was relieved to see that Jack hadn't touched her. Other than being chained to a wall, Raven appeared unharmed physically.

So where was Lucy?

Another cry of pain.

Hearing Lucy again, Mara whirled around. In a dark corner on the other side of the room. Jack Franklin towered over Lucy with a crowbar in his hand. He swung down, hard, and Lucy's arm cracked. He was breaking bones.

Lucy screamed in agony.

Raven yelled from across the room, "Get away from her, you son of a bitch!"

Jack hadn't bothered to cover his face this time. He completely ignored Raven, keeping his eyes only on Lucy.

Lucy stared up at him, crying. "Why are you doing this to me?"

"To toughen you up! You fell apart like a weakling when Samantha apologized to you. You should have made her earn your forgiveness; instead you let her have it like everything she had ever done to you was nothing!" Jack hit Lucy's leg with the crowbar this time.

Lucy's voice was raw from screaming so long, so all that came out was a loud croak.

Raven yelled again, "I swear to God I'm going to kill you!"

Jack didn't acknowledge Raven yet again.

Lucy's eyes turned defiant. "I'd rather be with Samantha than you. You're worse than she ever was!"

Jack stumbled back from the words as if they physically shocked him. "I am nothing like Samantha. I'm the one who will teach the both of you the lessons you'll need to survive."

"Survive what? Right now, it doesn't feel like I'm going to survive at all. And Samantha looked half-dead when they found her. You're nothing but a psychopath dressed up in what you think is justice, but you're just a loser and everyone knows it," Lucy spat.

Jack almost hit her again from rage but stopped himself. "You've had enough for today."

"Mara will come, and she'll take you down," Lucy said through bloody teeth.

Jack took a deep, calming breath, then answered, "Mara and her friends are idiots. They'll never find this place."

"What are you planning to do with us?" Raven asked, probing.

But Jack didn't answer. He simply walked up the stairs and shut the door behind him. The locks clicked into place.

Mara rushed over to Raven. "Raven! Can you hear me? Raven!"

Terry appeared next to Mara. "I've been trying since she got here. She can't hear us because she's not like us." At least Terry appeared calm, not angry and frantic. *This* Terry Mara could work with.

Mara eyed Lucy. "What about her? She seemed like she might have some kind of sixth sense."

Terry shook her head. "Not enough to see a ghost or someone in astral form."

Adam materialized next to them, and Terry barely acknowledged him.

Adam blinked rapidly, flustered. "I had trouble finding you. I never have trouble finding you."

Terry shrugged. "I may have interfered, but not on purpose."

"Oh." It was obvious Adam wasn't sure how to respond.

"We can't communicate with either of them," Mara informed him. Then she nodded toward Lucy, who cried softly in the corner. "He broke her arm. I heard it. Adam, he was hitting her with a crowbar."

Adam clenched his jaw, then seethed, "How are we going to find this guy?"

"We have to see if the FBI will help." Mara was desperate for a solution.

Terry appeared to agree. She turned to Mara and said, "You two go. I'll stay with them. I can manifest to you, if things get bad." Her eyes turned distant. "Not that you can help."

Terry waved her hand in front of Mara's and Adam's faces.

***

Mara and Adam woke up at the exact same time in bed.

They must have made some kind of noise, because Kimiko jumped up in bed as well. "What? Did you find them? Where are we going?" She was obviously still a little out of it, but Mara appreciated her enthusiasm.

Glancing out the window, Mara could see that they had slept the whole night through, though it had felt like seconds. "What time is it?"

Kimiko answered, "It's 8:13 a.m."

"I'm calling the FBI." Mara wanted to get going on any possible lead. She called the field office, and this time the receptionist put her through to Agent Joseph Torley.

"Agent Torley. How can I help you?" His voice sounded friendly at least.

"Hi, Agent Torley, this is Mara Johnson. I've worked with Agent Piper in the past?" Mara tried to sound as upbeat as possible.

"Ah, the psychic. Yeah. I heard you called the other day about Agent Piper," he responded.

"I know you might not believe in all that, but Agent Piper and Lucy Tildon have been taken by Jack Franklin. He's a teacher at Everett High School. He was the man responsible for kidnapping Samantha Perkins." Mara took the honest approach.

There was a moment of silence, then Agent Torley finally replied, "Jack Franklin?"

"Yes," Mara confirmed.

A long sigh. "Okay, well, I'll certainly look into it. Is the number you're calling on the best number to reach you?"

"Yeah, it's my cell phone," Mara answered.

"I'll call you if I find anything. Is that all I can help you with?" Agent Torley suddenly sounded like a customer service representative.

"Um, that's it. Thanks," Mara said lamely as Agent Torley hung up.

“Well?” Kimiko’s eyebrow lifted with a twinkle of hope in her eyes.

“He said he’d look into it.” Mara wanted to be hopeful too, but her gut told her Agent Torley was a waste of time.

Mara was about to call back when the phone rang in her hand. She answered it on the first ring. “Hello?”

“Mara? This is Dr. Laurence.”

“Oh, hi, Dr. Laurence. What’s going on?” Mara asked, thinking her teacher sounded frazzled.

“It’s your tests, Mara. I think I may have discovered something that . . . I can’t say over the phone . . . but this is big. This is very big. Can you bring Adam and Kimiko and meet me at the Sleep Lab as soon as possible?”

“We’re on our way,” Mara responded, then hung up. Turning to Kimiko and Adam, Mara announced, “Dr. Laurence says he found something in our sleep results, and he wants to go over them with us right away.”

Mara couldn’t explain it, but she had a feeling that whatever Dr. Laurence found just might be able to help them find Raven and Lucy.

Dream Entry #13

Dr. Laurence is so excited right now, it'd be cute if I wasn't so stressed about Lucy and Raven. He says he needs a few more minutes to put all his research together and that he hadn't expected us to come over so fast. He genuinely seems shy and flabbergasted. It's the complete opposite of the first few weeks of his class. I like this Dr. Laurence way better.

I'm writing while I have the chance because I need to get a few thoughts down. I don't mean to sound ungrateful, but sometimes having this gift of mine seems like a colossal waste of time. So I can see things? What good is it if I can't help anyone? And now, having two people I know locked up by a psychopath and there's nothing I can do about it except watch? I can't even communicate with them! Maybe if I could talk to one of them, Raven especially. She's an FBI agent. She would know things that I could look for to help. Or something. I don't know, I'm feeling so foolish, like I'm running around with my head cut off, not really getting anywhere, but I'm too freaked out to stop running. I'm not making any sense.

My dream last night was so vivid. I can still hear the crunch of Lucy's arm. What if she's bleeding internally? What if she's dead already? What if I'm too late? I know I shouldn't put all this pressure on myself, but I can't help it. Adam, Kimiko, and I are the only ones who know what's going on, or I should rephrase that, we're the only ones who believe what's going on. I told Agent Torley about Raven and Lucy, but he thinks I'm a quack. I can tell. Just like Dr. Laurence used to. Maybe if Dr. Laurence found definitive proof that psychics are real, he could show it to the FBI and they'd have to listen.

I'm trying not to be too depressed, even though I know that the world doesn't work that way. Even if Dr. Laurence finds proof, most people still wouldn't believe. It's the way things are. People will always look down on the word "psychic" because to them it's all make-believe and doesn't exist.

Tell that to Samantha and Lucy and their broken bodies.

Ugh. My heart hurts.

***

"Okay, come here. Let me show you what I found." Dr. Laurence motioned Mara and the others over to the desk filled with monitors.

Tucking her journal into her bag, Mara took Adam's waiting hand, and they both sat next to her professor while Kimiko stood, observing from a higher view.

Dr. Laurence pressed play on the computer, and they all examined the largest computer screen in front of them. He pointed to two horizontal lines that moved continuously across the screen like a heart rate monitor. "You see these lines?"

When everyone nodded, Dr. Laurence continued, "This top line is Mara, and this bottom line is Adam. They represent your REM states."

Mara remembered this from class. REM stood for rapid eye movement: the stage of sleep where dreams happened.

"Shouldn't it be more . . . squiggly?" Mara didn't know the proper term for it.

But Dr. Laurence didn't mind her terminology. "Normally, yes, but watch what happens when your body temperature drops."

Mara's eyes were glued to the screen as Dr. Laurence fast-forwarded slightly ahead. The lines stayed steady—until Mara's suddenly made three-inch zigzags up and down the screen while Adam's line then intertwined with the zigzags almost as if his line were trying to steady her zigzags. In awe, Mara recognized that she was observing a line interpretation of what had happened to her. The zigzags were when Terry yelled at her and made her blood go cold, and it was Adam who held her tight just like his REM line was doing with Mara's zigzags.

Then Adam's line was yanked away from Mara's zigzags, and the test ended.

"I've never seen anything like this. I've never heard of anything like this. I don't know what to make of it, but I have some theories. I wanted to talk to you two and find out what *you* make of this." The professor rambled with excitement. For him, this was the discovery of a lifetime. For Mara and Adam, it was a Wednesday.

But Mara explained to him everything that had happened during that time.

Dr. Laurence nodded emphatically. "That makes sense. Adam held onto you, which means your REM states . . . combined . . . this is unprecedented. This means that you two shared a dream together. That you were in the same dream state."

Mara would have loaded him up with a big old "duh," but she wanted the professor's help. If he was finally finding the science behind what had been happening to Mara her entire life, that made her thrilled beyond measure.

"But that's not the most fascinating part!" Dr. Laurence was so animated it was hard not to smile at his enthusiasm. He pointed to the two lines at a place before Mara was attacked by Terry. "Like you said earlier, you thought the lines should have indicated more activity."

Mara had said "squiggly," but she let it slide.

He continued, "You're absolutely right, especially when you see this." Dr. Laurence brought up a piece of footage of a close-up of both Mara's and Adam's eyes while they were sleeping. Their eyes were shifting back and forth as if their eyeballs would fall out of their heads. "You see your eye movement? It's off the charts, but the lines are steady as if you were in a deeper stage of REM sleep. I had to make sure I had the footage matched to the lines. I couldn't believe it myself."

"What does that mean?" Adam asked, genuinely curious. This was the first time he'd ever learned about his gifts as well, and Mara could tell he was just as fascinated.

"I'm not sure, but I think it means what you've been trying to tell me since you started my class. I think you two aren't in your bodies." Dr. Laurence shook his head. "I know it sounds crazy. My colleagues are going to laugh me under the table, but by God, Mara Johnson, I owe you a huge apology."

"Oh, well, thank you . . . I mean . . . apology accepted . . ." Mara wasn't sure how to respond to the energy coming off her teacher. She would have thought he had downed forty Red Bulls before they arrived, but she knew as a scientist, he was excited because he truly felt he had discovered something new.

Dr. Laurence rolled over her apology acceptance, he was so excited. "The possibilities of what this could mean are endless . . ."

Kimiko stopped him short. "Listen, Dr. Laurence. We're all very glad you're finally on the psychic train, but the three of us have been dealing with this our entire lives. So, much as we share your enthusiasm on finding what you hope is 'proof,' we need your help here and now."

Mara paused at that. Mara could tell Kimiko had an idea.

Dr. Laurence wasn't offended at all by Kimiko's outburst. If anything, he heard the words *need your help* and perked up even more. "Anything. What do you need?"

"You said this is proof that they're somewhere else. Is there any way to find out where they were?" Kimiko asked.

Mara's pulse raced. "Do you think we could find Raven and Lucy by going there hooked up to these machines? We wanted to do that last time, but it didn't really work. Or we didn't know how to work it. Do you have an idea?"

Dr. Laurence's eyebrows crinkled, but he answered Kimiko's question. "A location, huh? I'm not sure how we could do that, but we could try." Then he asked more seriously, "I thought they found that girl you were looking for. Are Raven and Lucy new victims?"

Mara nodded and figured she had nothing to lose and only

potentially something to gain by telling Dr. Laurence the truth. So she told him everything, right down to Raven and Lucy being held against their will in Jack Franklin's basement.

Then Kimiko's eyes widened and she clapped her hands together, then pointed to the screens. "What if we were able to bring me along to Jack's basement? My gift is different. I'm a telepath of sorts. Sometimes I can read a person's mind, as you remember from outing you and your sex dream in class," Kimiko said.

Dr. Laurence blushed slightly. "Yes, I remember. But what are you asking?"

Kimiko turned to Mara first. "What if there was a way that *I* could communicate with Raven or Lucy. Dr. Laurence just said that by you two combining, there may be a way to communicate through dreams. So if Adam brings me in, and we all go to Jack's basement . . . ?"

Mara finished her thought, "Your telepathy might be enough to communicate with Raven."

"Nothing may happen, but it's worth a shot, right? And if Dr. Laurence can somehow figure out where we are, then we can call the cops and get Raven and Lucy home safe."

Dr. Laurence's face tightened in determination. Two people's lives were at stake, and he obviously wanted to help. "Let's get you three hooked up to the monitors."

They each went into a separate room, where Dr. Laurence hooked them up with sensors. Mara wasn't sure how she was going to fall asleep, considering it was still morning and she had just downed a cup of coffee, but Mara knew she'd have to try. They were running out of time, and as each minute passed, she was growing more and more afraid that Jack would find the killer inside himself and beat Lucy to death.

Mara meditated and did her breathing exercises.

This was going to take a while.

The more Mara tried to relax, the more her mind wandered. She kept reminding herself of how important it was that she fall asleep. Raven and Lucy depended on her. They could be dying . . .

Stop.

Panic wrapped around Mara with its familiar embrace. What if she couldn't fall asleep? What if she lay here with her eyes closed all day?

Hearing the soft snores of Adam and Kimiko from the other rooms only made her anxiety grow. At this point she just wanted Dr. Laurence to hit her over the head with a club or something. Mara's brain was doing her no favors at the moment. Adam and Kimiko were in dream-land-limbo waiting for her . . .

Deep breaths.

Deep breaths.

Slowing down.

Relax.

Sleep.

Breathe.

***

"About time." Adam smiled at Mara as she materialized in front of him.

"That was so horrible," Mara vented. "I didn't think I'd ever get to sleep."

Adam kissed her gently, then motioned to the darkness around them. They stood in a room with black walls, ceiling, and floor.

"We need to pull in Kimiko." Adam got down to business.

"She's not here yet?" Mara had thought that she herself would be the final member to join their party.

"I don't have enough of a connection to her. I need you to channel her here." Adam gently took Mara's hands. "Concentrate on Kimiko, and I'll try to pick up her essence."

Mara nodded and focused on all the good things Kimiko had done over the last few days. She supposed remembering her bullying years might bring Kimiko in as well, but Mara wanted this to be a positive experience, and she wasn't sure what would happen if she thought negatively.

After a few moments, Kimiko popped into existence in front of them.

"This is insane," Kimiko said with admiration. "I can't believe we're asleep. Everything feels so real."

Though there were no details to take in, Kimiko kept searching her surroundings like she was in some kind of scenic setting.

"Take our hands," Adam instructed.

Together, the three of them joined in a circle, their hands clasped tightly together.

Adam addressed Mara. "I'd say concentrate on Raven, but I think your dream connection is stronger with Lucy."

Mara nodded agreement. "We'll try Lucy first. If that doesn't work, I'll concentrate on Raven."

Thinking only of Lucy, Mara allowed herself to be taken away from the darkened room but kept a tight hold on Adam and Kimiko. The darkness slowly began to dissipate, transforming into a swirl of color. Kimiko's eyes widened with awe as she took in the cyclone of colors surrounding them all. Mara knew this was new to Kimiko, and she suddenly wondered how different their lives would be if Kimiko had listened to her grandmother and chose to be her friend rather than her bully. It was pointless to think about, but in a fantastical moment like this, it made Mara ponder if she would have been able to stop Adam from killing at all if Kimiko had been her friend. They might have been able to save Colt as well. It was a painful thought, but Mara couldn't help but speculate.

The colors began to take form—until they stood in Jack's basement within inches of Lucy's body.

She was still chained to the wall, her arm completely black from the bruising where Jack had broken it. Sweat beaded down her forehead, and her eyes fluttered between open and closed.

"She has a fever. It's probably an infection." Mara didn't have to be a doctor to figure out that Lucy didn't have much time unless she got medical help.

Keeping their hands locked, Mara turned her head to make sure Raven was okay.

The FBI agent was also still tied to the wall, but she was in much better shape than Lucy.

"We should try Raven first. I don't think Lucy will be of much help in her condition." Kimiko said what they had all been thinking but didn't want to say aloud.

Walking as a circle (and feeling really awkward doing it), they made their way over to Raven.

Raven's attention was focused on Lucy, her eyes filled with worry and fear. Just like Raven to be more concerned for someone else than for herself. She obviously didn't see the trio in front of her.

"Do we still need to hold hands?" Kimiko asked.

"I don't think we should risk losing you," Adam answered. "Since we have to stay in a circle to keep our connection strong, let's put Raven in the middle."

Positioning themselves like a ring of protection around Raven amplified how strange this whole experience was. But they were here, and they needed to know where *here* was located. That either meant Kimiko being able to communicate with Raven, or Dr. Laurence figuring out how to use the dream monitors to track down where their astral forms flew to.

So weird.

Since Kimiko was the only one with a shot at communicating with Raven, she stood in front of the agent while Adam and Mara stood behind.

Taking a deep breath, Kimiko kept her gaze pointed at Raven, then turned to Mara, a note of panic in her tone. "What should I call her? Agent Piper? Raven? Ms. Piper?"

Mara steadied her voice to help calm Kimiko. "Call her Raven."

"Right. Raven." Kimiko nodded in agreement.

Raven's eyes flew up, as if she had heard her name.

Kimiko, Mara, and Adam all shared a hopeful expression.

Plowing forward, Kimiko stared down at Raven as if she were a bull's-eye target. "Raven? Can you hear me?"

Raven's eyes darted from side to side. She whispered, "Yes, I can hear you."

The trio sighed and laughed slightly in relief.

Kimiko spoke clearly. "Listen to me carefully. I'm not sure how long I can keep this connection up. This is Kimiko, and I'm standing here with Mara and Adam on the . . . astral plane . . . or whatever. We need to know where you are. Can you tell us anything?"

Raven nervously glanced over her shoulder. Then she nodded. "He took me at the hospital. He knocked me over the head, and I blacked out for a few minutes. I woke up as he placed me in his trunk, so I was able to pay attention to a few things. I counted the seconds and minutes, and it took two hours to get here. We went over a bridge, and there was a ferry near the end. I'm on one of the islands. I'm sure of it. I just don't know which one."

Kimiko informed Raven, "Jack Franklin knew your sister. Mara saw one of Terry's memories, and they were friends before she was killed. Did you know him?"

Raven's head reared back slightly. "Terry knew Jack?" She shook her head. "I didn't know. I've never seen him before. At first I thought maybe he could be my sister's killer, but Jack's MO targets bullies and their victims, and Terry was neither. Plus, we have no proof Jack has killed anyone . . . yet."

Mara wanted to brainstorm with Raven, but she didn't know how much time they had before the connection might break or before Jack came downstairs and interrupted them.

As if reading Mara's mind, Raven said, "You should go. Jack comes down at the top of every hour. Find us. Lucy is dying, and Jack is in denial or he doesn't care. Or worse, he's enjoying it. Mara, if you can hear me, go to Jennifer. She'll help you. Jack knows someone on the inside at the FBI, so I don't know who you can trust. I'm sure it's the reason I had so much trouble classifying Samantha's case as a kidnapping."

Detective Jennifer Nicholson.

Mara had mixed feelings about the detective. She was on a first-name basis with the detective now, but it hadn't always been such a peachy relationship. Jennifer had originally thought Mara was guilty of all of Robert and Adam's crimes. But the detective had surprised Mara during Adam's trial. She had even testified on his behalf. Showing up at the pier where Robert had held Mara and seeing that Adam had taken a bullet to save Raven and Mara, then hearing his story, Jennifer wanted to destroy Robert. She had seen too many kids like Adam being influenced by either their environment or extreme abuse like Adam.

After that, Jennifer blamed Robert entirely.

Why couldn't her parents do that?

Shaking useless thoughts from her head, Mara nodded to Kimiko.

Kimiko focused on Raven and said, "We'll contact Detective Nicholson, and we're going to find you." The conviction in Kimiko's voice brought Mara chills.

Nodding solemnly, Raven's eyes showed her fear but also her hope.

Mara needed to save the FBI agent.

Just like Raven had saved her.

They needed to find Jack's hideout. Now.

Taking charge, Adam tightened his grip on both Mara and Kimiko, and the colors around them began to shift once more.

***

Waking up, Mara pulled off the sensor leads on her head and chest as Dr. Laurence walked into her room. "We found Raven and Lucy. Raven is pretty sure she's on an island in the Puget Sound. Were you able to locate them?"

He shook his head. "I'm not sure how these tests will help me find a location. But I can try. I need some time."

Kimiko and Adam came up behind Dr. Laurence to sit next to Mara.

"I'm not sure how much time they have." Mara cringed from the thought. "We have to call Detective Nicholson."

"Who?" Dr. Laurence raised an eyebrow.

"Someone who can help." And Mara hoped that it was true.

Dr. Laurence walked them down to the outside quad, still excited by the discoveries he had made. He was in the middle of brainstorming how he would try to use the data to find Raven and Lucy—

—when Mara's mother and father suddenly blocked their passage.

Mara nearly stumbled from the shock of it, but the police officer standing next to them immediately brought up her defenses.

"That's him." Ben Johnson pointed at Adam with disgust. "We've talked to our lawyer, and she says that Adam is violating his parole by staying in a college dorm without permission. She said that any convict released on parole needs to be in a halfway house or a place with adult supervision."

With two women's lives at stake, this was the last thing Mara had anticipated. "What's happening?" was all that could come out of her mouth.

"We're sorry, Mara, but this has to be done," Claire said with defiance.

Adam stood frozen, shock and shame written all over his face.

The police officer addressed Adam. "Is this true? Are you staying in a dorm and not a supervised location?"

Mara's blood boiled to the point of a fury she had never experienced before. "How. Dare. You."

"Mara, stay out of this," Ben chided his daughter.

"Is it true?" the officer asked again.

But before Adam could confirm or deny living in Mara's dorm room, Dr. Laurence spoke. "Adam Layton is staying with me, a tenured neuroscience professor. I can acquire the proper paperwork if needed."

Mara's whole being surged with love for her professor.

The officer shook his head, giving a disapproving glance at Mara's parents, then turned to Dr. Laurence. "No, that's not necessary. I'm done here." He nodded to Adam. "Stay out of trouble."

With that, the officer turned to leave, but Ben grabbed his arm. "You can't let this murderer get away with that. I don't know who this man thinks he is, but Adam is staying with my daughter. He's lying to you!"

The officer removed Ben's hand from his arm forcefully. "You're lucky I don't arrest you for assault. I understand you don't want your daughter with an ex-con, but this isn't the way to handle it. Good day, sir." The policeman walked away.

Ben whirled on Dr. Laurence. "You do realize you're protecting a serial killer and allowing him to potentially murder my daughter!"

"SHUT UP!" Mara screamed at the top of her lungs.

But Ben and Claire ignored her completely.

Claire pleaded to Adam, "If you truly love Mara, you'll stay away from her. Please. Just leave her alone."

Mara couldn't see straight she was so angry, but her voice was steady when she said, "I don't ever want to see either one of you ever again." Then she made sure her eyes met each of theirs. "I *hate* you both."

Her parents froze, eyes round with shock.

They had just lost their daughter.

Adam's face was wracked with guilt. Gently he reached to touch Mara's arm. "Mara . . ."

But it was Dr. Laurence who spoke up. "I will give you a pass on insulting my integrity and calling me a liar because you're obviously concerned for your daughter's well-being, but I assure you Adam Layton is not a risk to anyone. Spending more than thirty seconds with the boy makes that obvious. Your brains are in a state of panic, so you can't see things clearly, but Mara, Adam, and Kimiko are in the middle of contacting the police to help two young women who are in a life-threatening situation, and they don't have time for your interference."

Hearing Dr. Laurence's calm, commanding demeanor helped Mara to relax slightly. He said everything so logically, she hoped it would get through to her insane parents.

It didn't.

"What girls?" Claire shrieked, then whirled on Adam. "Are you killing more people again?"

"And last time people were being murdered, this boy you are so fond of was making out with my daughter in OUR HOUSE!" Ben raged.

As if they didn't exist, Dr. Laurence turned to Mara. "Their brains are in a rotating state of fight-or-flight. Nothing we say will reach them. You three get out of here. I'll hold them off."

"You're not holding anyone off!" Claire reached to grab Mara, but Mara pulled away in time.

"Go!" Dr. Laurence urged.

Mara grabbed Adam's and Kimiko's hands and ran in the opposite direction. Adam tugged at first, obviously not wanting Mara to pick him over her parents, but she yanked hard enough for him to follow.

Looking over her shoulder, Mara saw her parents trying to get past Dr. Laurence, but he held them back calmly, motioning with his head for a couple of campus security guards to help him out. Mara was feeling all the feels for Dr. Laurence. Her teacher had stood up for Adam and covered for him without knowing that Adam had permission to stay with her from the dean and the district attorney. It made her trust him even more.

Mara's heart ached, but Raven and Lucy were more important than her parents' freak-out. They would die if they weren't found in time.

Kimiko separated from Mara and led the way toward her car.

Tightening her grip on Adam's hand to comfort him, Mara stared at Kimiko's back, following closely.

Mara had been nervous about going to talk to Detective Nicholson. Now it would be like nothing after the confrontation she just had with her parents.

Ugh.

Dream Entry #14

I'm trying so hard not to think of my jerk parents. We're at a hotel because I don't trust them not to have the police show up at my dorm to arrest Adam for some made-up crime, and we had nowhere else to go. It's annoying that they didn't bother to check to see that he has *permission to stay at my dorm from his doctor, the dean, and the freaking DA! It was supposed to help him acclimate. Fat good that's doing him with my parents trying to send him back to the psych ward every five seconds. I don't care that they think they're doing the right thing. The fact that they could look at Adam's destroyed face and STILL act the way they did makes me despise them. My chest aches thinking about how I no longer want them in my life. I always thought of myself as lucky to have the parents that I do, but not after today. Not after the last couple of months! They've been acting completely insane! Adam keeps telling me I should listen to them, that he's not worth coming between me and my parents. But I hope I made it clear to him that my parents are the bad guys in this situation, not Adam! I kept kissing him and reassuring him, but if Raven and Lucy weren't in a life-threatening situation, Adam would probably do something crazy and try to leave me. The fact that Adam is sticking around to help find Raven and Lucy just shows what a good person he is.*

Hello, parents? Blind much?

They're so stupid. And cruel. And . . . I can't think about them anymore. They're distracting me from what's truly important: finding Raven and Lucy.

Raven said they were on an island, which makes me instantly panic. I really don't want it to be Lopez Island, but my gut tells me it is. I can't think about that place without getting a little nauseous. I haven't been back there since I was a kid. Since before Great-Uncle John was murdered. I've never wanted to go back there. I never wanted to be anywhere near where he was killed. I'm scared of what it'll do to me mentally. Look what it's doing to me right now and I don't even know if that's where Jack is holding them! It's not like there aren't a ton of other islands around the Sound. What are the odds that it would be Lopez?

I can't stop the memories from flooding back into my head. I can see every detail of Great-Uncle John's body being severed and burned. The blood. The fire. I'm writing this now just to stop myself from crying.

I can't rely on the hope that Dr. Laurence will find a way to find the location. I hope he figures it out, but even he seems skeptical. How could the recording of brain waves show a location? He said he'll try, but Lucy and Raven are running out of time. And fast.

Kimiko and Adam are talking strategy at the table. Well, they're drinking coffee anyway, and Kimiko is trying to make Adam feel better, which doesn't seem to be working. Kimiko is going to stay with us in the hotel tonight. I'm not letting her out of my sight. Jack Franklin has a bully/victim complex, and I can't risk him taking Kimiko. He's way out of control at this point, and that scares me more than anything! He kidnapped a federal agent, for God's sake! And plus, if he is disgusted and fascinated by Lucy forgiving Samantha so quickly, he must think a fully changed Kimiko is his unicorn.

Please don't let it be Lopez. I feel like if I step foot on that island, Great-Aunt Eleanor will somehow steal my soul or something. Totally irrational, but completely how I feel.

We tried calling Jennifer as soon as we got in Kimiko's car. I had hoped she'd be working during the day, but apparently she has the night shift. So we're stuck waiting for her to call us back. I told the receptionist that the detective could call as late as she wanted.

I failed Terry. She asked me to protect her sister, and I failed. I even failed at what I thought *she had asked me to do, which was protect Lucy.*

I recognized the danger too late.

It feels like the story of my life.

But not again.

And I'm going to make it right.

I have to.

***

Mara placed her journal next to her bedside as her cell phone rang.

Looking at the caller ID, Mara said, "It's the FBI." Feeling a surge of nerves, Mara answered the phone. Hearing Raven admit that there might be someone working with Jack, or at least unaware that Jack was a kidnapper and helping him out, brought out all of Mara's paranoia.

"Hello?" Mara answered, putting the phone call on speaker so everyone could hear.

The voice on the other end was male. He sounded agitated. "Is this Mara Johnson?"

"Um, yes. Hi—" Mara began.

He cut her off. "This is Agent Phillip Bascow. Agent Joseph Torley passed your information on to me. I'm the one that's been officially assigned to Agent Raven Piper's cases. I hear you think something has happened to Agent Piper?"

"Yes, she's been taken by Jack Franklin. He's taken Lucy Tildon as well . . ." Mara knew Raven had told her not to trust anyone, but this wasn't new information she was telling them.

Mara didn't get to finish her sentence before Agent Bascow cut her off yet again.

"I don't know what kind of a relationship you have with Agent Piper, but your call is bordering on a criminal offense. Accusing innocent people of crimes is something the FBI has zero tolerance for. Agent Piper may have indulged in your . . . *talents*, but I assure you, I don't need any *make-believe* help."

It felt as if Agent Bascow had punched Mara in the face. She wasn't sure how to respond, her fear of being arrested kicking in. In a quiet voice, Mara couldn't hold back her defiance. "He's not innocent."

Agent Bascow didn't hide the loud, exasperated sigh he let loose over the phone. "I don't make threats idly, Ms. Johnson. If you accuse Jack Franklin again, you will be arrested by the federal government. Next time you try to pick a *criminal* for the FBI to pursue, make sure he doesn't have a squeaky-clean record and dozens of raving referrals. Also, we received word from Agent Piper this morning, and she's doing just fine on her personal leave. Now, if you call here again, I will press charges. You got me? Agent Piper may be naïve enough to believe your stories, but I see you for what you really are: a young lady who had her fifteen minutes of fame and wants fifteen minutes more. Good day."

Click.

Kimiko gritted her teeth as if she wanted to jump through the phone and throttle Agent Bascow. "What a dick."

Adam walked over to Mara and sat next to her on the bed, placing his arm around her. "We still have Detective Nicholson. She's used to our kind of crazy," he said with a smile.

Mara snuggled in close to him, fully realizing Adam was pushing down his own stress to comfort her.

Kimiko took a sip of her coffee and sighed. "This is why Grams never spoke to anyone but family about her visions, because of reactions like that douche nozzle. How many people have died because some person in authority is too closed-minded to believe in something they know nothing about?"

"Let's make sure it's not Raven and Lucy," Mara said quietly. But she completely understood where Kimiko was coming from. Reactions like Agent Bascow's and Dr. Laurence's were the reason Mara hardly ever told anyone about her gifts. It was only because of Robert and Adam that people found out about her.

Feeling Adam's chest vibrate as he talked was the most comforting sensation she'd felt in a while, and Mara wished she had some book she could make him read to her all day, but his words rang true. "We should go on the assumption that Agent

Bascow may be the inside man for Jack. If Jack is his friend, he won't consider his guilt and he'll bury this case."

A knock on the door caused Mara to jump to her feet. She was more on edge than she thought, but no one knew they were there, so Mara's fear levels were at an all-time high.

"Do you think it's room service?" Kimiko asked, doubtful.

"At a Motel 6?" Mara answered.

"Well, I'm kind of freaked," Kimiko defended herself. "I'll get it, though. You stay there."

Kimiko walked over to the door and opened it. Upon seeing whoever it was, Kimiko opened the door further so Mara and Adam could see who it was.

Detective Jennifer Nicholson.

"Detective!" Mara couldn't hide the relief and gratitude from her voice.

Jennifer smiled almost sheepishly, which was not like her at all—or, at least, not like the pit-bull detective Mara was used to.

"I tracked your cell phone to find you," she started with a guilty expression. "I wouldn't normally do that, but I called the FBI to get more information on Raven and got the standard 'she's on personal leave,' then called her parents and they had no idea what the FBI was talking about. Add that to your phone call to the station, and I knew something was seriously wrong."

"Can I hug you?" Mara asked, feeling a surge of warmth for the detective.

Walking into the room, Jennifer hugged Mara with a smile. "I'm just glad you're not angry I tracked your cell phones." The detective carried a messenger bag that bumped into Mara as she pulled away from the hug. "I brought my computer." Sitting at the table, Jennifer pulled out a small black pouch from her bag. "This will block the GPS signal from your phones so no one *else* can track you down."

Gratefully, Mara, Adam, and Kimiko handed the detective their phones, and Jennifer dropped them in the pouch.

Then Detective Nicholson eyed each of them. "So what have you got for me? Is Raven in trouble?"

Nodding, Mara sat across from her while Adam and Kimiko sat in the other two free chairs. "Jack Franklin. He's a high school English teacher. He's the one that took the girl from the news: Samantha Perkins." Images of lit matches being shoved down Samantha's throat flashed in Mara's head as she spoke. "He tortured her . . . horribly. Now he has Raven and a girl named Lucy Tildon."

Jennifer sat back, eyebrows furrowed. "Why would he take Raven or this Lucy girl?"

Kimiko answered, "It seems to be some kind of bully/victim cycle. Take the bully, beat them until they submit and have to beg their victims for forgiveness, then take the victim and beat them for forgiving too easily. The guy is sick."

Mara finished their theory. "And Raven, her sister Terry is a ghost who has been warning me this entire time about Jack, though she didn't know who he was at first. Her mind was all jumbled, but she knew him before he started kidnapping people. I saw it in a vision. Jack also knows I'd tell Raven he was the kidnapper when we figured it out."

"A ghost, huh?" Jennifer leaned back in her chair. After a moment she nodded slowly, appearing to process all the information. "And do you have any idea where he is?"

Holding on to any shred of hope, Mara explained, "All three of us were able to communicate with Raven through dreaming, and she said wherever it is, it's a couple hours away and the last chunk was by ferry. So she knows she's on one of the islands."

"That's a great start," Jennifer began as she pulled out the laptop from her bag and set it on the table. "I'm going to do a deep dive into Jack Franklin and see if we can track down any properties he may own on the islands, but also name changes, past cover-ups, local kidnappings, and murders where he grew up, anything that stands out. It's good to know he and the Piper sisters lived near each other. Maybe there's a connection we can find from that. I'll also have my techie search traffic cams for Jack and his car, though he possibly used a rental or someone else's. Face recognition software might work, but it can be spotty." Jennifer got to work, calling her colleague about the traffic cams and enlisting other cops to help with the search for anything involving Jack Franklin.

Without her phone, Mara felt helpless in aiding with the search, but after Jennifer delegated all the police-specific tasks, she focused back on Mara. "Why didn't you call me sooner? I know we've had our differences in the past, but I thought we'd come to an understanding."

Mara answered, "I just wasn't sure how you'd react to Adam helping."

Jennifer's eyes flicked toward Adam. "I'm sorry I gave you that impression. I'm a bit awkward with . . . people . . . outside of a case." Then she made sure Adam's eyes met hers. "I believe you are rehabilitated. I want you to know that. *Robert* is the guilty one. I know I made that clear in court, but I never said it to you in person." She paused, then nodded. "I'm very happy they let you out."

"Thanks." Adam's voice was small and humbled.

"We should tell you every detail we can remember. Maybe you'll pick something up that we didn't," Mara suggested.

On Jennifer's nod, Mara proceeded to tell the detective everything she could remember, with Adam and Kimiko chiming in with small details Mara had left out.

Thoughtfully, Jennifer seemed to be taking in everything she heard. "Should we be worried about your professor? You don't think he's out for a quick buck because you two are in the news?"

"I truly believe he's genuinely on our side, and he did stand up against my parents to protect Adam." Mara didn't want Dr. Laurence to be bad, but she always knew it was a possibility.

"He could have done that to secure his asset." Jennifer added, "I'll have my guys look into him as well. There are other things to be protected from than just psychopaths."

Kimiko seemed to be on board with Jennifer. "We want to trust him, but yeah, he was a total unbelieving dick before, so he could be up to something. Although at this point, I do think he wants to help Raven and Lucy, no matter what he really believes."

Mara agreed with Kimiko's assumptions but only trusted the people in that room.

And the people in Jack's basement.

Jennifer's phone rang, and she picked it up quickly. "What do you got for me?" The detective began to type down everything the person on the other end was saying into her laptop. "Okay. Really?" A beat went by. "Interesting." Another beat. "Are you sure about that? That could be vital." Nodding, Jennifer listened, then responded, "Excellent. Thanks, Roger, I owe you one." She hung up the phone.

Mara's heart pounded in her chest.

Delving straight in, Jennifer raised her eyebrow with curiosity. "Looks like your 'ghost' source was right: Jack Franklin lived in the same city as Raven and her family: Mukilteo." Skimming through her notes, Jennifer continued, "The only news story from the time of Terry's death was of a local boy who committed suicide. No murders, kidnappings, or beatings, so if kidnapping and torturing bullies was Jack's modus operandi, he didn't start that until later. And there's no reports from the school or the police that Jack was ever bullied or attacked in any way. But you saw him shoved in that locker in your dream and Terry helping him out, so it obviously just wasn't reported. According to Roger, they went to separate high schools a few miles from each other. And since you said Raven didn't recognize him, Terry obviously kept her friendship with Jack a secret."

With each new piece of information, Mara felt more confused. Jack was bullied. She *saw* that. But who murdered Terry? Terry was certainly angry enough at Jack to make Mara suspect he had been the culprit, and even though Mara never saw his face, she felt the love from Jack when Terry had rescued him from that locker. Mara couldn't imagine the young Jack whose body she inhabited in the past would ever hurt Terry. It left Mara feeling confused, and worse, doubting herself.

But no.

Jack was guilty. Of kidnapping and torture at least.

A ping on Jennifer's laptop.

"We got a hit on a traffic cam." Jennifer pulled up the footage.

Mara, Adam, and Kimiko leapt out of their seats and crowded around Jennifer's laptop.

The video clip was short, but it *was* Jack driving onto a ferry.

"Looks like a rental car," Jennifer noted and then pointed to a small sign on the boat in the far-right corner of the screen.

Mara nearly puked. The sign displayed the ferry's destination: Lopez Island.

Lopez Island.

Before Mara's brain could explode, Jennifer's cell rang again and she picked it up. "Detective Nicholson. Yeah. Copy. I'm on my way." Hanging up the phone, she turned to Mara and her friends. "I have to get back to work." Then she eyed Mara with the seriousness of a thousand suns. "Don't you dare go try to hunt Jack down. I don't want any of you to step foot on Lopez. You hear me? I'll go with cops I trust. If Jack has an insider in the FBI, he sure as hell has an insider on the police force. Agreed?"

Mara nodded to the detective. "We'll wait for your call."

"Good." Jennifer seemed convinced. Then she handed Mara the bag holding their cell phones. "Only take them out to make emergency calls. I don't trust anyone at this point, and I don't want you hurt."

Mara nodded again.

It was nice having Detective Nicholson on her side, and Mara knew she needed to trust that Jennifer would get the job done and bring Raven and Lucy home.

Jennifer packed up her laptop and left the hotel room.

The three of them stood there until her car drove away and was out of view.

The rest of the day and evening was spent watching television and trying not to jump in the car to try to find Jack Franklin's crazy-basement-of-torture on Lopez Island. Part of Mara didn't care that it was on Lopez anymore. If it meant saving Raven and Lucy, then Mara would set up house and live there forever.

It was getting late though, and they still hadn't heard a peep from Detective Johnson. Not that Mara had expected Jennifer to lead the calvary right away, but . . . yeah . . . Mara had kind of expected that.

"We should get some sleep. I don't think anything is happening tonight," Adam suggested.

"I guess." Mara wasn't convinced but also knew she needed her rest.

Cuddling up to Adam on the bed, Mara rested her head on his shoulder and closed her eyes. There was no way she could fall asleep right away, she was too wired for that, but taking a deep breath, Mara tried to calm herself . . .

***

Oh.

That was easier than she thought.

Mara didn't remember feeling tired, and now she was fully asleep, dreaming and completely aware.

The young boy from the cement room with blood was back.

And now she knew who he was.

It was Jack.

Fourteen-year-old Jack, but now that she'd seen his eyes in person, she'd recognize him anywhere.

Mara and Jack both stood in a crowded hallway. She knew this hallway. Mara remembered it from the kidnapper's memory when Mara had been shoved into a locker. Now she knew for certain that Jack was both the boy from the locker and the boy from the blood-filled cement room. This was his high school.

The students were loud, talking and laughing, heading to class, completely unaware of Mara.

Jack walked away from Mara, and she followed. Mara knew no one could see her, not even Jack, but she kept a bit of distance between them to be safe.

Swinging the exit door open, Jack walked through, but Mara could see that it was black fog beyond.

The students disappeared around her in puffs of smoke, and the school hallway melted down to smolders as if a giant had decided to burn down its doll house. There was no heat, but the remnants of what was left of the high school glowed red like drying lava.

Jack was still ahead of her. He didn't look back—which, now, Mara was grateful for. The last thing she wanted was a confrontation with a kidnapper, especially if he was in dream form. He may be his fourteen-year-old self, but in dreams, that hardly mattered. Fourteen was possibly the age something traumatic happened to him to make him the way he was in the present. Was he leading her to that moment? Maybe she'd find out what happened to Terry? Any information would help at this point, so Mara kept focused.

Hurrying to catch up, Mara followed Jack through the molten mounds that used to be a school. Reds swirled into greens until Mara was now walking in a thick green forest made up of ancient pines with trunks the size of small cars, moss growing on the sides. Jack stayed ahead of her, trudging over the wet, sodden leaves and thick layer of pine needles on the ground.

Ahead, a bright green light shone through the trees, and it seemed to be Jack's destination. At this point Mara wasn't sure what was happening or where they were going, but she figured she should keep following. Maybe he'd lead her to his house on Lopez Island, and she could tell Detective Nicholson. She knew there weren't any trees this big or this old on the island, so they were definitely in Jack's subconscious, but sometimes the subconscious rooted itself in reality, maybe enough to at least narrow down the location.

Trying not to be too hopeful, Mara kept her distance but continued forward.

The silhouette of fourteen-year-old Jack paused in the green light, standing between two ancient trees. Whatever his destination, he was there. Mara stopped as well, not wanting to catch up with him. She didn't have to wait long, as Jack began walking forward again, past the strange gateway. Once Mara was sure he wouldn't see her, she arrived at the two trees and almost stumbled from what she saw in front of her.

The forest was gone. In its place was a field of the brightest fluorescent green grass Mara had ever seen in or out of dreams. But the disturbing part was the line of buried bodies with only their decaying heads popping out of the abnormally green grass. They were laid out horizontally, as if they were a row of cabbages in a garden. Though it was difficult to differentiate male from female, Mara could tell there were both.

Fourteen-year-old Jack was there, and he now had a watering canister in his hands. He still paid no mind to Mara as he began to water each head. Even though Mara was dreaming, she could feel the bile build up in her throat as instead of water pouring out of the canister, it was blood.

And Jack looked absolutely thrilled.

Happy.

Proud.

It was too much for Mara. She knew she was in his head now.

In Jack's head.

He wasn't just a kidnapper.

He was a killer.

And if the grinding in the pit of Mara's stomach was correct, he'd been one for a very long time.

These were his victims.

Jack was a murderer.

Which meant Raven and Lucy may already be dead.

Ice flowed through Mara's veins from the shock of it.

She had no idea why he hadn't killed Samantha if he'd killed all of these people. Something must have tipped him off or spooked him to let her go free. Or maybe he always let them go free to see if they would change, to not be bullies anymore, but when they failed he'd murder them and bury them in his backyard at Lopez. Mara wouldn't be surprised if a version of this green grass existed at the house where Jack held Raven and Lucy.

Because this was how he saw his victims, as things he could change and grow, just like he kept saying to Samantha, which explained the rhetoric she spouted in the hospital about change and becoming a better person. Mara knew then that Samantha wasn't safe.

Samantha was on a trial period.

But if Mara was inside Jack's head, maybe she could figure out where his house was by seeing through his eyes? Normally, this was exactly how her visions worked: through a killer's eyes. It was what made her dreams so terrifying. It was still difficult to handle it when she'd remember witnessing Adam killing three people.

Shaking the thought from her head and focusing on saving Raven and Lucy, Mara concentrated as hard as she could to force herself to see out of Jack's eyes.

When nothing changed, she yelled, "Where are you?"

Still the garden of rotted heads.

"Tell me where you are!" she screamed.

With a flash of black, Mara was in a car.

And looking at her brown-leather-gloved man-hands clasping the steering wheel, she knew she had succeeded. Mara tried to see as much as she could through Jack's eyes, but he was only focused on the traffic light in front of him. The light turned green, yellow, red, but Jack stayed parked through the entire minute-long cycle. There were no cars behind him: at least none that Mara could hear or see. She imagined that if anyone had been behind Jack's car, there would have been a few honks or angry drivers passing by on a green light.

Green, yellow, red. Green, yellow, red. Green, yellow, red.

What was he waiting for?

He didn't move, his hands securely on the wheel, ready for something?

Mara tried to search for street signs, since Jack was so focused on the lights, but nothing was close.

A siren in the distance.

Finally, Jack's grip tightened on the steering wheel. Whatever he had been waiting for, it was coming.

The siren grew closer, definitely a police car.

Were they coming to arrest him? Had they found out where he was?

Jack's eyes went toward the siren. Mara could see the flashing police lights radiating from the top of the oncoming cop car. It was coming, and it was coming fast.

Timed to utter perfection, Jack hit the gas pedal.

SMASH!

Jack's car hit the police car full force on the driver's side.

Mara barely had time to react as she recognized who drove that car.

Detective Jennifer Nicholson.

Dream Entry #15

I watched Jennifer get hit by Jack's car.

My brain can't comprehend it.

It felt as if I had hit her. I was in his body, so seeing it like I did . . . I can't get her face out of my head. She hadn't seen it coming at all.

She's alive, thank goodness, no thanks to me, but Jack obviously knew what he was doing in the way he hit her car, because he didn't have a scratch on him and his car was working enough to take off away from the site.

Apparently, Jennifer had been on her way to a crime scene, but it had been a hoax.

Set up by Jack.

I told the officer that called us, Detective Nicholson's partner, Roger Wilkins, what I dreamt. It wouldn't help with tracking the car down, but at least they knew it was Jack.

It's almost midnight, and I'm sitting in the back seat of Kimiko's car on the way to the hospital to see how Jennifer is doing. She's not in critical condition, but she broke her arm, leg, and a couple of ribs, so she's not going anywhere for a while.

But why Jennifer? The jig was up, the cops know Jack is behind the kidnapping, so what good would it do to take Jennifer out of the picture? And now that I've seen Jack's psycho garden, I know he's a killer, not just a kidnapper. I told Roger that. He acted as if he believed me, but really, the only person I trust in the police department is Jennifer (which is kind of crazy in and of itself considering how I used to feel about her).

Honestly, I couldn't wait to see her. I needed to get that image of me smashing a car into hers out of my head. Maybe we can brainstorm Jack's motivations at the hospital if she's up for it.

I'm so happy and relieved she's okay.

Something else I need to admit to myself: we were willing to let Jennifer take the reins on arresting Jack Franklin before, but now? Now that the detective can't go herself? My gut says we need to go after Jack. Maybe my dream will help us locate his house. I mean, Jennifer will want to send the calvary, but will they go? Will they believe her when they find out her "source" is me?

I haven't talked to Adam or Kimiko about any of our options. I only told them about the rotting head dream and Jack being a murderer and not just a kidnapper. But as of now, we're focused on getting to Jennifer to see how she's doing.

Oh. We're here at the hospital. Write more later.

***

Mara stuffed her diary into her bag and exited Kimiko's car. They were on the top floor of the parking garage because Kimiko wanted to get in and out easily and there were hardly any cars parked up that high.

So far, no one had spoken in the car.

The call from Detective Wilkins only made their situation more real. If that was possible. Mara had just been grateful for his texts on the ride over, which consisted of updates on Jennifer's condition and what room she was in.

Finally, it was Kimiko who broke the silence. "Do we know what floor she's on?"

Nodding, Mara said, "Ninth. She's not in the ICU, but she's pretty messed up."

"Yeah." Kimiko appeared genuinely shaken.

"Do we have any theories on why Jack would do this?" Adam voiced what they were all thinking.

"Not yet," Mara admitted.

"Aside from being a dick? I got nothing." Kimiko sighed. "Though if he planned on finishing her off, he obviously didn't know Jennifer very well. She's tough as nails."

Mara had to agree. If Jack's plan had been to kill the detective, Mara was glad that Jennifer had proved him wrong.

Arriving at the automatic sliding doors, the glass barriers opened as they stepped foot on the rubber mat just outside the entrance.

Hitting the welcome desk first, Mara, Adam, and Kimiko received visitor sticker badges that they wore on their chests.

Samantha was still in the ICU.

For some reason, Mara hadn't thought about that fact, she was so worried about the detective.

But the idea struck her as important somehow.

“I don’t know if this is going to mean anything, but I had a weird feeling about the fact that Samantha is still in this hospital,” Mara confessed.

Both Adam and Kimiko seemed surprised by this, then Adam proposed, “Maybe one of us should keep an eye on her?”

Nodding, Mara said, “Let’s check on Jennifer first.”

Taking the elevator up to the ninth floor, once they stepped off the platform, Mara, Adam, and Kimiko were greeted by three police officers. The officers nodded a hello, expecting the three of them, presumably on Jennifer’s orders. Walking closer and closer to Jennifer’s room, Mara smiled at the fact that there were so many cops stationed on the floor. They weren’t about to let anything more happen to one of their own.

Finally, they reached Jennifer’s room, and she waved all three of them in. Jennifer’s leg was in a cast and elevated above her bed, her arm was in a sling, and two black eyes stared at Mara with an expectant expression. Surrounded by six more officers in the room, including her partner, Roger, Jennifer motioned that some of them could leave to make the room a little more comfortable. It was small, but at least it was a private room consisting of one bed, one armchair, and a couple of fold-out chairs that had been brought in for Jennifer’s security detail.

“Are you okay?” Mara raced to Jennifer’s side.

“I’m on some serious painkillers, so I don’t feel much.” She motioned the three of them closer. “I didn’t see him. The car came from nowhere. Roger said you saw it though?”

Mara nodded, guilt coursing through her. Though, logically, she knew she wasn’t driving the car, just being in Jack’s body and witnessing it created a knot in her stomach.

Jennifer seemed to pick up on this, as she said, "It's not your fault, Mara. Jack is off the rails if he was willing to do something so publicly to a police officer." Shaking her head, she added, "He made sure he wasn't on any traffic cams, and the plates on the car trace back to a woman named Emily Thompson, who said her rental car was stolen, so we can't prove it. Roger here and the department are still trying to track down any property on Lopez Island that ties to Jack, but we're not having any luck. Nothing in his name, nothing in his relatives' names. Just a whole lot of nothing. He's good."

"But why did he go after you if he has his trail covered so well?" Kimiko asked, frustrated. "He had no idea Mara would dream about him."

"He must have thought I was onto something. Maybe I was. We'll have to go through everything over and over until we figure it out."

Mara was about to respond when Terry suddenly appeared next to Jennifer's bed, her eyes round with fear. The ghost kept opening and closing her mouth as if trying to speak but unable to, just like the first time Mara had seen her.

"Do you see her?" Mara asked Kimiko and Adam.

They shook their heads.

Jennifer motioned for Roger to stay, but nodded for the remaining two officers to leave the room.

"Who do you see, Mara?" Detective Nicholson asked in a calm and soothing voice.

"It's Terry. She's standing right next to you," Mara answered. "She wants to say something, but I think it's hard for her to manifest like this." Mara desperately wanted Terry to say something, anything that could help them find Raven and Lucy.

"Sam!" Terry's voice finally screeched out. It sent instant chills down Mara's spine like broken glass shredding bone.

"What about Sam?"

Terry reached out and touched Mara's hand before Mara could react.

SWOOSH!

Mara was no longer in Jennifer's hospital room. She was in the basement of a house. It was dark, with only a single dangling light bulb hanging from the ceiling to light up the large room.

The hair raised on her neck and arms.

Her dream.

The cement room with blood and the light bulb and young Jack.

Even though this room was obviously a basement with an actual exit, Mara knew her past vision had been a symbolic representation of this very space.

An old wooden table was shoved up against a wall, and pieces of an airplane model kit lay strewn across it, half finished but meticulous in the work that had been done so far. Other than the table, the room was empty, just a long wooden staircase leading to the main floor of the house.

The door at the top of the stairs opened, and Mara saw Terry walk down, alive Terry, the Terry that existed before she had died, the same Terry that helped Jack out of his locker. Could this be the same day? Or was this days or months later? Mara couldn't tell. Terry looked the same age whenever she'd seen her.

Another memory.

This time it was Terry's.

Though Mara's pulse raced from hearing Terry scream Sam's name, she hoped that this memory would help her somehow figure out what was happening.

Going back to the memory, Mara could see that "alive" Terry was upset as she hurriedly walked down the stairs, just as she did the day she pulled Jack out of the locker.

"Jack? Are you here?" Terry whispered loudly.

"Yeah, I'm here," a small voice spoke from the shadows.

Terry stepped off the last stair and hurried over to the corner of the room where the voice came from.

Jack walked out into the dim light.

His hair and clothing appeared disheveled—and he held a crowbar in his hand.

His weapon of choice.

But the Terry in the memory didn't show any signs of fear at all of the dangerous stick of metal, she simply seemed more concerned. "Did he attack you again?" she asked with anger in her tone.

Jack nodded. "I think he broke three ribs. I've wrapped them." Jack took his free hand and lifted his dirty shirt to show the bandages wrapped around his torso.

"Oh, Jack." Terry's face fell with deep concern. "What are you going to do with that crowbar? You're not going after him, are you?"

"Yes, I am," Jack said with determined fury. "He deserves to die."

Terry stepped closer to Jack, touching his arm. "He does. But you don't deserve to have your life ruined because you murdered someone."

"I know how to make it look like an accident. Or suicide," Jack protested.

Terry sighed, incredulous. "With a crowbar? Think this through, Jack."

Tears began to flow down Jack's cheeks. "I can't take it anymore, Terry. The fear. The anticipation of him showing up everywhere I go. I can't live like this."

"You're fourteen. Three more years and you're out of here. I can protect you until then. My dream saved you the last time, didn't it?" Terry tried to sound hopeful.

Terry's dream . . .

Mara kept watching to find out what that might mean, because she knew being stuffed into a locker wouldn't equate to death. Terry must have had another vision of Jack being hurt, seriously hurt.

Jack shrugged. "You saved my life because of that dream, but it doesn't mean he won't succeed at some point. You could miss it, and then he gets to live and I don't. That's not fair. The universe shouldn't work that way."

"But it doesn't work that way, Jack. It's how I found you. My dreams led me to you and saved you from that creep. Obviously, the universe wants you alive," Terry pleaded.

"To punish the guilty," Jack agreed.

"Jack." Terry sighed again, exasperated. "You're not a murderer. Please just sleep on it. For me?"

Jack exploded as he yelled, "I haven't slept in two weeks! I can't! I'm too terrified all the time. I need to end this. Please don't stop me."

"If you haven't slept, that's why you feel this way. Trust me,

Jack. You need to force yourself to sleep. I'll stay with you. I'll keep you safe. If Doug tries anything, I'll dream about it first. We can avoid him by using my gift." She reached for the crowbar.

Jack yanked it back. "No. I have to end this."

Terry tried to pry the weapon out of Jack's hand, using her bigger size for leverage. "Jack. You're going to thank me for this later. Just let go."

Jack's face snarled in anger and panic at Terry trying to take the only thing that apparently made him feel safe. He yanked the crowbar back out of Terry's grasp, and before he could stop himself, Jack smashed the steel bar against her head.

Terry crumpled to the floor. Mara could tell she had died instantly.

Jack dropped the crowbar and fell to his knees, terrified at what he'd done. He kept trying to wake Terry up, calling her name, shaking her, then finally cradling her in his lap, crying in loud aching sobs.

"I remember now," Terry's voice cut into the memory, and when Mara blinked, she was back in Jennifer's hospital room. By the way everyone stared at her, Mara could tell only seconds had gone by instead of the amount of time it felt like it had taken when experiencing the memory firsthand.

Terry's icy hand left Mara's arm, and she stared at Mara, still frightened. "I'm responsible for the monster he became."

"No, you weren't. You tried to stop him." Seeing Jack kill Terry, even if accidentally, made Mara truly understand that if Jack could kill a friend, he could kill anyone. And now remembering that there had been a reported suicide in their town, Mara would bet money it was this Doug guy who had tortured Jack.

"He's killed so many since then. And he was right. He's never been caught or been a suspect." Terry leaned forward. "But he's doing it right now. Sam. He's going to make it look like she died of complications."

"Like right now, right now?" Mara asked in a panic.

Terry nodded. "He just walked into her room."

"What's happening?" Jennifer asked, though she was growing more and more groggy from her meds.

Mara answered quickly, "Jack is here in the hospital. Terry says he's going to kill Sam right now if we don't stop him."

"I thought there were cops protecting her room." Kimiko's eyes widened.

Jennifer turned to Roger. "How many men on Samantha Perkins's room?"

Roger swallowed hard, knowing they were in trouble. "I pulled everyone off her room to protect you."

"Which is why Jack hit your car without the intent of killing you," Adam said.

Roger tried explaining further, "We thought he'd come back to finish the job."

"Go! Room 238. Code two-one-seven!" Jennifer ordered Roger, and he motioned to four cops outside her door to go down to Samantha's room and protect her.

As Mara, Adam, and Kimiko moved to follow the policemen, Jennifer shook her head. "You three have to stay up here where you're safe!"

But Mara shook her head. "If Terry manifests down there, I have to be there. We'll be okay. We have five cops with us."

Before Jennifer could argue, Mara, Adam, and Kimiko joined

the assigned officers at the elevator as the doors opened for them to enter.

Roger motioned to the three of them. "Get behind us and don't provoke him. I know Detective Nicholson trusts you and . . . whatever it is you do . . . but I'm not going to be responsible for any of you getting hurt."

Mara and the others complied and stood behind the five cops as the elevator descended to floor two, where Samantha's room was located.

When the elevator doors opened, the five police officers drew their guns and moved down the hallway toward Samantha's room.

Mara noticed that the floor was almost empty. Only a single nurse sat at her station, alarm written all over her face when the gun-wielding cops came her way. With one finger to his lips for silence, Roger successfully conveyed to the nurse the need to keep quiet.

Arriving at Samantha's room, Roger motioned for the others to stand ready as he went for the door. But when he tried to turn the knob, it was locked. Very carefully, he glanced quickly inside Samantha's room through the small rectangular window built into the door.

Whatever he saw there made him yell, "Jack Franklin, step away from the girl!"

From the expression on Roger's face, Jack didn't do as he was told. Waving to the sitting nurse, he shouted, "Keys, now!"

The nurse stood from her station and tossed Roger a ring of keys. His face furious with frustration, he yelled, "Which one?"

Practically tripping on her own feet, the nurse made her way toward Roger.

Mara felt completely useless, standing there doing nothing while Jack was murdering Samantha.

Terry materialized in front of her. "I can help," the ghost said, then disappeared.

Screams from inside Samantha's room sent chills down Mara's spine, but it wasn't Sam's screams, it was Jack's.

And Mara knew in that moment, Terry had somehow been able to manifest in front of him so he could see her.

The nurse pointed to the correct key, then backed away, letting Roger and the other cops do their job.

It was almost over.

Jack had no way out.

Roger kicked the door open so he could keep his gun level.

Before Mara could see what was happening, Roger shouted orders. "He's on the fire escape! Get as many as you can on the ground! We can't let this creep get away!" Then he turned to the cowering nurse as he left the room. "Samantha seems fine, but make sure."

The nurse ran into the room to help Sam.

Roger's eyes found Mara's. "Get back up to Jennifer's room. It's the safest place for you three."

Mara nodded, and the three of them walked toward the elevator.

In her gut Mara knew that Jack wouldn't stop until he satisfied his urge to kill. She'd seen it in her dreams of other killers before. Their compulsion and need to finish the job.

Which only meant one thing.

Raven and Lucy were running out of time.

Dream Entry #16

We left the hospital after all the mayhem died down. Shocker: Jack got away. Roger is organizing a blockade, but I just know that Jack will be able to get around it. The police can't even find Jack's address. I can't really blame them for that. We can't rely on "normal" investigation methods to find the house, but Dr. Laurence thinks he may have found a way, and right now we need to find them fast. Then we can tell Roger and pray that they get there in time. I desperately want to go myself, but I'm pretty sure cops with guns is a far more effective way to take Jack down. But finding the place is the priority. Now that Terry has been manifesting all over the place, I feel like she might be able to help us.

Three teenagers and a ghost. What's a better combo than that?

Ugh.

We're headed to the Sleep Lab now. We told Dr. Laurence everything we knew, which wasn't much, but at least we have it narrowed down to Lopez. He thinks he has a way to make his machines help us find that house. He didn't give details, but he seemed beyond enthusiastic.

At this point, my terror of revisiting Lopez is on the back burner behind my terror of losing Raven and Lucy. If we could just, I don't know, float above the house somehow. See it in some way! I never thought Lopez would feel huge, but when there's two thousand people living on it and twenty-something square miles to cover, it's still too many houses to go door to door. I honestly think that's what Roger is going to do though. He seemed as frustrated as I am when we left him.

Gee, if only the FBI had listened to me.

But I knew that didn't matter anyway. Jack had an inside man there. What did that mean anyway? A fellow serial killer? What inside man would allow a psycho to kidnap and kill kids? I have to hope his inside man truly believes Jack is innocent, or my head is going to explode. Way too much conspiracy-theory for my brain. When we left, supposedly Roger was going to call the FBI office, so we'll see how far he gets. Roger was a witness, that has to mean something. Jack may not have been caught on camera, but a cop saw him with his own eyes.

It was over.

Jack had to know that.

I just want him caught already.

Maybe Roger will catch him before he takes the ferry back.

Maybe we can find where Raven and Lucy are being kept and we can go get them because the police will have already arrested Jack and they won't be in any danger.

Maybe I could have a good ending for once in my life.

A lot of maybes.

We're at the campus. Write more later.

***

Mara tucked her diary into her bag and exited the car with Adam and Kimiko. They parked near the science buildings so they wouldn't have to walk far to Dr. Laurence's Sleep Lab. The campus was empty, peaceful, not even a security guard in sight. Mara figured it must be at least two in the morning by now. They had left the hospital at one thirty, and it only took about twenty minutes to get back to school.

Glancing over her shoulder every few seconds, Mara was more paranoid about her parents sending spies than she thought. Or worse, popping out in the flesh. The last thing she needed was Ben and Claire Johnson trying to stop them from helping Raven and Lucy. Again.

But they made it to the building with the Sleep Lab with no issues. Dr. Laurence happily buzzed them in, and Mara led the way up the stairs to the safety of the lab.

Dr. Laurence's face lit up as if he were going to hug them all, but he settled for a friendly wave and a smile. "Any news?" he asked, after Mara and the others awkwardly waved back.

"Nothing new. Still haven't caught him and still have no idea where his house is," Mara informed him.

"That's where I think I can help." Dr. Laurence walked over to his desk with the computers arranged in a neat row underneath and five monitors on the surface. Also on the surface was what looked like a couple of helmets made of wires and sensors. "Grab those, we're going to the Med Lab where the MRI machines are."

There were three head devices, and each of them took one.

Mara examined it more carefully, realizing it was more like a swimmer's cap with holes all around it where the leads must be placed. Next to the stationary desk was a mini desk of sorts on wheels and another stand on wheels that had a large panel attached to it that looked as if that was where the wires from the strange helmet would plug into. And the wires. There were nine of them coiled up and hanging from the side of the stand, but Mara was shocked at how long they appeared to be. At least fifty to eighty feet in length from the bulk of the coil.

Dr. Laurence explained, "It's an EEG machine. A colleague of mine said he was acting on the research of a private company that claimed they could visually record dreams by having the subject hooked up to an EEG then placed in an MRI machine. Yours are no ordinary dreams, so I have no idea what we'll be able to see, but it's worth a shot if we can find this location, right?" He seemed so hopeful and proud that he had possibly figured out a solution.

Kimiko gave Dr. Laurence a placating smile, then said, "Explain in English please."

"Of course." Dr. Laurence didn't seem fazed at all by Kimiko's snark. "You're already familiar with the EEG, electroencephalogram machine. It's how we recorded your brain activity before. But MRI stands for magnetic resonance imaging, emphasis on the imaging. My colleague said the combination of the two gave him real-life images of the subject's dreams! We'll possibly be able to see everything you three do!"

Excitement filled Mara. "It's worth a shot! Yes! Thank you. I think Terry is a lot stronger now. She's able to manifest without attacking us. Maybe she can finally jump outside the basement where Raven and Lucy are being held, and we can see this place."

Dr. Laurence positively beamed. He grabbed the mobile desk and motioned for Kimiko to get the stand, leading them to the elevator. "It's not far. It's on the basement level."

Hearing "basement level" at two o'clock in the morning put Mara on edge. It sounded like the perfect setting for a horror movie. But then again, *her life* was a horror movie most of the time, so she decided to go with it.

The wheels of the two carts were the only noise that welcomed them as they walked down a long hallway that led to the elevator. There wasn't much to say. Mara was going into battle, at least that was how it felt. She had no idea if Dr. Laurence's idea would work, but she had to hope for the best. The four of them in the elevator would almost be comical if two people's lives weren't at stake. But looking over at Dr. Laurence, Mara could tell his mind must be racing a mile a minute by the fact that he kept mouthing random words as if the three of them weren't there.

When the elevator doors opened, they were greeted with another long hallway.

"It's only a couple doors down. Room 104," Dr. Laurence informed them.

Reaching the door, Mara opened it as if she were entering a high-security science experiment, which essentially she was.

Inside, the front part of the room was a waiting room, which made sense since patients came here to use the MRI machine. But being so late at night, Mara knew they wouldn't have any interruptions.

Past the waiting room were seven open doors, and glancing inside, Mara could see that there was an MRI machine in each room. It was such a sterile environment, Mara didn't want to touch anything.

"Let's get you three hooked up." Dr. Laurence practically skipped to the first of the MRI machines.

"I'll go first," Mara volunteered, wanting to start this experiment as quickly as possible.

Time was ticking, and this was their last hope.

Dr. Laurence placed the EEG cap onto Mara's head, then Mara saw the reasoning behind the absurd length of cables. The professor planned on plugging each one of their EEG caps into the one machine they brought down, and the wires had to reach from three different rooms to the center, where Dr. Laurence planned on sitting behind the mobile desk.

Three wires plugged into Mara's cap, then her professor motioned for her to lie back on the MRI machine. "You're not claustrophobic, are you?"

Mara gulped.

"Kind of?" Mara flashed back to her childhood, hiding in a doghouse when her great-aunt came after her with a knife. She wasn't full-on claustrophobic, but small spaces and crowds did tend to freak her out.

Dr. Laurence's brows furrowed, but Mara shook her head. "You don't need to worry about me. I can handle it. I *have* to handle it," she said with more confidence than she had.

"If you need me to pull you out, just shout. I'll get you out right away," he reassured her.

It helped.

A lot.

Mara still couldn't fathom the turnaround in her teacher. It was nice though. Something she had wanted from the start.

As Mara lay down on her back, with the three wires gently lying next to her, Dr. Laurence pressed a button, and the slide Mara was on moved back into the machine. Breathing deeply as the rounded walls of the MRI enclosed her, Mara pushed out any thoughts of panic. Trying to hold back the feeling of wanting to push herself out of the tube encasement, Mara had more self-control than she thought she was capable of. Closing her eyes and concentrating on her breathing calmed her down. She needed to fall asleep as quickly as possible, so Mara began meditating to speed up the process.

Listening to Dr. Laurence hook up Adam and Kimiko put the pressure on to fall asleep, but Mara erased that from her brain and focused on her breathing . . .

***

"Mara?" A voice in the darkness.

Opening her eyes, Mara could see only blackness, but she recognized Terry's voice.

As soon as the thought entered Mara's head, Terry appeared in front of her.

Searching the inky blackness, Mara asked, "Where are we?"

"This is where I am when I don't have enough energy to manifest," Terry answered.

Instantly, Mara's insides squeezed in sympathy. It was so dark and empty here. No wonder Terry was so angry at first when Mara couldn't understand what she wanted. "Is this where you've been since you died?" Mara asked, terrified of the answer. Thinking of anyone in darkness for years on end, with no closure, with no peace, hurt Mara to the core.

But Terry shook her head. "I honestly don't know where I was . . . before . . . I awoke in this place when Sam was kidnapped. But then I saw a flash in my mind of Raven being murdered by the same masked man that kidnapped Sam, and I used every ounce of my power to try to help her. I didn't know it was Jack. My brain wasn't coherent enough to remember him at all." Her eyes met mine as she said, "*You* were the one I could reach because you're connected to Raven. I tried to warn you. Tried to tell you to keep her safe. But . . ."

"I failed. I know. I'm so sorry." Mara had no words to help ease Terry's pain.

"You didn't fail. *I* failed. If I could have just remembered him and told you about Raven . . . I just couldn't think clearly at first."

"But we can help Raven now. We just have to find out where she is."

Terry glanced over her shoulder as if something were there. "Your friends are asleep. They're trying to find you."

"You have to let them, Terry. We need to find Jack's house so we can tell the police where he is and rescue Raven and Lucy." Mara tried to get through to Terry. The ghost stared in the distance, lost in thought, or worse, like they had already lost, which scared Mara more.

Terry ignored Mara's request as if she didn't hear her. "I made Jack see me." Then she nodded. "I'm glad I scared him. He deserves it."

"Terry, listen to me." Mara waved her hand in front of Terry's face to force her to focus on Mara. When she was sure Terry was listening, Mara spoke slowly and clearly. "We need to find Jack before he kills Raven like he killed you. Do you understand?"

Terry nodded, expectation filling her features. "Yes," she agreed.

Mara prodded. "I think my friends can help us. Will you let them in here?"

Terry nodded again, jaw set in determination.

In a flash, Adam and Kimiko stood with Mara and Terry inside the darkness. It looked as though they were both about to ask questions, but Mara silenced them with a quick shake of her head. They got it and let her lead.

"Let's bind ourselves together." Mara reached one of her hands out to Terry and motioned for Kimiko to do the same since she was standing on Terry's other side.

Slowly, Terry took both their hands, and Kimiko and Mara took Adam's to complete the circle.

A rush of energy flowed through Mara.

"Now take us to Jack, Terry. Focus on his energy like you did in the hospital room and take us there." Mara made sure her voice was as commanding as possible so Terry wouldn't flinch.

Terry's nostrils flared in anger, and the blackness around them began to swirl like dark fog.

Mara exchanged hopeful glances with Adam and Kimiko.

Pinpoints of light came into focus, and Mara recognized them as stars peeking through the clouds in the sky. As the world took form in front of them, they were in the sky over the Puget Sound.

Mara was a little disappointed that she wasn't staring at a house or Jack's face, but it was closer than they'd ever gotten before at least.

With a loud swooshing sound, a small floatplane flew past

them on its way to land in the water.

"That's him." Terry nodded toward the plane. "The ferries have been shut down, but Jack can fly."

Dread filled Mara.

Jack was returning home.

The police hadn't stopped him. Hadn't found him. Didn't even think about the idea that there were other ways to get to Lopez, or if they did, it wasn't enough time to shut down all private airports and airplanes.

"Follow him!" Mara yelled, and Terry yanked them all forward, flying fast toward the landing seaplane.

It didn't take long as Jack landed on the water, then taxied to a long dock along the coastline.

Mara held back her feelings of terror at seeing Lopez Island this close again. It was too important that she pay attention. She couldn't lose focus. There was a house up the lawn past the dock. It was Jack's. Mara was certain. She could see the faint light coming through the painted windows from the basement. They had found the location.

Jack jumped out of the plane and secured it to the dock, his face set in determination.

"He's going to kill her!" Terry exclaimed in panic. "I can see it in his eyes!"

"We don't know that." Mara tried to calm her, but she knew it too.

Mara had seen killers like Jack before in her dreams.

He had been blocked from killing Samantha, so Raven would no doubt be his substitute-Samantha. And if Jack thought the cops were closing in now that he had officially been identified . . .

He'd kill Raven and Lucy as soon as he could.

Which meant . . .

Now.

Terry screamed an ear-splitting shriek until Jack whirled around and his face turned white.

"Terry." Jack uttered her name, his hands shaking.

"YOU WILL NOT KILL MY SISTER!" Terry yelled.

Then Jack's eyes suddenly met . . .

Mara's.

"You," he said accusingly.

Oh boy.

Jack could see her. He whirled around as if realizing in that instant that Mara now knew where he lived. Then he turned back to her. "If you tell the cops where I am, I promise you Raven and Lucy will be dead as soon as you fly back to your body or whatever it is you do."

Mara wasn't sure if he'd be able to hear her, but she tried anyway. "Please. You don't have to do this. Raven did nothing to you, and Lucy is innocent. A victim like you were."

Jack heard her.

And he didn't like what he heard.

"You and Kimiko come. Alone. Yes, I know about you two. I did all my research as soon as I figured out who you were, and it looks like you two are . . . friends." He said it as if he couldn't stomach saying the words. Then he continued, "I promise I won't hurt Lucy or Raven if you two come alone. I have questions."

He seemed sincere.

A squeeze of Adam's hand reminded Mara that there was no way Adam was going to let her go alone, but Mara nodded. "You promise you won't do anything until we get there?"

Jack nodded. "I promise. But if you bring the cops, I *will* kill them, and I'll start with Raven."

His words caused Terry to scream again, and she yanked her hands away from Mara and Kimiko.

***

Mara bumped her head on the MRI machine as she was slammed back into her body. "Let me out! Let me out!"

She could hear Kimiko and Adam screaming the same thing.

Poor Dr. Laurence hit all three buttons to slide them out of the machines as quickly as he could.

Mara yanked the leads off her head and raced to Dr. Laurence. "We found the house! We just need to Google-Earth it or something. It's right on the coast!"

"Calm down, calm down." Dr. Laurence tried to remain calm himself as Adam and Kimiko raced to Mara's side as frantic as she was. He continued before they could object, "Breathe for one second. Guys, we were successful! I recorded the entire dream. I can take the images and put them directly into the computer. I put software in that would match geographical similarities of the San Juan Islands and specifically Lopez, so it should be quick."

Mara was beside herself with panic. "Do it, then!"

Dr. Laurence knew the stakes. He hurried to the computer. The picture was rough, almost blurry like an old film, but everything they had just seen—the dock, the hill, the house—was on the screen. He put it through his program, and within seconds there was a match.

A match.

It was the exact dock, the exact inlet, the exact house.

With a couple of clicks, the address popped up on screen.

"Let's call the police and let them know." Dr. Laurence smiled triumphantly.

Mara was about to tell him Jack's demands when Kimiko stepped in with her phone in hand. "Dr. Laurence, you're a savior! I'll call Roger right now!" Kimiko threw Mara a knowing glance, and Mara kept her mouth shut.

Kimiko put the phone to her ear. "Roger? Hi. Yeah, it's Kimiko Thompson. We know Jack Franklin's address. Yes. He used a seaplane to get there. You have to hurry. We think he's going to kill Raven and Lucy now. Yes." She examined the computer screen. "Yes. It's 4487 Turnpike Road. Good luck. And call us as soon as you hear anything. Yes, thank you. Bye." Taking the phone away from her ear, she smiled at Dr. Laurence. "We're so exhausted. Do you mind if we leave and talk about all this in the morning?"

Dr. Laurence was absolutely elated by the footage he captured of the vision. "Of course. I'll be examining this all night. I can hardly believe this really happened."

"We'll call you as soon as we hear anything," Kimiko added and hugged Dr. Laurence.

Mara followed her lead, shocking their teacher, but he nodded, and Mara hoped he had been properly placated. Adam simply nodded, not one to hug.

As soon as they left the room, Kimiko showed Mara her phone. "You know I didn't call Roger."

"Yes." Mara could barely think straight.

"You know we have to go save them," Kimiko said, looking as freaked as Mara felt.

"Yes," Mara responded.

"Okay." Kimiko nodded. "Let's go, then."

"How? The ferries are closed, and I don't know how to fly a plane." Reality hit Mara hard.

But Adam walked down the hallway, leading the way. "You're not going without me, and I know how we can get there."

Mara and Kimiko followed, not arguing about Adam inviting himself along for one second.

As they climbed the stairs to reach the main floor, Mara kept thinking . . .

What had Terry done to Jack when they broke communication with her?

She really hoped the ghost had done some damage, because Mara couldn't shake the feeling that Jack wasn't going to keep his promise and that she and Kimiko were heading toward their own deaths.

#17

It's freaking freezing out here, but at least it's starting to get light out. It took us a while to get ahold of Adam's contact, and now it's close to six a.m. We're currently on a tugboat in the middle of the Puget Sound headed toward . . . I don't even know what. It's completely irrational. We should have called Roger, but I've had enough dreams of killers in my life to know that Jack would make good on his promise and kill Raven and Lucy if he saw cops coming his way. He'll do it anyway. But I have to try to stop him. So I'm stuck: I can't call the cops and also I can't sit around knowing that I know where Raven and Lucy are.

So we're on a boat, a very smelly boat, going to the island where my great-uncle John was murdered. The island that starred in my very first vision. I'm shoving my emotions down because if I stop and think about them, I'll probably pass out and be useless. Or I'll huddle in a ball and be just as useless. But it's there. A tap, tap, tapping of overwhelming emotions that keep trying to break my thin wall of composure.

I need to stay strong.

I need to save Raven and Lucy.

Even if it means I die.

I hate thinking like that, but what else can I do?

At this point, I'm going, so I might as well come up with a strategy.

Come on, brain, think.

***

"We're almost there." The captain's voice broke through Mara's concentration. His name was Chris, and he was a family friend of Adam's. Adam hadn't been sure if Chris would help, but when Adam called, Chris said he'd do anything for him. Adam told Mara that Chris had been friends with his mom, so when everything came out about her being murdered, Chris felt somehow responsible for leaving Adam with his abusive dad.

Adam had laughed when he thought of Chris, thinking he'd never need the use of a tugboat for anything, but the Universe worked in crazy ways.

Mara nearly choked from nerves. She was headed back to an island where she witnessed her first murder from a vision and would possibly be murdered herself. It was weirdly fitting. But also terrifying.

With the directions given directly to Chris, the tugboat pulled up to a dock a half a mile away from Jack's dock.

As Chris jumped off the boat and secured the boat to the dock, he turned to Adam. "You sure you don't want me to take you to the exact address?"

Chris was entirely clueless as to why they were headed to Jack's house. Adam had lied and told him that his mother's sister lived there and he needed to see her. With the police blocking all ferry traffic, Chris was reluctant at first, but Adam pressed all the right guilt buttons. Plus, it did help that the cops weren't being forthcoming about why the ferry ban was happening. So Adam pushed the idea that it could be something non-dangerous, like someone might have had a heart attack on the ferry or some kind of crime occurred on the dock. After easing Chris's mind and making him feel sufficiently guilty, he agreed to take them.

Adam answered Chris, "No. I want it to be a surprise. I mean, she's expecting me, but she probably thought I canceled because of the whole ferry thing. And it's so early. I don't want to wake her up."

Chris nodded, and Mara couldn't read his expression. Was he going to turn them in? Did he believe Adam? It was past six in the morning at this point. Early, but not that early. She looked to Kimiko to maybe pull off a mind-reading thing, but Kimiko seemed focused on getting off the tugboat. Her face did look a little green.

Jumping off the boat herself, Mara joined Kimiko on the dock, then Adam joined them.

The sun was above the horizon at the point, but just barely. The air was crisp, and Mara knew her cheeks and nose were red from the cold. The blades of grass past the dock were covered with a light layer of frost but were already starting to sparkle from the sun melting the frozen tips.

Awkwardly, Adam hugged Chris goodbye, and Mara and Kimiko waved their thanks. Throwing the docking rope back onto the boat, Chris hopped on the ship and gave them all a quick wave before he puttered back out to the Sound.

"You think he's going to tell the cops?" Adam asked what Mara feared.

"Oh, definitely," Kimiko confirmed. "Wouldn't you?"

Mara agreed with Kimiko's assumptions. "He might not know what's going on. In fact, I'm sure he doesn't, or he'd never have taken us, but he cares enough about you to be doubly sure you're okay."

"Then we have to act quick," Adam said. "I'll stay back and let you guys go in. Make him think you came alone. But I won't let you out of my sight for a second." Adam's eyes met Mara's as he held her cheek in his hand.

Kimiko shifted from the obvious third-wheel feeling, but then shook her head. "Adam, we can take care of ourselves. You need to break into that basement and get Raven and Lucy out of there. Mara and I are very capable of stalling him."

Mara nodded. "Our mission is to save them."

Adam shook his head. "I can't leave you with him. He could kill you."

Kimiko forced eye contact with Adam. "He'll try to kill me first since I'm the Samantha in his equation."

"Is that supposed to calm me down? We can't let him hurt any of us!" Adam's voice raised in panic.

Mara had to agree. Hearing that Kimiko would be Jack's first target sent her heart racing.

But Kimiko quickly explained, "What I was about to say is that I can handle myself. Six years of self-defense classes has to be good for something." Then she said to Adam, "I won't let anything happen to her."

"I can take care of myself too." Mara was defensive. But really, Mara was good at hiding, not fighting. It was how she'd survived with her great-aunt and even Robert.

Because yeah . . .

She'd had experience with serial killers.

She was dating one in fact.

Oof.

Adam sighed deeply, his hands fidgeting. Finally, he nodded. "As soon as I free them . . ."

"You'll get Raven's ass up to help us. She's trained for this crap." Mara finished Adam's sentence a little differently than he perhaps intended.

But Adam smiled. "Yeah, you're right. She's our best asset against Jack."

"And hopefully her sister will help too, if she hasn't already," Mara said, thinking again of the last time they saw Terry as she manifested to Jack.

With nothing left to say, the trio carefully made their way over the frosted grass and through the tree coverage that separated this space from Jack's house.

Trudging through the dense trees, Mara tried not to think about the fact that she felt as if she were walking down a very long plank. Jack would be ready for them, most likely preparing some elaborate trap, or a simple crowbar to the head, which was more his MO.

Up ahead, Jack's house came into view through the tree line.

Mara motioned for the others to stop. "You stay here, Adam. When we're inside, make your move."

Adam nodded and kissed Mara as if they'd never see each other again.

And maybe they wouldn't.

But Mara couldn't think about that. She had to move forward. She had to confront a killer straight on.

Not like Robert, who kidnapped her at knifepoint.

No.

Mara was going to ring the killer's doorbell.

Grumbling to herself, Mara and Kimiko left the tree cover and walked across the lawn that led to Jack's front door. As the frosted grass crunched under their feet, Mara saw the large, manicured backyard and recognized it from her dream. Luckily, there weren't rotting heads popping up like cabbages, but Mara could sense that all his victims' bodies were there, buried deep. She wasn't sure how that would be possible considering his victims had been construed as suicides or accidents, but she had never been surer of anything in her life. Jack had taken them from whatever graveyard his victims had been buried in and reburied them here. His trophies.

Mara shuddered as they walked up to Jack's front door.

From what Mara could remember from her architecture class in high school, the house had been built in the forties or fifties. It wasn't in the greatest shape: broken shutters, chipped roof shingles, wooden siding that had lost most of its paint from age and saltwater. Mara would have thought it was abandoned it was in such ill-repair.

The door was large and sunken into the porch. If Mara didn't know any better, she'd think they were about to enter a killer's home.

Oh wait.

Sighing, Mara and Kimiko exchanged one last nod of support before Mara knocked on the front door.

It opened at her knocking.

No locks, not shut properly, the simple force of her knuckles on the surface had pushed it inward.

"Yeah, that doesn't scream trap," Kimiko said under her breath.

Mara didn't answer as she carefully pushed the door the rest of the way open and entered the house.

The interior was much nicer than the outside. It was difficult to survey the details, as Mara was afraid that Jack would pop out from every corner. A large living room welcomed them first, neat and orderly, two floral couches positioned across from each other with a handful of antique shelves and display cases arranged against the walls. The far wall was made of glass with a sliding door leading to a side deck and another forest as the view. Two hallways led in opposite directions, and from what Mara could see, the left hallway led to the kitchen and the right to a set of rooms.

"Which way?" Mara asked.

But Kimiko shook her head, grabbing a metal bookend off one of the shelves, then handed Mara the other one on the opposite side of the shelf. "We can't let him sneak up on us. Better to be offense than defense." Moving to the sliding door, Kimiko unlocked it and slid it slightly open. "Quick getaway if needed."

Mara nodded, holding the hefty bookend like a rock. They were on the same page.

Raising her voice, Mara yelled, "We're here, Jack! Show

yourself!"

Nothing.

Silence.

Mara didn't want to move, but she didn't want to set Adam up for failure if Jack was downstairs waiting for an escape attempt.

A voice came out of an unseen speaker system: Jack's. "You two actually came."

Searching the room for a speaker, Mara spotted it on the side wall above one of the shelves. For some reason, she talked to it as if it were Jack himself. "We came. Now, let Raven and Lucy go."

A low chuckle. "No. I don't think I'm going to do that."

"Shocker," Kimiko grumbled under her breath.

Mara had to stall, give Adam time to help Raven and Lucy escape.

Feeling the cool breeze of freedom behind her, Mara stepped away from the sliding door, but only a few feet. "Show yourself! You coward! Terry told us you always hid from Doug like a sniveling weasel! You couldn't even confront him! You had to kill an innocent girl who was just trying to help you! Real brave!" Mara taunted, both scared and hopeful that it would lure Jack out.

It did.

He came from the direction of the hallway with the rooms.

Nostrils flared and hands clenched, Jack snarled, "Your little light-show tricks are fooling no one!"

Mara had his attention. And this was her arena. "Light show? What, with flashlights and the massive amounts of special effects I've learned in college? Then how do I know that you killed Terry with a crowbar? Just like you've been beating Lucy with one too?"

In a pouncing stance, Jack kept about ten feet between them. Mara had no doubt he could leap toward them, quickly and efficiently.

In angry bursts, Jack answered, "Oh, I know you're psychic like Terry was. I figured that out quickly enough, so I *know* that's how you found out about me and my past. It's why I wear a mask, so people like *you* don't see me."

Finally, the answer to why he wore a mask even though his victims already knew his identity. He'd been protecting himself against psychics, so afraid that people like Terry and Mara would see him in one of their visions.

Jack continued forward. "But ghosts? That's a stretch. And why now? If ghosts were real and she was angry, why didn't she haunt me years ago? What is it? Some kind of hypnosis?" His head cocked to the side, curious, as if he had to find out how Mara somehow made Terry appear.

"Why is she haunting you now and not back then? Are you serious?" Mara asked incredulously, then brought out her sarcasm. "Um, I don't know. Maybe it's because you kidnapped her sister? I didn't realize you were a moron too." Mara provoked him, she had to keep him distracted enough to give Adam time.

Jack flinched when Mara said "moron." "It doesn't matter, because ghosts don't exist."

One thing Mara knew was that Terry must have disappeared when she went after Jack without them. Terry must have needed Mara's energy to manifest.

Mara thought to herself, *Well, Terry, if you need my energy . . . take it! And take this idiot down while you're at it.*

Nothing.

Thanks, Terry.

Jack turned to Kimiko, his expression one of frustration. "I need answers from you."

It was as good a stall as any, and Kimiko picked up on this as well when she said, "What do you want to know?"

Jack slitted his eyes as he sized up Kimiko. "What happened to you to make you stop being who you are?"

"Stop being an a-hole like you, you mean?" Kimiko's grip tightened on the bookend.

Nostrils flaring, Jack answered, "I'm nothing like you or any of the others. You seem to have changed without reason though, and I have to know why!" There was desperation in his voice now.

Was it because his main mission was killing bullies because he thought they were incapable of change? And to have Kimiko stand in front of him, side by side with the girl she used to bully, was possibly causing him some kind of brain hemorrhage.

Kimiko took a purposeful step forward, confidence oozing off her. "I stopped being mean because I knew what I was doing was wrong. I was cruel for no reason except to make me feel powerful. I didn't want to be that person anymore, so I changed."

Jack didn't like that answer. "It's not that simple. You can't just *decide*. You were born that way, and you'll go back to your old self someday."

"Nope." Kimiko shrugged, knowing full well that an off-handed *nope* would only infuriate Jack.

And it did.

"You will!" he screamed.

Kimiko readied her bookend. "I have a question for you now."

Jack's curiosity calmed him enough to nod for her to continue.

"If you really cared about helping the helpless, then you never would have taken Lucy or Raven. Raven's entire life is dedicated to helping people, and Lucy has been tortured by Samantha for her entire high school existence. Why?"

If a person's forehead could have writing on it, Jack's would say: *Does not compute. Does not compute.*

"Aaaahh." Kimiko smiled in understanding. "Denial. I know that look well. You took them because you didn't want to get caught, and you just used Lucy accepting Sam's apology *too early* as an excuse to take her. Your self-preservation overrode your supposed *mission* or *code*." Kimiko grimaced in disgust. "You're worse than any bully, and I should know, I was one of the worst."

That did it.

Jack pounced.

Kimiko's quick reflexes kicked in, and she threw the metal bookend with all her strength, hitting Jack square in the forehead.

Jack fell back, but it didn't knock him unconscious like Mara hoped it would.

Kimiko grabbed Mara's hand and pulled her through the sliding glass door and out into the morning cold, slamming the door shut.

As they ran across the deck, Mara glimpsed through the glass wall to keep an eye on Jack.

He was gone.

Not following. Not in the living room.

Just gone.

This scared Mara even more. She kept her hand clamped to Kimiko's as she said, "He's not in the living room. He's probably going to cut us off somewhere. We need to do something unpredictable."

Nodding, Kimiko stopped as they went down the three steps that led to the side of the house. "We should go back in and help Adam."

"Will he expect that though?" Mara's mind raced trying to figure out which way Jack's head would go. Her biggest fears were coming to fruition. The scariest moment of her life was when she hid in that doghouse, and her great-aunt, holding a butcher knife, found her there, ready to kill. It was scary because she had hid and she'd been found by a killer.

This house was Jack's. Where could they hide that he didn't know about? There was a part of Mara that wanted to desert everyone and run, her fear was that strong.

But seeing Kimiko's terrified eyes—a girl who had been her enemy for so many years—Mara found that she couldn't leave. She had to stay. Nothing would keep her from helping Raven and Lucy. Two people who were in exactly the same position she had been in with her great-aunt.

Fighting through her paralyzing horror, Mara said, "We need better weapons." Her other hand still clung onto the bookend, but seeing as how Kimiko's direct hit didn't even slow Jack down, they needed something better.

Walking around the deck while keeping her eyes on the

glass walls, Mara still didn't see Jack. Heart racing, she almost wanted to scream at every footstep, just anticipating Jack jumping out at her. But they had to get back in the house. They had to get to the basement.

Mara led the way this time, moving around the perimeter of the house, searching for the painted basement windows that were in her vision while also searching for any kind of new weapon. Kimiko held on tight to her free hand though, and Mara took great comfort in it.

Seeing the first painted window, Mara decided to go for it. "Let's just get in there. Even if he's down there, I'd rather take him out before he kills any of us." She didn't know what she was saying, but it felt right.

Kimiko's hand was sweating. She was a lot more scared than she was letting on.

Mara's overprotective nature swept through her like wildfire. "We got this. Okay?"

Nodding, Kimiko's hand began to shake. "I hit him in the head," was all that came out.

Mara could tell Kimiko was going into shock. She needed to snap her out of it. "We need Terry. Can you help me concentrate on her? Manifest her? It's the only thing that scares Jack."

Seeing Kimiko's eyes glaze over, Mara gently dropped the bookend, took her hand away from Kimiko's grip, and cupped both her hands around Kimiko's face. "Kimiko. I need you. I can't do this alone."

Kimiko seemed to hear her. She took Mara's hands in hers and brought them down off her face, squeezing them. "Yes. Okay. I'm here. I can help."

Before Kimiko could go into shock again, Mara took the bookend from the ground and began breaking the glass in one of the windows, carefully, slowly, and in perfect chunks, so as not to make as much noise and to get rid of any large shards of glass that could cut them. "Terry, if you can hear me, we need you right now."

"Mara!" Adam was down below in the basement, steering clear of the broken glass.

The window was clear at that point, but Mara stripped off her jacket and placed it over the bottom edge of the window so they wouldn't cut themselves. "Adam! We're coming down. Do you have the girls?"

"They're not here," he said in a panic.

"What? Let us get down there." Mara moved to drop herself down into the basement.

"No. Don't. I can't find a way out of here. Get me up." Adam reached up with his arms for Mara to grab.

Though the knowledge that Raven and Lucy weren't in the basement crushed her, her need to get Adam to safety overrode any concerns. Kimiko leaned down as well, grabbing Adam's other arm, and the two girls quickly pulled him up to safety.

Adam rolled to his feet in a defensive position. "Well, Jack knows I'm here. I hope that doesn't mean he . . ." Adam couldn't finish the thought. No one wanted to think of the possibility that Raven and Lucy were already dead.

"No. He's hiding. He's playing games with us. Raven and Lucy are the bait, and we're the mice. We just have to be a few steps ahead of him," Mara reasoned.

"I can't believe I'm saying this, but we should split up. It's our only advantage," Kimiko suggested with a slight shake in her voice.

"He'll pick us off that way." Mara couldn't be alone. Not like when she was a kid. Not so Jack could find her . . . with a knife . . . Shaking her head of the memories, Mara regained her focus. "If we do that, we need a plan."

Kimiko nodded, taking each of their hands. "I think I have one."

#18

I'm in a closet.

Hiding.

I fully plan on writing down everything that happens when I get back. If *I get back. I have to stick to my end of the plan. I needed someplace to be that I could feel somewhat safe. Getting in here took about three seconds. I ran in the front door and pretty much dove straight into the closet. Kimiko's and Adam's missions were to divide and conquer, with each one taking a respective hallway.*

No one wants to kill Jack. We just need to knock him out. Which is a lot harder than it sounds, because Kimiko hit him really hard with that bookend and he got up and ran away quickly afterward.

At this point, I've never been so unsure in my life.

Sitting here in this closet, I have to admit . . .

I want Jack dead.

I hate that my mind is thinking that, but it's true. I don't want people like this to exist in the world. I just don't.

Feeling like I am, and it's not the first time, hiding from my great-aunt, being tied up and tortured by Robert . . . people like that shouldn't exist. They should all just go away.

I know I'm thinking all these things because I'm so freaking scared, but it doesn't make them any less true. And it makes me know in my heart of hearts that this is where Adam was coming from when he killed those three men. He didn't want them to hurt anyone else, kill anyone else. They were ticking time bombs that could murder innocent people at any moment, and Adam stopped them from ever having the chance to do that again.

Adam could do it.

But could I?

The hard truth hit me in the chest, and it made me even more terrified, and I knew with absolute clarity . . .

I could never kill anyone.

I know I couldn't.

I'm scared for my life in a closet, but if Jack was in front of me and I had a gun, I wouldn't shoot.

I couldn't.

I physically wasn't capable.

Mentally, I'd shoot fifteen holes in his chest, but physically *I'd never be able to pull the trigger.*

I need to not think about this.

I need to do my part of the plan.

I need to get Terry's butt in this house.

***

Mara took a few deep breaths and focused as hard as she could on the ghost-that-wouldn't-go-away-but-now-wouldn't-show-herself, Terry. It was difficult not to be bitter when Mara had been scared to death by the ghost and extremely annoyed with her pulling Mara into visions and yanking her awake, but now when they needed her most, Terry was a no-show.

There had to be a reason.

Last she saw Terry, the ghost had been so angry that she had rushed Jack and broken the connection between herself and Mara, Kimiko, and Adam. A horrid thought hit Mara: Would the fact that they were hooked up to an EEG and an MRI at the time permanently sever their ties to Terry?

No.

That was paranoia. If Terry wasn't showing herself, there was a reason. Mara needed to be open to it, needed to help her manifest into this reality.

Closing her eyes, Mara thought only of Terry, only of her voice, her face, how she resembled Raven, how she had been cheated out of life by a psychopath.

"I'm here, Mara." Terry voice was right in front of her.

Mara's eyes flew open, and she'd never been more relieved to see a ghost in her life. "Terry, thank goodness. We need your help."

Terry peered over her shoulder, seeing something Mara couldn't. "I was with Raven, though she can't see me. I don't think I can manifest without you. You're my link to this reality." Her eyes glossed over with sadness, as if it was hard to admit when she said, "I didn't want to leave Raven, but your call was strong."

A pang of guilt. "Is Raven okay? Is Lucy?"

Terry nodded. "Jack has them in a hidden room. Kimiko is

closest. Should I show her?"

"Yes. And Terry, Jack doesn't think you're real. Show him how wrong he is." Mara hoped Terry would get what she was asking her to do.

Terry said, "I'll give him a show he'll never forget. I need you though. I'm stronger when you're near. I don't know if I can be at full power unless you're next to me."

Gulp.

But fine.

Mara was ready.

This was the plan.

Terry was the plan.

"Let's do it, then. Where is Jack now?" Mara asked, hoping Terry could give her his location.

"He's in another one of his hidden rooms. Watching," Terry informed her.

"Watching? He has cameras?" The idea that Jack was able to see them sent shivers down Mara's spine.

"Everywhere."

"Here?" Could he see them, or her, to be specific?

"He knows you're in here from the hallway camera, but there's no camera in here." Terry seemed to be becoming more comfortable "existing" the longer she stayed with Mara.

Mara stood up and opened the closet door. "Lead the way and tell me if he's coming."

"I can't see everywhere at once, but I can sense him. If he comes for you, I won't let him hurt you." Terry's words were tinged with bravery.

It was time.

"Let's go."

Mara nodded for Terry to lead the way, and she walked down the hallway toward the kitchen. Glancing over her shoulder, Mara worried about Adam, who had gone the other way, but Terry assured her that Jack was in the same direction as the secret room holding Raven and Lucy, so for the moment, Adam was safe.

Also, the fact that Jack stayed in his little private room spying on them all and not attacking wasn't lost on Mara. He was biding his time. Like a lion with his prey.

Could he see Terry on camera? Did it look all creepy-distorted-footage-horror-movie-like? Mara hoped so.

Passing the kitchen, Mara barely noticed the clay-tiled counters and dark wood cabinetry. She was only focused on following Terry.

Motioning to a wall with light wood paneling, Terry said, "There are three doors." She proceeded to point to each. "Here, here, and here. Jack is behind the one furthest to the right, and the girls are in the middle."

Mara needed backup, the human kind. There was a smaller hallway that led past the fake wall of doors, so Mara decided if she was on camera anyway, what did she care, and called out, "Kimiko?"

A few moments later, Kimiko walked around the corner, eyes wide and scolding. "I thought you were going to . . ." She seemed to finally see Terry. "Oh, good. Do we know where psycho is?"

Glancing at the wooden wall, Mara answered, "Three hidden doors. Three hidden rooms. Raven and Lucy are behind door number two."

The third door swung open suddenly and slammed against the wall.

Jack's face was crazed with anger and frustration, and he held a crowbar in his hand. "How did you know that?"

He couldn't see Terry.

Or he would know how Mara knew that.

Time for some concentration.

Mara focused all her energy into Terry, really seeing her, making sure all her thoughts were on the ghost and willing her into existence for Jack.

It worked.

Jack stepped back, almost tripping on himself. "How are you doing that?"

Terry stepped forward, confident. "You will suffer for everyone that you killed, Jack."

"No! You're not here! You're not real!" Jack swung his crowbar at Terry, but it passed harmlessly through her.

Mara nodded to Kimiko to go through the middle door while Jack was distracted.

Kimiko moved without a word, feeling the wall for the hidden entrance to the second door. She popped it open and disappeared inside.

Mara kept her concentration on Terry, making sure she stayed in this realm.

Jack was going berserk, swinging left and right, trying to somehow erase the ghost from his past.

Terry laughed, and it chilled Mara to the bone. "Now that I'm back, I'll haunt you forever for what you did to me, Jack. You're worse than any bully you murdered."

Shaking his head, Jack screamed, "I'm making the world a better place! You were an accident, but your death gave me the courage to start my mission! And I've done so much good! Ended so much suffering!"

Terry's ghost shook from his words, then she stuck her arm in his chest. He screamed. Mara knew the coldness of that touch and watched as Jack's lips turned blue.

In a frightened rage, Jack's eyes met Mara's. "You!"

Mara took a step back, not knowing why he was suddenly focused on her.

"You brought Terry here!" Jack yelled.

True. Also the expression in Jack's face caused her whole body to tremor. He had the same cold, dead eyes her great-aunt had. Jack wanted to kill Mara. And he wanted to do it now.

Pushing through Terry as if she were made of fog, Jack raised the crowbar and slammed it down toward Mara's head.

Mara was too shocked to move out of the way. Too surprised by the sudden attack.

But the crowbar never hit her.

It crashed down on Adam's back as he leapt to intercept the blow.

Mara screamed and wanted to charge Jack with her entire body and strangle him, but Adam pushed her down, protecting her with his body.

Feeling every painful thud like a vibration of anguish as the crowbar smashed into Adam's back, Mara tried to flip Adam over so she could take some of the blows herself. But Adam stood strong. He wouldn't let anything happen to her. His eyes stared into hers with all the love that he had.

"Adam." Mara whispered through tears as each thud to Adam's back broke her.

"I love you," Adam said as blood began to drip down his neck and body.

Mara struggled to save him, but Adam wouldn't budge.

"Adam, please! Please let me save you!" Mara screamed.

"You already did." His voice was raspy and choked, blood coming out of his mouth now.

Mara had never known a pain that deep. When she screamed, it felt as if every part of her soul was breaking into a thousand pieces.

The pounding stopped.

Adam's body collapsed onto Mara's, no longer tensed from being beaten by Jack, simply limp.

Mara saw past Adam's head to see Raven, freed by Kimiko and ready to fight. She took another swing at Jack with a skillet in her hand. Apparently, the first swing had pulled his attention away from smashing Adam's back with the crowbar.

Jack swung his crowbar at Raven, but she was an FBI Agent (and frankly, a badass) so his swing went wild.

Kimiko ran over to Mara and Adam, carefully lifting him off of her body, trying to help Adam get clear of Jack's radius. Adam was barely conscious at this point, but he let Kimiko lead him to a chair near the kitchen. Mara went with them.

Raven managed to smash the skillet into Jack's jaw, and a loud crack of bone snapped. If it wasn't such a horrendous sound, Mara might have cheered.

Jack's lower jaw hung loose as blood poured from his mouth. He swayed for a moment, dazed from the shock and pain of it.

"That was for my sister, you son of a bitch!" Raven's eyes were wild and angry as she hit Jack again, but this time in the shoulder.

Crunch.

The bone snapped again, this time his collarbone.

Jack still swayed like a zombie. He swung his crowbar at her, but it was weak and aimless, easy to avoid.

Mara could tell he'd been hit too many times in the head for him to function properly at this point.

Raven sensed this as well, but instead of trying to subdue and arrest him, Mara could see the agent was going for the kill.

And Mara found that she wanted her to.

As Raven lifted her arm to give Jack the killing blow, Terry suddenly appeared in front of Jack.

Mara was about to yell to Raven that Terry was there when she saw the expression on Raven's face. "Terry," Raven said.

"Don't. Don't become him," Terry pleaded.

"But he killed you," Raven argued, her body beginning to slump in exhaustion.

"You'll make him pay, just not this way," Terry replied.

Raven slowly lowered the frying pan.

"I love you," Terry said.

"I love you, too," Raven choked, her emotions catching up to her.

Terry disappeared, and all that was left was Jack, dazed, swaying, half-conscious.

With surprising ease, Raven yanked Jack's arms behind his back and tied his hands together with the handcuffs that had held her earlier.

Shoving Jack onto the couch without a care for his injuries,

Raven hurried over to Adam and Mara and examined the damage to his back. It was bad. His shirt was ripped open from the crowbar, deep gashes pouring out blood.

"We need to get him to a hospital." Kimiko was on the verge of tears.

Mara held Adam's hand, panic threatening to overtake her. His eyes could barely focus, but he managed a small smile for Mara. "My dad's done worse. I'll be fine."

But she knew he wouldn't be fine if he didn't get help.

And the fact that he'd made the comparison to his father's abuse made Mara want to scream all over again. Adam deserved so much better in life.

Then he smiled again and said, "I could have killed him, Mara. But I didn't." His eyes beamed with pride, happiness, and relief. "I didn't kill him. Even when I could have. I'm not a killer." His face was full of so much joy at the revelation despite his injuries, Mara almost wanted to smile with him, but her pain was too deep that she might lose him forever.

Kimiko placed Lucy on the chair next to Adam, and she was barely conscious. Sweat dripped from her forehead, the infection getting worse. "Help is coming," Kimiko said to Lucy, wiping her head with a napkin that had been on the table.

Lucy nodded, teeth chattering.

Mara could already hear Raven on the phone calling Roger after Kimiko had given her the scoop on who was in charge, and soon the sound of helicopters filled the air. Though it felt like hours, it had only taken minutes for the paramedics to storm into the house, immediately helping Adam and Lucy.

It was all a whirlwind of motion and noise that Mara couldn't comprehend, her only thoughts were of Adam and hoping he'd survive his injuries.

Kimiko's arms wrapped around Mara, supporting her, helping her walk, but her voice sounded warbled, like she was underwater. "Mara? Did Jack hurt you? Are you okay?"

But Mara couldn't find the right words. The only thing that came out was, "Adam."

Kimiko's face dropped, tears in her eyes. "They're doing everything they can. Mara, I'm so sorry. I couldn't get the stupid cuffs off Raven and Lucy fast enough. I'm so sorry."

Mara didn't want Kimiko to blame herself, but she still couldn't form the right words.

Terry was gone.

A ghost wasn't enough to save Adam.

She had disappeared after stopping Raven from killing Jack.

Mara didn't even get to say goodbye.

Having Raven find her killer after all these years and seeing that her sister was safe . . . there was no more reason for Terry to stay.

Police ran rampant through the house and only added to the confusion in Mara's head.

Her vision began to shrink, like a tunnel closing in around her until there was only blackness, and she fell into Kimiko's arms, unconscious.

***

"She's waking up," a familiar voice rang in Mara's ears.

It was her mother.

For a moment, Mara thought she was back at her house, in high school, and the last two years had been just one of her awful dreams.

But when she opened her eyes, she was sitting on the steps of Jack's side deck with a blanket wrapped around her, cradled in her father's arms with her mother looking worriedly down at her.

And everything that had happened rushed through her like bile.

Adam!

Mara pushed out of her dad's embrace with disgust. "Get away from me! Where's Adam?"

Claire's face was stained with tears. "Mara, he's fine. He's going to be okay . . . and Lucy too. Please, you need to sit down and rest. You're in shock."

The words flowed through her in waves of relief. "He's okay? And Lucy?"

"Well, not *okay*, but he'll live. Seven ribs were broken, and he has some damage to his spine, but nothing permanent, and Lucy is responding to the antibiotics." Claire paused as if she wasn't sure how she should say the next sentence, but finally rushed through it. "Adam will need you for his recovery."

Mara stood in mute shock.

Her chest squeezed in guilt and horror at hearing the extent of Adam's injuries, but also Mara couldn't quite comprehend what her mother was saying. Was Claire Johnson trying to be supportive? Of Adam?

Ben took this as his cue to stand up and lightly touch his daughter's arm. "That psycho recorded everything. We saw what Adam did . . ." Tears fell from Ben's eyes, and Mara felt tears of her own pouring down her cheeks as well at the memory. Ben's voice cracked with emotion. "He could have killed that monster . . . *I* would have killed that monster. But he didn't. He . . . saved you instead."

A sob broke from Claire, and she wrapped her arms around Mara. "I'm so sorry, Mara. I'm so sorry. We were just so scared for you."

"We're still not comfortable having you around any of this, including Adam, but we're willing to try. It's all we can promise right now." This seemed to pain her father to say. Then he added, "And we're paying for all his medical expenses . . ." Ben was at a loss. Mara could tell he wanted to make up for everything by helping in the only way he knew how but at the same time still wasn't willing to fully accept Adam.

Maybe in time.

But Mara couldn't care about her parents at the moment, and she didn't really want to be around them. She knew she'd forgive them eventually, but she just wasn't there yet. Not after what had happened to Adam.

Raven stepped into view as if hearing Mara's thoughts. "Can I see Mara for a moment?"

Ben and Claire nodded and walked toward Roger and the other officers on the lawn.

"You'll find all his victims buried in the backyard." Mara suddenly remembered.

"I'll have a team excavate the site today," Raven said. Her eyes met Mara's, and she placed her hand on Mara's shoulder, squeezing slightly. "Thank you, Mara. You, Kimiko, and Adam saved my life and Lucy's."

"We couldn't have done it without Terry." Mara wasn't sure how to bring up Raven's sister.

Raven fought off emotion and nodded. "I can't believe I saw her. I actually saw her. And I know that's because of you." She paused, trying to regain her composure. "Thank you, Mara."

"She's at peace now," Mara told her, not sure where the thought came from. But she knew it was true in that moment. Terry was gone. And she was at peace.

"Terry was Jack's first victim. Terry had tried to help him hide from a guy who was hurting him . . . with her dreams, but he ended up turning on her." Mara was finally able to give Raven the answers she'd been searching for her entire adult life.

Shaking her head, Raven answered, "I can't believe it's finally over." Then she reached down and hugged Mara tightly. "Really, I can't thank you enough." Pulling back, she smiled at Mara with affection. "You remind me of her, you know. It's what drew me to you in the first place."

A few days ago Mara would have taken that as an insult, but now that that she'd spent time with Terry, the real Terry, her chest filled with warmth.

Raven sighed and glanced over Mara's shoulder to Jack's backyard. "I'll call in the excavation team." Then she nodded toward the area behind her. "They're going to evacuate Adam and Lucy in the helicopter. You better hurry, if you want to go with."

As if seeing the scene before Mara for the first time, it was utter mayhem. Cops, paramedics, and FBI swarmed the lawn and house of Jack Franklin, serial killer. A helicopter was parked on the flat end of the lawn, and Mara could see the two gurneys being transported inside.

Mara went in for one more hug from Agent Piper, then ran up to Adam. Kimiko was there, holding his hand. He was asleep.

Kimiko sighed in relief as Mara approached. "I wasn't sure when you'd wake up. I was going to go with him just in case."

Mara hugged her fiercely, and Kimiko hugged her back. "Thank you."

Kimiko nodded into Mara's shoulder.

Pulling away, Kimiko's eyes were shining with fresh tears, but she smiled. "We got that bastard."

"And saved the damsels." Mara smiled back, though she didn't feel it yet. Not with Adam in the condition he was in.

Kimiko eyed him thoughtfully. "I'll let you two be alone."

The paramedics loaded Adam's gurney into the helicopter, next to Lucy's. The color was back in her cheeks, and she was sleeping, but they needed to get her to a hospital to check for internal injuries. Mara sat next to Adam, holding his hand while he continued to sleep as well. He lay on his chest, since the gashes were too deep and wide for him to lie on his back.

Loud thumping filled the air as the helicopter blades spun until they were airborne.

Adam's eyes fluttered open at the movement. Mara leaned down so her face was right next to his.

"You're going to be okay," Mara said through tears.

Adam smiled softly. "The meds took away most of the pain."

"That's good." Mara tried to take comfort in that.

"We got him though? And Raven and Lucy are safe?" he asked.

"Yeah, everyone is safe." Mara kissed Adam gently. "I love you."

"I love you, too." Even Adam's eyes smiled. "Meet me in my dreams? I want to go to our Disneyland."

Mara laughed, and it felt so good.

"Of course. Go back to sleep and I'll meet you there." Mara kissed him again.

Adam nodded and closed his eyes.

Mara watched him sleep and knew everything was going to be okay.

Other Books

The Riser Saga:

Riser

Reaper

Ripper

The Atlas Series:

Atlas

Grigori Returned

The Underworld

Riser Saga/Atlas Series Finale:

Atlas Rising

The Dream Diaries:

The Dream Diaries

The Dream Diaries: Blood Ties

Jeraline's Alley

Alexis Tappendorf Series:

Alexis Tappendorf and the Search for Beale's Treasure

Alexis Tappendorf and the Search for Atlantis

Love & Dark Series (with Hina McCord):

Vessel

First Born

Gutian Code

BIOGRAPHY

Becca fell in love with storytelling at an early age. The first book she read was The Lion, The Witch and The Wardrobe and she's been looking for the door to Narnia ever since! Becca is a passionate reader, consuming anything sci-fi or fantasy. Mix it in with YA and she is a fan for life. So it's no surprise that she writes in these genres as well. When Becca isn't writing, she loves to sew. From Mortal Instruments rune pillows, to elaborate Firefly/ Serenity bags, Becca loves to create!

www.ingramcontent.com/pod-product-compliance
Lightning Source LLC
Chambersburg PA
CBHW030527310726
48979CB00010B/1826/J

* 9 7 8 1 9 4 9 8 7 7 3 8 0 *